THE WINTERMEN

Also by Brit Griffin,
co-authored with Charlie Angus

We Lived a Life and Then Some
(Between the Lines, 1996)

THE
WINTERMEN

by
Brit Griffin

ScrivenerPress

Library and Archives Canada Cataloguing in Publication

Griffin, Brit, 1959-, author
The wintermen / by Brit Griffin.

ISBN 978-1-896350-65-3 (pbk.)

I. Title.

PS8613.R535W56 2014   C813'.6   C2014-905476-9

Book design: Laurence Steven
Cover design: Chris Evans
Cover photo: Loyola Santa Valentina
Author photo: Loyola Santa Valentina

Published by Scrivener Press
465 Loach's Road,
Sudbury, Ontario, Canada, P3E 2R2
info@yourscrivenerpress.com
www.scrivenerpress.com

We acknowledge the financial support of the Canada Council for the Arts and the Ontario Arts Council for our publishing activities.

Canada Council   Conseil des Arts
for the Arts   du Canada

ONTARIO ARTS COUNCIL
CONSEIL DES ARTS DE L'ONTARIO
an Ontario government agency
un organisme du gouvernement de l'Ontario

To mom and dad

Thanks always to
Charlie, Mariah, Siobhan and Lola.
And cannot forget Anthony.

THE INCIDENT

JOHNNY SLAUGHT LOOKED UP when he heard the kid say, "Put them back? You gotta be kidding."

He'd noticed the young guy earlier, the kid maybe eighteen or so, wearing a green and black skidoo jacket. It had the head of a big cat on the back. A classic. He remembered maybe selling that jacket to the kid's dad a few years back. Slaught was pretty sure the old man's name had been Cooper. Had a short fuse, that Cooper. Guess his kid did too. The security guy and the kid were eye to eye now.

"Sir, I am going to ask you one more time. Return the gloves, they're the property of Talos."

"Don't be an asshole," the kid said. "I've been freezing out here with these crappy things." He said it like the conversation was over, holding up both his hands to show the thin work gloves they'd all been given. A few of the guys had been complaining about them over coffee break.

Slaught thought maybe the kid was handling it wrong, sounding a bit too cheeky, the security guy starting to look seriously pissed, sort of leaning into the kid, "Those are standard issue work gloves you have, like all the workers. So quit whining. The sooner you're back to work, the sooner you're done."

The kid rolled his eyes. "I've been loading truck after truck of your shit for the past two months, all for a lousy food voucher and heating allowance. And as far as I can see, you and your buddies are just fucking the dog. So tell you what, I'll keep the gloves, and you can have this job, okay?"

Slaught could see the back of the security guy's head and the kid's face. The kid's face was red. Slaught figured it could be the cold or the kid might just be ready to blow a gasket. The security guy was wearing the dark green Talos uniform with an army style parka and the yellow happy face badge on the sleeve. Christ, those badges.

"No. I'll tell you what, you little shit," the security guy said, not raising his voice but quickly sounding nasty, surprising Slaught, "put the gloves back in the box or I'll have you arrested. Then you'll be doing the same thing without the three squares a day plus that fuel."

Slaught put down his wrench and moved forward so he could hear better. He looked down the platform to where most of the guys were loading crates onto a waiting truck. The truck was running, coughing out a greasy trail of grey onto the snow, sending the stink of diesel up along the cement platform. Arrested? Slaught figured the guy must be bluffing. Slaught wasn't even sure Talos actually owned any of the shit they were taking out anyway, also not really sure whether they were a private company or some kind of government agency. What the fuck was Talos anyway? Last month the guy who owned the hardware store in town had told him that Talos had come along with official looking requisition forms, said they had the right to take what they needed and then had proceeded to empty the store. When Slaught heard that he'd moved his snowmachines out of his showroom to his hunt camp, hiding them under tarps and brush. He'd already sold off most of his stock, there'd only been a dozen or so snowmachines left, but sure as shit Talos wasn't getting them.

Then the kid said, "Arrested, as if," and kept moving, but the security guy was barking, "This is your last warning, put the gloves back in the crate and get back to work."

By now several of the guys on the loading dock had stopped working and were watching. More security types were also moving forward. Slaught saw a big man with a pockmarked face approaching, also in uniform but with some sort of extra badges on it. Looked official.

"What seems to be the trouble?" It was the pockmarked guy. He was the kind of guy his ex might have found attractive if his face wasn't blasted to shit by scars. She wouldn't have gone for that. The security guy said, "Sir, this civilian has taken Talos property and is refusing to return it."

"Hey, we have a right to be as warm as the next guy, none of us have proper clothing here," started the kid by way of explanation, sensing maybe the new guy was important, but the pockmarked guy raised his hand to silence the kid.

"Your name?"

"Darren Cooper." When the kid said his name he sort of straightened his shoulders, like he was standing to attention or something, the pockmarked guy being the boss. Slaught wondered whether if the guy asked him that same question he'd stand at attention when he said 'Johnny Slaught'. Not fucking likely.

"Well, Mr. Cooper, I'm Ted Reitman, Talos's man on the ground here. I'm sure you know how much we at Talos appreciate you volunteering."

"I didn't volunteer," Darren Cooper said. "I was pretty much dragged out of my house."

Slaught figured the kid wasn't exaggerating. He'd volunteered himself, but he'd seen those recruiting teams strong-arming more than one guy. Since the government had contracted out civilian security, these Talos guys were passing through all the towns on a regular basis. It was different for Slaught; his wife had walked out on him a few years back, no kids, his business in the shitter, didn't matter much to him. Help out the Security Services? At the time he thought why not, he was eating hamburger helper solo most nights anyway. He was seeing it a little differently right now though.

Reitman looked pissed. "Cooper, these supplies are going down to the City—there are areas down there that are desperate. You have no idea what it's like down there."

The kid laughed. "Hard for people down there? That's bullshit, what about us?"

"Talos's priorities are to ensure the rational allocation of resources and oversee public safety. You, Mr. Cooper, are getting in the way of both objectives right now. I would be well within my jurisdiction to haul you off to a security facility. If you want to avoid that, return to your work station."

"Does rational allocation mean the City gets everything? Is that what you're telling me, that we don't count for shit?"

Slaught could see other guys nodding, agreeing with the kid. Things were just getting too hard in the north, lots of people had already left. It hadn't taken long, started with the weather being way out of whack for a few years, storms, flooding, tornadoes, you name it, everyone was getting whacked with something. Then that long, hard winter that just wouldn't let go. At the time he thought it was some lame-ass version of global warming. Crops tanked, there were food shortages, Christ, you were paying a fortune for a fucking apple.

But then the following year, there was a blistering hot summer. The government was scrounging power anywhere they could to keep things cool. In the heat of that short summer, there was no rain, and lots of bush burnt all over the north. Everyone started talking about cloud seeding, trying to get rain to the droughts that were all over the fucking place. All the scientists were saying different things, and all the governments were saying different things, and no one seemed to know what the fuck was going on.

So the government started to just let some areas burn, saying they couldn't afford the fire-fighting costs. Rumor was that if a town didn't have a school, it was going to burn, because the government thought it just wasn't worth saving. People had to scramble to get south of the fire zones, and nothing was moving up the highway, no food, no gas, nothing. It was suddenly like they were living in another country.

Then the bridge on the main highway collapsed and that was pretty much it. Never really did rebuild it, just jimmy-rigged it on a temporary basis that became permanent. And the government, facing food shortages and riots in the City, put Talos in charge. Talos was some sort of corporation, had their fingers in a million pies, everything from farming and food processing right through to pharmaceuticals. They owned everything, and nothing went in or out of the north except on Talos's trucks or buses. Folks said they even owned the highways and roads.

Next thing you know, Talos started centralizing all government services in the southern part of the region. Apparently, most of the provinces were doing the same, pulling out of the rural areas and consolidating their urban areas. And around that time, the Feds brought in the Emergency Measures Act and things started to look a whole lot different.

And then it started to snow.

That was over a year ago and it hadn't really stopped. It just kept snowing, staying cold all the time, getting a few weeks of warming up but not enough.

That's all it took, a few years of seriously pisspoor weather and it was all fucked up.

Now, they were shutting down the last of the government service depots. He hadn't really thought about it, but it was Talos's trucks that were hauling everything out, goods, people, machinery, everything on that last scrap of rat's ass highway heading south. Guess Talos was totally in charge now—it was some bullshit.

As if reading his mind, the kid said, "I don't give a shit about the City, or Talos. Hard to believe, eh? Fuck the City, and fuck Talos."

"How come," asked a thin man, talking calm, maybe trying to slow things down a bit, "all of this stuff is going down south anyway? What are we going to do when all the food and supplies are gone?" He was middle-aged, wearing bulky garage coveralls that said 'Harv' on the pocket. He had bushy eyebrows along with a drooping mustache and dark hair that fell over his collar in the back.

"This is none of your business." Reitman said, but a couple of the guys laughed, probably thinking it was pretty rich that he would say it had nothing to do with them when it was their chunk of real estate that was being gutted. That was how Slaught was seeing it anyways.

The same guy in the coveralls said, "Well, it is our business, of course it is, because once everything is gone, we'll still be here."

Slaught, for one, was willing to take his chances up here. Talos had offered folks a relocation package, trying to get everyone out, money for moving, six months living expenses and then you were on your own down there. Slaught wasn't buying it. A couple guys Slaught knew had actually come back up north, saying it was shitsville down there, crowded, no work, line ups for everything.

"Cut the bullshit and give the kid the gloves, come on," said one of the workers standing near the back of the small crowd that had gathered.

The older guy with the mustache nodded, said, "Why don't we just hand out the gloves to everyone, so we can all do our jobs better. We'll load your stinking trucks, you can take more shit away, and everyone will be happy, how about it?"

Another security guard started to move up. Slaught counted four men in uniform plus Reitman.

One of the other guys nearby said, "C'mon, its cold, these things they got us wearing are crap."

Slaught could feel his own hands, cracked and raw from the cold, bunched into fists and jammed down into his pockets. That guy was right, just hand them out to everybody, why not?

"Gentlemen, last warning. These supplies are the property of Talos and there will be consequences for all of you if this disturbance persists."

"That's it," the kid said, "Fuck you cop wannabees, I'm taking the gloves, plus I'm going home. Just wanted to keep my hands warm by grabbing this four dollar pair of gloves, but screw you buddy, I'm out of here."

With that the kid turned and headed for the parking lot.

"I can't allow that," Reitman said.

The kid was smiling, glad to be finally going home, Slaught was sure he'd been thinking about it long enough, they all had. "What are you going to do," the kid shouted over his shoulder to Reitman, "shoot me?"

"If I have to."

The mustache guy said, "Whoa here, I think we just need to step back for a minute and stop with that kind of talk."

Reitman said, "Back off buddy, I've just about had it with you."

Slaught's eyes followed Darren, picturing him swinging onto the snowmachine, gunning the engine and pulling out of there, a perfect fuck you to Talos.

The mustache guy persisted, "Maybe you're over-reacting a bit here, really, it's just a pair of gloves."

"Yeah, you want to see over-reacting, keep it up," and Reitman drew a semi from inside his coat. He held it so everyone could see it, then let his hand drop to his side, just holding it loosely and pointing it downwards, like he was holding a hot dog or something. Christ, Slaught didn't know these guys were armed.

Everybody on the platform froze. One of the young guys said, "Darren, the guy's got a gun." Darren glanced back over his shoulders, sort of gave his head a shake like he couldn't believe it, and then kept going.

Reitman said, "Mr. Cooper, return the gloves to the crate and get back to work. Now."

Slaught noticed one of the other security guys drawing his gun. Another one had his hand resting along the edge of the parka, getting ready.

Then someone said, almost as more of a question, like they couldn't believe what was going on, "It's just a pair of gloves."

"Now," Reitman said quietly.

The kid turned to face Reitman and said, "No, I won't. I'm outta here," seeming pretty sure the guy was bluffing. It did seem crazy, shoot someone over a pair of gloves? There was no way. Slaught figured the gloves were made in fucking China anyway.

Cooper moved to the edge of the platform, ready to jump down and head for his snowmachine. Reitman raised his gun and shot the big cat on the back of Cooper's jacket right between the eyes.

The men on the platform watched Cooper fly forward and hit hard against the hood of his machine. He crumpled up, blood seeping out from below him and running down towards the head-lights.

"The fun is over gentlemen," Reitman said, and then to the security guard closest to him, "Get that guy out of here. And load his machine onto the truck. Hose it down first."

More incredulous than anything, the guy with the mustache said, "What are you doing? You can't go around shooting people."

"This is Talos country, asshole. I just did."

Slaught noticed the security guy who was trying to pull Cooper off the sled was struggling with the weight. Slaught himself was having a hard time breathing, watching as the security guard resorted to sliding young Darren Cooper face down off the hood and dragging him over the snow by his boots, yelling at one of the other guards to help. A security guard joined him and took hold of one leg, hauling him like that, the sound of the jacket skidding on the hard crust of the snow. He couldn't believe they were all just standing there, watching. No one was making eye contact, just staring as Darren Cooper went by.

"Now all of you move away from here and get back to loading the truck."

Slaught picked up his tool kit and slowly walked back inside the warehouse. He was shaking. He could hear the rest of the guys muttering, looking scared but mad too, trying to make sense of what had just happened. A few of them headed into the warehouse to tell some of the other guys working way in the back, everyone saying pretty much the same thing. Un-fuck-ing believable.

Slaught leaned up against the workbench. He was trying to slow down his breathing, think straight. Picturing them all stand-ing there on that hard grey cement, not looking at each other. What the fuck?

He took a look around the warehouse, stacks and stacks of

crap still to be loaded. Crates piled high on skids, almost reaching the roof. Quite the operation, there was everything in here anyone would need to get by. In his head he could see Darren Cooper sliding off the hood of his snowmachine. Thinking about why no one had done anything. Then thinking why he hadn't done anything. Thinking then maybe he would.

It had taken a while for his hands to stop shaking, but when they did, Slaught headed back out to the platform. In the fifteen minutes or so he'd been in the warehouse thinking about exactly what he could do, most of the guys had gotten back to work. Slaught was thinking that most of them were probably trying to figure out how to get the hell out of there when their shifts ended. He doubted many of them would be coming back.

He noticed the crate of gloves had been moved further down the platform so he headed that way, no one really taking any notice, not seeing the pump action he was carrying down at his side. He couldn't see Darren Cooper anywhere, Slaught wondering what they were going to do with the body, take it down to the City? Burn it? Return it to Cooper's girlfriend over at her shack? Were there other bodies? Slaught was beginning to wonder what the fuck Talos was that they could get away with this, and the main guy, bending his head to light a cigarette and waving away the smoke with his hand, was definitely acting like he was getting away with it.

That pissed Slaught off, the guy's arrogance. And the shrill red smears left from dragging Darren Cooper across the snow, that pissed him off too. He hadn't known the kid, but Christ, face down in the snow, like a slab of meat, the green eyes of the cat on the back of his jacket just staring up at them, all fierce. It was enough, he guessed, to explain why he was about to plunge himself into some major fucking mayhem.

Slaught felt the metal of the gun bumping against his leg,

reminding him it was there. He took a deep breath, and reaching the boxes, slid the crowbar off the top of the crate and with his free hand pried open the lid. The screws squealed in the cold as the lid popped up. A security officer standing at the side of the truck glanced up, and then Reitman turned to look.

Grabbing a pair of gloves, Slaught said, "I think these are mine."

Reitman rolled his eyes, looked to the security guy beside him and said, "Deal with this asshole, in fact shoot anyone you want, just leave enough to load the truck. I'm sick of this bullshit, I have a schedule, and I have clients waiting for their merchandise."

"Sorry buddy, shop's closed," Slaught said evenly, pulling up the pump action up and pointing it down at the guy's head, almost seeing himself doing it, like he was in a movie, playing a role. He hoped it had a fucking happy ending. "Just toss your semi on the ground—all of you. And then get your boys to start unloading these trucks. I think we'll be needing some of this stuff."

The men were all looking now. Slaught said, "Nice eh?" holding the gun up a bit higher so they could see it, "There's a whack of them at the south end of the warehouse. If you want one, I'd get it now, there could be a fire sale on this shit," and then to Reitman, "Are you going to listen to me or you gonna stand there waiting for me to add another crater to your face?" thinking as he said it that he was sounding a bit like he belonged in a schoolyard.

"Nobody move," Reitman snapped. He was trying to stay calm looking, but he was facing a pump action and a couple of other guys were muttering 'Fucking A' and heading for the warehouse. Reitman turned to Slaught, "What's your name?"

"Frosty the Snowman, now get your ass in gear." Slaught was gesturing with the end of his gun to all the crates now stacked at the end of the loading dock, "All this stuff? Right back here where it belongs. Then get going and don't ever come back."

Reitman took a minute, tossed his cigarette down in the snow, a brief faint sizzle in the dead silence as everyone watched it extinguish itself, then said, "There is no way that is going to happen. You're making a big mistake."

"Yeah, well, my ex-wife said I've been making mistakes all my life," said Slaught, "one more isn't going to make much difference. So toss your weapons and start giving back all the shit that you're stealing from us."

"Men, hold your ground," he said, and then to Slaught, "You are in way over your head."

"The only thing I've ever shot before now was a black bear climbing in through my basement window to get at my chokayecherry wine. I didn't know jackshit about shooting a man before today, but I just got a first rate education from you."

"Don't do this."

"Too late pizzaface."

The man half turned, moving as if he was lowering his weapon, then brought it up fast. Slaught fired, spinning the guy around, thinking that the recoil on the pump action was tougher than he thought it would be. Thinking too that he hadn't really planned this whole thing out, and his heart was pounding hard and fast, but other than that he was feeling pretty good, surprised it was so easy. He'd have to think about that later when he had some time.

There was silence for a few seconds as everyone watched Reitman fall. The snow gave underneath his weight, crumbling to outline his body that was now lying across the path, open-mouthed, eyes staring upwards. Slaught had his gun on the security guard who was standing over the body of Reitman, looking surprised more than anything.

Finally the man with the mustache said, "OK, now what?"

"Now we take charge," the kid standing beside him said. He

was a bit stockier and with close cropped hair, but definitely the guy's young lad.

"That's right," Slaught said. "First job is for you Talos boys to put down your guns and get over against this wall. Come on, move it." And then to the man with the mustache he asked, "Who are you?"

"Harvey Larose. From V-Town."

"Well Harvey, think you could empty them crates out, we gotta send these young men home in style."

Larose shrugged, so Slaught tossed him a pair of gloves from the crate. Slaught could see his hands were shaking a bit too. A couple of young guys moved up to help. Some of the other young ones already had guns. Slaught asked Larose's young fella if he and his buddies could round up the guards and their weapons and keep an eye on them till everything was ready. Sure as shit they could.

"Hey, you sure you know what you're doing?"

It was the big native guy asking, the one who was always going on about war and history at lunchtime, had a long braid hanging down his back. One day at lunch he'd explained that he was an Algonquin, said that his people had lived in this area for over six thousand years. Six thousand years, he'd said, think about that. One of the young guys had said, shit, that's older than Jesus, and the Algonquin guy had just said, "That's right, and dollars to donuts we'll be here for another six thousand years, makes no difference to us what you white guys do." Then the young guy asked him what he was doing there, why wasn't he on the rez, and he'd said "Trying to get you people the hell off our territory once and for all, that's what." Slaught put him in his early thirties, a few years younger than himself. Few inches taller too, big enough fella. He was standing with a Remington resting in his crossed arms, looking pretty comfortable with the thing. Slaught could tell the guy was sizing him up.

Slaught answered, "I'm beginning to get some idea, yeah."

"OK, good enough for me."

"Your name?"

"Chumboy Commando."

Slaught gestured to the crumpled up body of the security boss down in the snow. "OK then Chumboy, if you want to lend a hand, could you put him in the passenger seat?"

"How come I gotta handle the dead white guy? "

Slaught wasn't sure if Chumboy was just giving him the gears so he didn't say anything. Chumboy said, "Well, at least give me some of those precious gloves for the job, I'm not getting blood all over these mitts, my Auntie made them for me." Slaught looked as Chumboy thrust out his hands, showing him a pair of red, purple and black knitted mitts, saying, "Maybe she'll make you a pair, you're a regular Dirty Harry, and my Auntie loves Clint."

Larose said the crates were ready. Two young guys moved the guards up onto the truck and one of the other men on the platform grabbed a hammer and some nails saying he wanted to make sure they were tucked in nice and comfy. Chumboy said it was turning into a fine community project.

The security guard looked wrecked as he climbed into the driver seat. Slaught asked, "You okay to drive?" and the guy just nodded, pale eyes rimmed red and watery. Slaught said, "You'll be alright. You got enough fuel to make it to North Bay. Now don't be coming back here and doing anything stupid, understand?"

He slammed the door shut and the men stood watching as the truck moved off slowly, getting some traction and then headed off down the snow-packed road.

Chumboy asked, "What's the plan Frosty?"

"We figure out a way to bury Cooper."

Chumboy nodded, said that was fine, but he meant something a little longer term.

"Thinking of heading down to the old Fraser Hotel."

Chumboy raised his eyebrows, "In Cobalt?"

"That's right, it's the old home patch, and I've been thinking after what's happened here today, some of us could use a beer."

"Hate to break it to you, but everyone's gotten the hell out of Dodge. Talos has been through these towns like a pack of hoover vacuums, went in there with their buses and transports and hauled everyone and everything away. Old Cobie Town was one of the first to be evacuated as far as I can recall, which means they've already cleaned that one out."

Slaught shook his head. "One of the security guys told me Cobalt was just a shithole, said they didn't even bother going through the town 'cause there was nothing there worth taking, said they weren't stopping until they got to North Bay. They've already pulled all their security off the Highway 11 corridor. Guess the liquor store wasn't on their radar. I say we head on down there, have ourselves a few rounds, check into the vacated Fraser hotel, and make ourselves a plan."

Chumboy asked, "What's your name?"

"Johnny Slaught."

"Well Johnny Slaught, first round's on you."

CHAPTER ONE

Two years later

"So, you're Grier Laskin," Captain Frank Muspar said, standing and extending his hand, "I've been anxious to meet you."

Muspar was thinking the guy looked all wrong, like he belonged in a goddam fashion magazine. Lean and well built, Laskin's blonde spiky hair was more rock star than Navy Seal.

"I know what you're thinking," Laskin said, grinning, "but don't worry, I got cojones the size of a T-Rex."

"You don't say? Well, let's hope that is what we need in this case Mr. Laskin."

"Trust me, it's what you always need."

Bob Scott, head of the Security Division of Talos, had told Muspar that Laskin was the answer to their problems in the Territories. What the hell was he thinking?

Scott came around from behind his desk, extending his hand, said, "Grier, good to see you again. This is Captain Frank

Muspar. As you may be aware, Talos is heading up security for the City and often works hand in hand with Captain Muspar's Emergency Police Services. As you may also know, Talos is responsible for overall resource allocation, both for the City and the Territories. Our problem today involves both components of our mandate."

Scott was leaning back on his desk as he talked, arms crossed, file folder tucked under his arm. Muspar figured his own office was maybe a quarter the size of this one. The desk was large, a deep red wood, and next to it a long couch and a coffee station. Stylish black and white photos along the far wall, showing cityscapes from back in the day. How the city used to look, all lit up at night, sweeping down towards the big lake.

Scott crossed to the coffee station, held up a mug and asked if anyone wanted a coffee. Muspar said no, he was fine, but then clearing his throat and nodding across the room said, "So Bob, this is a classified briefing. Maybe Mr. Laskin's friend could wait outside until we're done?"

"Outside," laughed Laskin, "no way man, Mitch is my right hand man."

"Mr. Laskin, I don't know about your arrangements, but as far as I know there've been no security checks on anyone else concerning this issue."

"Relax Capitano," Laskin said, shrugging good-naturedly, "she's a Talos girl, got clearance up the ying yang. I'm sure Bob here can straighten this out, but, just to let you know, if she's out, I'm out. I don't work without Mitch Black, that's just the way I roll, comprende?"

Muspar looked to Scott. He could tell Scott was ready with the bullcrap. "That's right Captain, sorry not to have mentioned it earlier, but Ms. Black has done numerous contracts for Talos.

Ms. Black and Mr. Laskin have a good deal of experience working together and it just seemed a good overall fit."

That had to be the fifteenth time in the last twenty-four hours Muspar had heard the 'sorry not to have mentioned it' shit. He'd found out about the proposed mission more by accident than anything else when one of his guys had said, "See you in the a.m. over at Talos, sir." Muspar had asked Private Pete Solanski what was going on at Talos and he'd said, "Well, you know, a few of us got seconded for that mission into the Territories."

Muspar had just said, "Oh yeah, that," and then made for his office, sending a blistering voice mail over to Bob Scott. His cell rang a few minutes later, Scott saying, "Frank, calm down," and Muspar cutting him off, "Why the hell wasn't I consulted about this mission to the Territories?"

"Why don't you drop in sometime, we'll have a drink..."

"I want an answer."

"OK Frank, you weren't notified because there was no reason to notify you."

"They're my men, that's reason enough."

"Frank, you know the drill, they're your men until we need to borrow them, then, technically, they become our men. After all, it's in our Memorandum of Understanding with you people."

Muspar was silent, thinking, then said, "I want to know what's going on Bob. I think that's also part of our Memorandum of Understanding. 'Informed cooperation' I think is the expression used."

Scott sighed, said, "You know I really don't have to tell you anything, but just to demonstrate our desire to have a collegial relationship, you can sit in on the meeting. Tomorrow, 10:00 a.m. sharp," then added, "as an observer. I'll send over the briefing notes for you. This is pretty sensitive stuff, not the kind of thing you want people hearing about on I-TIME."

"I thought Talos controlled all the programming on I-TIME, it's your networking service after all."

"Frank, what I am saying to you is that this mission is not for public consumption."

"What's this about?"

"Frank…"

"I can be over there in ten minutes."

"Alright, calm down. We're going in for the Wintermen. See you tomorrow," and the phone had gone dead.

Muspar now realized that he should have blocked the secondments then and there. He didn't like getting mixed up with Talos. When things blew up, it was always the Police Services that ended up wearing it. He knew Talos was desperate to get the Wintermen under control, and the damage was getting expensive. And public. The recent border raid that had turned up a trade in raw silver for black market gasoline had renewed questions about Talos's control over the Territories—the huge swath of land that ran east from what used to be the Saskatchewan-Manitoba border over to the James Bay ice fields.

Scott passed a mug of coffee to Laskin, "Heard of the Wintermen?"

Laskin sipped the coffee, said, "This tastes like crap, where are you getting this shit, those tax-free zones in Mexico?" then added, "The Wintermen, yeah, I've heard of them, who hasn't, they've been on I-TIME's most wanted often enough. Hillbilly renegades right? Some guy went berserk at a government depot a couple years back, been holed up in the Territories since, rumours about illegal trading, poaching, all that kind of shit. What about them?"

"Talos wants them gone."

Laskin said, "I figured you guys would have deep-sixed them long ago."

Scott shook his head, said at the time it didn't seem worth it, there was no real civilian population left, just a few holdouts, and there was enough to do elsewhere. "At the time of the incident at the government depot a team went in and did a recon, but they were long gone by then and we didn't have any resources to spare. We tried rousting as many holdouts as we could during Operation Clean Sweep but the evacuations were massive, it was chaos up there. And after we pulled out it didn't take long for it all to turn into a no-go zone, its just too goddam difficult to do anything up there. It took about six months for the phone lines and cable lines to go, the weather just did everything in. We've only maintained our communications infrastructure as far as the border with the Territories. We can barely keep up with the maintenance on our network to that point, beyond that, there's literally fuck all."

"So why go back in now? No one really gives a shit what goes on up there anyway."

"To be blunt, the vision for the Territories has always been 'people out, Talos in.' As far as we are concerned, with no civilian populations, we can focus on re-establishing resource security and exploitation. The City is facing a crisis, our emergency measures are stretched to the breaking point, too many extended brown outs and blackouts, shortages of everything, our surveillance and financial infrastructures need major investments, we're into food rationing, we need more of everything or we won't be able to maintain order. Simple as that. Right now, our strategic corporate agenda is poised to ramp up power production and mineral extraction, but we got these yahoos riding around like cowboys fucking up the works."

Grier seemed skeptical. "Yeah? A few cowboys and the cavalry can't handle them?"

"Listen, it's anarchy up there, no police, no army, no food, no supplies, nothing. Not even roads anymore. Zip. We've targeted three sites to launch fly-in mining operations over the next three years, but we just can't get the resources in there to ensure their security. The logistics are overwhelming enough without this other shit to worry about."

Grier ran his hand through his hair, giving his spikes new life, checking his hair in the reflection of one of the big black and white photos, said, "You think this guy and his drinking buddies pose a real threat?"

Muspar could see Scott tensing up, looking pissed. Scott said, "Yes, I do."

Shrugging, Grier said, "Well, I'm not convinced."

Muspar winced. He was sorry this wasn't his show, he'd toss the smug little shit right out on his ass.

Scott said, "Murder of a law enforcement officer not enough for you? They've got weapons, food, fuel, everything they need for a serious insurrection. Then there is the illegal trading, poaching? Worst, there's been a disturbing trend over the last year, civilians trying to get back up into the Territories, they've heard of these yahoos living up there, re-creating the goddam frontier, and they start thinking, yeah, I can make a go of it too."

This was the first Muspar had heard of this, said, "Why weren't we apprised of this, what kind of numbers are we talking about here?"

"A few stragglers here and there at first, now it's steady, we're hauling in dozens every week. Some are probably slipping through, after all, it's not exactly the most effective border, there are gaps all along the perimeter, only the travel corridors are under adequate surveillance. Now we have an illegal trade in snowmachines—any idea of what one of those is worth on the black market? And a few enterprising sonsofbitches are smuggling people up into the Territories, we have no idea what happens to them. All of this shit is costing us time and dollars. And these Wintermen, word is getting out, the public starting to think they're some fucking freedom fighters or something. These guys are terrorists, and they're acting like they own the Territories. It's time to teach them otherwise."

Laskin nodded thoughtfully. "You need some guerilla action out there."

"Which is why," Scott said carefully, "Talos wants you in on this. There is nothing conventional about this operation, and nothing that we really want out there on the radar. We just want it dealt with."

Muspar watched Laskin smirk, was surprised at his tone when he said, "Yeah, I've dealt with a few things for Talos before haven't I?" like he was sharing a private joke or something, then back to business, saying, "So how do these guys keep going, I mean, supplies are short even here?"

"Stealing. Anything that was left up there. We tried to get out as much as we could, but the in the case of the areas furthest north that were cleared first, there was tons of stuff left behind, partly because there was just too much shit to move out and also we thought we could repopulate those areas when things settled down. But things didn't settle down and we never went back up. So everything from fully loaded hospitals to industrial plants to the mom and pop stores were just left as is. Now we know the Wintermen have to be getting around mostly by snowmachine. Fuel must be an issue, but they are still looting everything from municipal garages to police stations and drugstores. Lately, there've even been a few raids on our border stations. Christ, according to our sources, they even hit some of our liquor shipments in the travel corridor."

"Cool, snow pirates."

They'd almost forgotten she was there. She swung around on her chair to face them.

Laskin laughed. "Yeah, I like that, snow pirates. I guess that sort of makes us like the British High Command huh, hunting these rogues down on Her Majesty's high seas."

"It'd be more fun to be the pirates."

"Can't have everything babe."

Muspar cleared his throat. He couldn't believe these two, thinking it was all a big joke. "Mr. Laskin, I don't have to remind you that this is a very serious situation."

"Chillax Frank, I've got this. Just give me the specs on this guy and some idea of what he's got, ammo-wise, where he's dug in…"

Scott stepped in. "Okay, we don't know a whole lot, but we've had a few reports about a group up in a old mining town, probably Cobalt from our reports, about an hour and half from the border. We have no idea what shape things are in up there. They might be holed up in one of the mines, a mill, might have taken over an entire town, we just don't know."

"Where's your last outpost?" Mitch asked, standing up and stretching. Muspar paused with the other two to watch her for a moment, the tight black wife-beater creeping up along the flat of her stomach. Her pale blonde hair was cropped short, her eyes almond-coloured. Some broad, he thought. She was putting it out like a cat in heat.

"Right at the Green Line, edge of the Territories. We have one main travel corridor running up there from the City and it's the last place with any maintained infrastructure, we're talking roads, bridges, communications networks and, of course, security. There's about a thousand people just south of there, a support community, guards, emergency workers, greenhouse workers, they stay put up there, no one gets in or out without special passes. And north of that, nothing."

"So how far south have the Wintermen come?"

"Recently we had action from them as far as that last outpost. They got a few generators, fuel, a whack of batteries, mostly that kind of thing. "

"And how many of these guys are we dealing with?"

"Anywhere between twenty and two hundred."

Mitch smiled. "Great intel."

Muspar saw Scott give her a look. She sighed, "Sorry. Out of line. okay, so you don't have much on these bad boys. Can you tell me what you do know?"

Scott snapped open the file and spread it out on the desk.

"Alright. Looks like a bunch of them are just local low-lifes, you know the type, 'nobody's pushing me off my land' kind of guys."

"What about indigenous populations?"

Scott looked at her blankly. "What do you mean?"

Grier answered, "She means Aboriginals, you know, the First People and all that? What about them? Are they whooping it up on the warpath too?"

Scott sounded impatient, "Don't know, don't care. Those communities had the same chance as anyone else to get out, who cares if they chose to freeze their asses off up there. Anyway, this is about eradicating the Wintermen, whoever they are, not cultural outreach, got it?"

Mitch said, "Got it, loud and clear. So let's talk about this berserker guy, the one who started things rolling, have anything on him? "

"We believe he's a guy called John Slaught, divorced, late thirties maybe, dark haired, just over six foot."

Mitch took the cup of coffee from Laskin and smelled it, made a face and passed it back to him, said, "So our boy is tall, dark and handsome."

Scott ignored her, continued reading from his file. "We have reason to believe he is originally from Cobalt. The last location we have on him is that incident report on the murder of a Talos officer from about two years back that Grier mentioned. That was at the depot in the Temiskaming region, close to Cobalt. There was also a significant theft of arms and militia supplies at that time. After that he seemed to disappear for a while until these border raids started about a year ago."

"So is he ex-military? From the cop shop, what?"

Scott, shaking his head, sighed and said, "Snowmobile dealer."

Mitch looked over at Laskin and they both cracked up.

"Look," began Scott, "I know it sounds ridiculous and at first we figured it would take us a few hours to round him up, but..." his voice faded out, then, exasperated, added, "I want this over, and I never want to hear about the Wintermen or this John Slaught again. Understand?"

In the silence that followed only Muspar's raspy breathing could be heard. Then Mitch swung her arms up, clapped her hands together hard, said, "Gentlemen, I need to meet your crew, check out your equipment, and I want your baddest sled. It's time to revoke this guy's dealership."

CHAPTER TWO

"YOU KNOW WHAT I'M THINKING?"

She shook her head. Just the big hood moved when she did that. Her parka looked too big, like it belonged to her old man or something, sloping off her shoulders and reaching down to her knees. And she was just standing there, leveling that shitass looking rifle at him.

Johnny Slaught was wishing he had taken his time coming in here. Should've known from the look of things, passing by the broken down school bus in the yard to where the building's windows were broken, thinking something didn't seem right but letting his guard down anyway, maybe getting too cocky, they'd all been doing pretty much what they wanted for the past year or so without running into any real trouble. This day was turning into a pisspoor event. "I'm thinking that if things get bad…"

"They are bad," she said. Slaught didn't like the flat quality in her voice, standing there, unsmiling, hand clenched white on the gun. Made him very nervous. He'd never really figured on running into any whackjobs. He'd barely said anything to her, just introducing himself and starting to ask if she was okay and then she was suddenly going full bore into rage mode.

"I mean worse, you know, the end times kinda of thing, if things get worse, maybe you and I could do the Adam and Eve thing, you know, do some serious repopulating?"

She stared at him. He could see her eyes were blue. Dark blue. Maybe teasing her was the wrong approach. Except he couldn't think of another one.

"Come on," he tried again, "just put the gun down. We'd make such beautiful babies together.

"Go fuck yourself," she said.

He was past pleading. She had the gun, waving it at him and shouting, not much he could do. Then she'd taken him further into the building, towards the back. He was worried she just might shoot him by mistake, waving the thing around like that, finger always jumping around the trigger. She was one twitchy woman.

Now she had him stashed behind some sort of service counter. Bound up his arms across his chest with duct tape while another woman, a younger one, held the gun. Then more tape around his legs, pushing him back onto the cheapest piece of shit office chair ever designed.

He couldn't believe he'd been so stupid to walk right into this. His snowmachine was way up the street, stashed in some cedars. He'd been out looking for some cows, a guy had told him there were rumours there was a herd out grazing on the old Clover Valley road, but there had been no sign of the goddam cows and he decided to head back. At the last minute he decided to head back through the string of towns along the lake rather than retracing his trail. That's when he'd seen the smoke, coming out the chimney on the large brick building tucked up on a rise just as the first town ended.

He hadn't taken this route through the towns in a while, but he sure as shit hadn't heard about anyone living twenty minutes up the road from them. Parked up behind the building was a yellow bus, big bundles strapped to the roof, looked like one of the evacuation vehicles that was surplus. Maybe there was something worthwhile there, it was surprising the kind of shit Talos had left behind. Between the smoke and the bus, he just couldn't help himself.

He thought he was being careful by making his way in on foot. But what a jackpot he was in now. Going in alone had been one of the most fucked up things he'd ever done, and it had a lot of competition. And now what? He was off the beaten track, pretty much hogtied and surrounded by the worst pile of crap he'd seen in a long time, kid's toys, bottles of shampoo, broken dishes, all jumbled up with clothes and maps and smashed computer parts. Jesus.

He could hear her behind him, maybe just outside the room over to the left, talking with the other woman, a young hippy girl with an oversized sweater and her hair pulled back in a braid who was saying, "We're not interested in him now, we got to get focused, okay? Don't worry about him, we can deal with him later."

"Hey," Slaught yelling over at them, "how about I make things easy for you and just leave so you don't have to deal with me at all..."

But then a scream, low, almost a moan, but too piercing, and the two women were moving, through the door and into the room, the door slamming shut behind them.

What the fuck was that? Slaught scrambled up as much as he could, hauling himself up, standing. Then leaning over the counter, he tried to shuffle down along it so he had a better look at the door. In the sudden silence he caught his breath, tried again to get his wrists free of the tape, but it wasn't budging. Then the moaning, Slaught straining to hear voices, anything else, and then there was that fury again, that fucking awful scream.

Slaught looked around, feeling panicked now. He tried to move further along the counter, lurching, his feet wrapped way too tight to move. Another scream, muffled and distorted by the door. Christ almighty, though, it sounded like they were tearing someone apart, sounded like a woman, but deep, from her gut kind of yell. He propelled himself a bit further along the counter, slipped, and hit the floor hard just as the door flew open and the blue-eyed woman came running out, stepping right over him, caught her foot on his parka, stumbled but caught herself, cursing. With the woman's moans coming through the open door behind him, the blue eyed one was already tearing through piles of crap along a metal shelf, tossing stuff aside, grabbing boxes, bags, clearly looking for something. She came up with a pair of scissors. Her parka was off, he noticed she was slim, long hair pulled back, sleeves pushed up.

"What the Christ are you doing in there?"

She stepped back over him like he wasn't even there. He could hear their voices now, but couldn't make out too much of what they were saying. He began to inch his way towards the open door along the floor.

It seemed to take hours for him to cover each small bit of ground. By the time he reached the opening there'd been three more screams, each one sounding worse than the last. He'd never heard anything like it. The other women were talking low, it was hard to hear, and his back was to the door, rolling over was almost impossible. He was thinking his situation was pretty fucked up right now, thought maybe that for the first time in a long time he was in some serious trouble. He wasn't sure why he needed to know what was going on in that room, he wasn't in much shape to help anybody, but still, he needed to know.

He began to try and rotate his body, and the screaming seemed to turn into some dark, deep yelling, and the other women were sort of yelling now too, and he managed to get on his back, push himself past the counter so he could see the door, partially open, and he turned his head a bit and then there was a thin river of blood running out the door towards him.

The backs of the two women, crouched on the floor, were blocking his view, but there was a body between them lying on the ground, and the blue eyed woman was at the body's feet, and she was saying things that he couldn't hear. And there was more of the deep yelling. What the fuck was happening? And then there was a huge, slurp of blood that joined the thin river and washed towards him.

Slaught yelled, and tried to scramble backwards, and only then did the younger woman look over her back towards him, barely acknowledging him.

"What the fuck?" he yelled, still trying to move back out of the way of the door, fishing his body back and forth. He moved maybe only a matter of a couple of feet back, all the while the women were bent over the woman on the floor, talking in hushed voices, Slaught couldn't hear them, straining, wondering if the woman was still alive, then some strange whisperings, and the hush in the room was suffocating to Slaught and he yelled again, "What the fuck is happening in there?"

The two women both turned. He could tell they'd been smiling, they looked at him and then each other and started to laugh, seeing his panic. The blue-eyed one stood up and came through the door, and she had blood on her hands, and he could see as she moved the body of a woman on the floor, turned a bit away from him, a bunch of sheeting underneath her, sort of a rose floral pattern, and it was soaked through with blood. He was trying to move away but his legs were jammed up against the counter, his feet now hitting the roll away chair, sounds of metal scrapping along the floor.

He was scrambling still when she leaned over and grabbed his coat, shouted, "Hey, settle down, enough of your shit, we'll figure out what to do with you later. And be quiet."

He was thinking she wasn't looking scared or unsure or anything. Not like him, not like he felt now, not like when he'd been on that loading platform, when he felt the gun and watched Reitman go down, and he thought, Fuck, I'm in it now, no going back.

"You sick bitch ..." Slaught shouted. It seemed to get her attention.

"Us?" she hissed, turning and landing a solid kick to his ribs, "Us? You would think that, wouldn't you," she was leaning down over him again, grabbing the back of his head, "you killed all those old people ... and I've heard about others, women, even their children, you taking everything from them, leaving them to starve," and she kicked him again, then yanked on the hood of his coat so it sort of pulled up over his head, catching tight under his arms, and she dragged him towards the door, stronger now than maybe she really was because she was so pissed off, and she dumped him on his side, so he could see into the room.

The other woman turned, looking a bit worried and said, as if trying to calm her down, "Susun, leave him, we need you here, okay, come on, we need to focus."

The woman stared down at him. "You bastard. Unlike you, we don't kill babies, we deliver them." And she kicked him again, with his coat half up over his face, right into his chest, sort of tipping him back, but he could still see it, right there, blood everywhere, spreading out now over the linoleum, and the mom on the floor, and there lying across her breasts, all wet and bloody and squirming, a baby.

Well, goddam.

"I mean, could this be any more boring and full of bullshit?"

The other guys knew Turner wasn't really asking a question so nobody bothered responding. He was an asshole anyway. There were five guys waiting together in the cafeteria, and sure they were bored, they'd been there for a few hours with a batch of lukewarm coffee and a few back issues of *Security Works* to read.

"I'm getting pretty sick of sitting around picking my nose." It was Turner again, talking for the sake of it. A couple of the guys knew him from the last time they had been seconded by Talos. Over a year ago they'd been brought together in order to crack-down on an organized syndicate that was siphoning gas and selling it on the black market.

"That's all you ever do Turner." It was the tall guy, Miller. Turner swung around and gave him the finger, and the chubby kid who was bringing in their third round of coffee and donuts sniggered. Turner pointed at the kid.

"Why don't you just shut up? You're pissing me off."

The kid shrugged and turned his attention back to the magazines he was picking up off the floor near Turner. He barely got them onto his cart when the door swung open and in came Captain Muspar with three other people. Turner whistled softly as Mitch slid onto the edge of one of the long tables directly across from them, but with her back to them, reading from a blue file folder.

"Gentlemen," Muspar said crisply, "your attention."

He waited while they straightened themselves up. Well, they weren't the best group he'd ever seen but they would have to do. As he had reminded Scott, his best were either busy down in the worst of the City's sectors, or were away on Foreign Border Rotation. The rotations were the jobs most of the guys dreaded, being stuck down in one of the outposts along the American border, dropped off with three months worth of shit food, staring out into the white expanse, hauling yourself out to monitor the state of the bridges, making sure no one was going across. Not like that was going to happen. The bridges were jammed up with snow and ice, it was barely possible to keep the one lane clear, and there were no real highways running off either end. The official line was that the bridges were symbols of hope that one day things could be normal again. But for the guys sitting in the isolated border outposts, that looked like a long time coming. Everyone was long gone, people cramming themselves into the cities, leaving all the small towns, the farms and factories, all the countryside, to the steady and relentless reach of the snow.

"Gentlemen, most of you know me, but for the benefit of those who don't, I'm Captain Muspar, Emergency Police Services. Mr. Bob Scott here is with us from Talos Civilian Security, he can fill you in on the secondment. Bob?"

Scott said, "This is Mr. Grier Laskin, you probably know him from I-TIME's Man Up program? He will be leading this assignment with Ms. Black. This task is going to take you deep into the Territories and Mr. Laskin, as you may know, is one of our few backcountry experts. Since the City established our borders, and the government withdrew from the northern regions, few people have had any on the ground experience. Mr. Laskin is one of the few."

A slightly nasal voice interrupted. "I'm from up there."

Muspar scanned the room. "Who said that?"

The kid in the back with the coffee cart put up his hand, looking like he was back in Grade One and needed to use the can. Muspar sized him up—what in Christ's name was this kid doing here?

"Who are you?"

"Uh, Ricky Skinner, sir, I work in your office."

Muspar could feel everyone now looking at him, Bob Scott rolling his eyes a bit, like let's get on with this please. Muspar remembered the kid now, some suckhole they sent over from Social Services. Work placement bullshit.

"Finish up and get out, this is classified Skinner."

"As I was saying," Scott continued, "Mr. Laskin and Ms. Black are taking the lead on this and it's an easy in and out task. The target is John Slaught and his associates, or as the press likes to call them, the Wintermen. I am sure most of you have read about them and are aware of their criminal activity and the threat they pose to security and safety. Your job is to put an end to that. You'll be heading up to the Temiskaming region, there is some Intel that suggests that is where the Wintermen are based." He paused and looked to Mitch, "Ms. Black, just to get to know everyone, do you want to go over the list?"

Mitch swung around, grabbed a chair with her foot, dragged it over and propped her feet up on it.

"Okay gentlemen, there are five of you who have been selected for this mission based on a range of required skills and background. Let's start with Solanski."

A lanky guy, around thirty, sat up wearing a long mournful face under heavy, sloped eyebrows.

"Right here. "

"Alright. You're from the Lands branch, is that right?" Solanski nodded and Mitch kept going, "Okay. Looks like you've got some experience in the backcountry, also some tech background. Good, you'll be backing up Grier."

"Actually, I'm from up there," Ricky Skinner said, leaning forward over his cart, his hand up again.

"Was I speaking to you?" asked Mitch, not bothering to even look up from her file.

"Well, no, but I thought I should let you know…" Ricky started, his face flushing as the guys shifted in their chairs to get a better look at him.

"Skinner? Is that your name?"

"Uh, yes, but…"

"Skinner, get the fuck out. Now." Mitch turned to Muspar. "Get that annoying piece of shit out of my face," she hissed.

Christ almighty. "Skinner," Muspar snapped, "get over to the stock rooms and start packing up all of the gear. Start with the food supplies that are there. Move it."

"Uh," Ricky protested, shoving his glasses back up along his nose, glistening with sweat, "but…"

"Now Skinner!" barked Muspar.

Skinner shuffled out, Muspar watching him go, feeling like giving him a kick in the arse as he passed by, but restraining himself, figured it might look bad in front of the guys.

He heard Mitch start up again.

"Okay, Solanski, make a quick list of everything you think we'll need then run it past Grier before you requisition it, okay?"

"I'm on it." Solanski edged past Laskin who glanced up and nodded, then returned to the file on Slaught.

"Okay, next up is Miller. Miller?"

"That's me. Kyle Miller."

Mitch looked over at the square built guy who was now standing at the back. Heavy set, not overly tall but all dressed up—even his boots were tidy and laced up sharply. Hair cropped tight.

"Some background in neighbourhood surveillance, corporate security. Great. Why don't you get your gear together and drum up a list as well. We're going to need some surveillance, but we've got to be mobile too, okay? Everything ready to go by morning, got it?"

"This is truly an honour. I just want you both to know that," he nodded respectfully. "I've watched Mr. Laskin on I-TIME and I'm a big fan, love the extreme challenges, how he tracks all those perps down when they try and hide out up along the border, it's great stuff."

Laskin didn't bother looking up and Mitch waved Miller out, saying, "Yeah right, Miller. Hope you're as motivated at 4:30 tomorrow morning as you are now."

"Next we have Burke and Leclerc—you guys are Talos, right?"

Muspar hadn't seen these two guys before, but they had Talos written all over them, both sitting at the side, quiet, tidy, non-descript, no bullshit, probably just how Talos liked them, nobody you'd remember, nobody you'd want to meet.

The one guy answered for the both of them said, "Yes Ms. Black, we're all set, gear's loaded and ready to go."

"Alright then gentlemen, check in for supplies and then hit the sack. Okay. Finally, Turner?"

Muspar wondering why the broad was even bothering going through the list, she barely looked at these guys, not seeing Turner smirking at her, a big guy jammed into the desk, eyes all over her.

"Last but not least," he said.

"Right," said Mitch. "You're the real deal, military training, a few stints on Foreign Rotation?"

"That's right, I'm the real deal."

There she was, rubbing her temples, Muspar figuring she was letting the guy know he was making her tired, she said, "Why don't you pull together a nice range of weapons, keep it light, lethal and useful, okay?"

"Want me to find a nice little action for you?"

Mitch looked up, stared at him for a moment, said, "Don't worry about me Turner, I bring my own."

Muspar had no doubt about that.

Mitch caught up with Laskin after she'd done a final check on the route and made arrangements with border security for their passes.

"Hey, thanks for leaving me with the dickwads."

"Mitch darling, you had them eating outta your hand."

She shook her head but accepted his pat on her ass. He could be such a tool. But she'd wasted too many years on men who were either so insecure they were needing to prove themselves all the time, or they were just plain terrified and eventually couldn't handle the relationship. But with Grier it was different. He could be a vicious prick but that was just the way she liked him. After all, everyone needed someone to screw at the end of the day, and he was it for her.

"So, how are things going so far?" he asked.

"We're pretty much loaded up, ready to go. Just have to do the final check."

"Right, I just stopped in, all the guys are there, but that tubbo was in there making life difficult for Solanski."

"Who, that Skinner kid?"

"Yeah, I guess he's, you know, like janitor or something, but he was asking all kinds of questions and shit. Demanding paperwork. Figured I'd butt out and leave that to you, you handle all that stuff better than me. It's the Talos touch."

She wondered what it was today that she didn't handle better than Grier. "Yeah, okay, I'll meet you later."

Making her way down the thin corridor of stairs that led to the storage and loading area, she was thinking that even Grier was beginning to get on her nerves. Lately, he'd been more of self-absorbed than usual. Everyone loved his new I-TIME slot, lots of action and all that risk-taking shit. He was getting off on it himself, told her he'd been thinking of bringing a film crew along on this gig. Imagine, he'd said, shots of him hauling in the Wintermen, people would go fucking mental. Scott had said no, sending Grier off the deep-end, complaining to her it was bullshit, he should try and get some footage anyway, never know how they could use it. She'd told him it seemed like a bad idea.

She found all the guys in the storage area finishing up. She read them the riot act, no booze, no drugs, no pranks and definitely no initiative. Turner gave her a bit of grief but she sent him off pouting. When she was getting ready to go, Ricky Skinner was still hanging around.

"Leave now Skinner, we're shutting down for the night."

Skinner didn't look up at her when he said, "I still have to make sure everything is signed out."

"I said beat it."

His head buried in the big bin behind the counter, Ricky answered something but it was too muffled. Mitch said, "Skinner, you're crapping up my night, okay?"

Ricky straightened up, pushing his glasses back up his nose

and peering through the mesh screen at her. "So you're heading up north tomorrow, eh? I figured you could use my help, I know that country like the back of my hand."

Mitch didn't answer, just stood staring at him. He added, "I'd be a real asset to your team."

He ploughed on. "I really know my way around up there, you might think about, well, maybe, bringing me along, I know lots of people up there, I could help out. My Uncle…"

"Skinner…"

But Ricky was looking excited now, "And Miss Black, well, you'd really like my Uncle and I bet he could help us out."

Mitch moved fast, standing right beside him, Ricky down on his knees looking up at her and her staring down at him. She could see the sweat creeping along his neck and under his glasses, him pushing them back up as they started to slide down his nose, blinking up at her.

"Who told you that you could touch any of the equipment down here?"

"My placement worker. She said I should start taking on more responsibility and Captain Muspar said I could keep things 'ship shape' in the Supply Room—well, that's what he said."

"What is your job here?" Mitch asked.

"I'm on the Custodial Team."

"The Custodial Team?"

"Yeah, that's right…"

"You know what it means to be on the Custodial Team Skinner?"

"Yeah, well, it means I maintain the offices and the yards and stuff."

"No, it means you're a fat piece of shit, and fat pieces of shit don't talk to people like me who are trying to get their work done. Can you understand that?"

She didn't wait for his answer. She threw open the door to the adjoining room where Muspar was talking with a couple of the guys and said, "Get this shithead out of here before I hurt him."

Muspar looked in and saw Ricky standing there. "For godssake Skinner, there's important work going on in here, now beat it, go clean somewhere else."

Mitch watched Skinner scramble out, his face flushed hot. She said to Muspar, "I never want to lay eyes on that little crud again."

Muspar didn't answer her but Turner leaned through the door, giving her a thumbs up, wearing a big shit-eating grin. She smiled back thinly. Christ there was a lot of dickheads in this world.

CHAPTER THREE

"IT'S TAKING HIM TOO LONG."

"Relax Larose. Me, I think Johnny's just pissing around out there, he'll be back."

Harvey Larose and Chumboy were in the workbay, doing some repairs on one of the snowmachines. It used to be the fire hall, a big shell of a building with a grey cement floor and a metal roof that made a steady din when there was sleet or wind. It was another cold one, so they had loaded up the wood boiler that was cracking and snapping in the corner. It wasn't helping. Chumboy had said that Larose's kid, Shaun, should hurry up fixing that goddam generator so they could have some proper heat. Larose explained it wasn't a fucking Tonka truck you could fix with duct tape or glue, but Chumboy said that's how Shaun had fixed it the last time. Larose said maybe that was the problem right there.

Larose said, "He should've been back by now."

"I'm telling you, you're worse than my mother…"

"You ain't got a mother."

"I'm telling her you said that."

Larose saw Chumboy glance out the small rectangle of a window at the deep turquoise sky.

"See?" Larose said. "He's late, okay? Now are we going?"

Chumboy set down the wrench he'd been using. Slaught was a little late, but then sometimes the guy just went off, did as he pleased without checking in or saying where he was going. Chumboy figured Slaught had some demons on his back but never said anything, no point, the guy wasn't exactly a great conversationalist.

Chumboy asked, "Know where he was headed?"

"Said he was headed north, just half hour or so up the line."

"Yeah? What's there? I thought we'd been over that ground way back when."

"Johnny said he thought there might be some cows, believe it or not. Last guy who came in, that Mowat guy, said someone told him a big farm had been there, figured there might still be some animals around."

"The guy said he saws cows?"

Larose shrugged. "That's what he said."

"Must've been into the homemade hooch him, probably just saw a moose."

"The guy was a farmer himself, you know, he said it was a cow. Some of these guys had barns full of hay when they up and left. Cows might have found a way to get it you know."

Chumboy said, "Me, I still think them cows would be ever goddam skinny by now."

"Well anyway, he said he was just going to check it out. Not as though we don't need it, eh? There's more people trailing in here almost every week now. You should hear Tiny griping, says he's going stop being camp cook, no flour, out of salt. Can't keep up. And Christ, did you see that last bunch that came in here, man, that broad must've had ten kids with her."

"Two. There were two kids."

"Yeah, well it seemed like ten, okay?"

"North, eh?"

Larose didn't answer. Chumboy looked outside again. Yeah, Slaught had left early this morning and where he was headed wasn't all that far. They'd put a few big maps up on the wall, sectioned off different areas and had been working their way through them all, seeing what folks had left behind. Now they were doing some backtracking. First time out they had most of what they needed and maybe weren't looking as hard. Now, they were looking hard.

He said, "Okay, let's go find our cowboy."

Chumboy figured it was better to check anyway, you never knew when you went out, you could run into any kind of shit. Last time out, he just missed going toe-to-toe with a wolf, scrawny but big enough, hungry enough too. Usually it was the weather blind-siding you, but it could be anything, some guy going postal, you just never knew. They'd been lucky so far.

Their breath hung in the cold air as they walked from the workbay to the hotel, the snow packed hard underfoot. Inside the main building, a young scrawny guy was sitting behind a table keeping notes on what had been hauled in yesterday. A girl around eight was helping, pulling some pink barrettes off their packaging. In behind them were huge racks and shelves that took up about a third of the big open space that used to be the bar area. It was one of the main storage areas in the place. At the other end, still using the little round red tables along with some big rectangular tables they'd hauled in, was the dining room. Chumboy had said they should keep the formica-topped tables that had been in the bar back in the day, said they must have good juju. A few kids were playing cards back there, laying the cards down on the round, cherry-red tops, and Chumboy could hear Tiny banging around the kitchen behind him.

Chumboy was watching the scrawny guy print painfully slow in the big ledger they kept. He leaned over and tapped his finger on the neat row of printing that said "barrettes, pink."

"I think that's a bit retentive, just keep track of the things we might need, okay? Oh, and let Tiny know we're heading out, should be back in a few hours."

"Hey, where are you guys going?"

"Don't get your shorts in a knot Sylvester, we're just heading out for a bit, going to check up on Johnny."

"Who is left then? Jeff is out, so is Shaun. You can't just leave the place like that. What if something happens?"

Chumboy looked at the kid. Maybe eighteen, skinny as crap. Hair cropped short above his ears.

"Calm down Sylvester. We'll be back just after supper. Nothing's going to happen, nothing ever happens."

"Uh, well okay, I'll keep an eye on things, uh, and, uh, you know, my name is Max."

"Yeah, whatever Sylvester, hold down the fort."

Larose tossed a helmet to Chumboy, said, "Why do you keep calling him Sylvester? It drives him crazy."

"You have to ask? Look at him. That kid ain't no Max. The Road Warrior was a Max. Him? He's a Sylvester."

Chumboy figured they only had a couple of hours before the dark really started to settle in. Already the lean shadows of the birch were reaching out across the snow, the streaks of lime on the aqua sky ebbing away. They headed out, across some farmers' fields, Chumboy picking up Slaught's trail, passing a string of lonely houses with snow drifted up over the front porches, up over the doors of the occasional pick-up truck left behind, up over dog houses and tool sheds. Then into the bush, cross-country over rough trails, taking to the bends and hills, ridges of snow hard-edged and sculpted from the wind.

Finally, there was a cluster of buildings, the neat row of houses surrounded by unbroken snow, and a drift of smoke up through the air over the bigger brick building at the far end. Chumboy moved up and spotted Slaught's sled sitting at the top of the street under a bunch of cedars. He cut his engine, waited for Larose to do the same.

"What's the building Larose?"

"The old town works building I think. Should we scout around the back, see what's up?"

They split up, circled the building and met back by Slaught's machine. Larose said, "All I got were a few dead pick-ups. What'd you get?"

"A school bus and tracks from maybe two sleds."

"Yeah? How old are the tracks."

"Well, I'd say a day or so maybe?"

Larose looked over his shoulder.

"Shit. That doesn't look good."

"Maybe, maybe not. Either way we should be careful, and get a move on."

"So, take the machines in?" Larose asked.

"The place gives me the heebs."

"Is that a yes?"

"I'm not walking in there me, you crazy?" Thinking that was exactly what Johnny had done, walked right in there, couldn't leave the guy alone for an afternoon without some sort of shit hitting the fan.

51

They decided to check out the bus first and then take a look at the set of tracks outside the building. Chumboy headed straight on, Larose skirting around and coming up from the opposite end of the bus.

They came in slow, Chumboy approaching the driver's side, now maybe ten yards away. Larose killed his engine as Chumboy reached behind his seat for his rifle.

Chumboy paused, seeing a set of footprints, almost up to the bus, but then backtracking. Snow was crusted up along the tire wells, drifted up onto the door.

"Looks like school's been out for a while."

Larose nodded, said "Let's hurry, I want to get the hell out of here."

Snow had filled in the bottom of the door and the first step. The door was frozen half open, enough for Larose to pry himself through, which he did.

"Shit. Holy Shit." Larose came backing out of the bus fast, the doors making a grinding sound then popping open.

"What? What is it?" Chumboy asked, but Larose was just staring up into the bus.

Chumboy moved cautiously past Larose and up onto the bus. Christ, it was like Madame fucking Tussauds in there. A scattering of waxen figures throughout the bus, some slumped forward, others leaning against each other in the seats, huddled under blankets. A pair of old guys with some candy wrappers in their laps, scarves bundled around their necks. A lady with tangled knitting stuck to her blue coat with frozen blood sitting behind the driver. He was hunched over the steering wheel. It was coated in red ice. So was the floor below. Chumboy couldn't budge him. Everyone was frozen solid.

"How many?" Larose asked.

"Twenty or so. Looks like most of 'em froze to death far as I can tell. Except the driver, looks like he was shot in the chest, must've splattered on this lady behind him."

Larose said, "Jesus. Anything else?"

"Maybe they tried to start some sort of fire. Some of the seats are scorched and there's ashes back here."

Chumboy climbed down, leaned against the bus, feeling the cold yellow metal through his parka. They'd come across some bodies before, a snowmobiling accident, another looked like a heart attack, but nothing like this. This was messed up.

Larose asked, "How long you think they've been here."

"Hard to tell. Could be a year or so? Maybe longer."

"So you mean the bus was here long before that set of tracks."

"No doubt about it."

Larose said, frowning, "Surprised we missed it, must have always come through here by a different route."

Chumboy nodded towards the building, a mess of tracks leading up to a series of partially broken windows. "Looks like somebody decided to start a party inside."

"Could be trouble."

Chumboy shrugged, "Then dollars to donuts that's where Johnny is."

They headed towards the windows, the snow deep, up over their boots. There was a series of windows, two were cracked, the third smashed through. Chumboy leaned in, jagged, crushed glass along the floor inside. Must've taken a run at the other two windows with no luck. He stood back. "There's no way I'm fitting through this window."

Chumboy backtracked to the door. It looked like who ever had gone in through the window had tried their luck with the door too but couldn't get it open. He looked around and saw a set of tracks

headed around the other end of the building, thinking they probably belonged to Slaught, maybe him trying another way in, worried
about the noise of busting in the doors. Chumboy wasn't worried
about that. He passed his gun to Larose then stepped back, gave
the door a couple of sound kicks—the cracking of ice along the
frame and it flew open.

Larose stepped in first and they made their way across the
open space. Looked like some sort of work area. Chumboy was
already taking inventory. A few plough blades, a truck. Along the
wall some oil cans. Shit, even a couple of generators on the back
of the pick-up. Now that was a find, wondering how they'd missed
this place. But there was crap too, scattered across the floor, some
pink slippers, a big bag of red curlers, a few books.

"Looked like something puked up a yard sale," muttered
Chumboy, pushing a pile with his foot, salt and pepper shakers
shaped like toadstools, a chipped coffee mug, couple issues of
National Geographic. He bent down to grab the issue on top and
then he saw the pair of boots, tucked in beneath the pick up, dead
ahead.

"What a bunch of bullshit, eh buddy?"

Larose looked over, and Chumboy nodded his head towards
the truck. Chumboy figured if the guy was armed, he would've
already dealt with them. He looked questioningly at Larose. Larose
shrugged.

"Hey asshole," Chumboy shouted, "do us a favour, we're cold,
tired, and hungry, come on out with your hands on your head and
let's get this over with, okay?"

Nothing.

He edged his way towards the truck. There was no real way to
get at the guy except straight on. Chumboy easing his way forward
now, shooting a look over at Larose who was on the other side of

the room, staring hard at the truck. "Come on, I'm not going to pulverize you or anything, just come on out slowly so we can have a look at you, okay?"

Larose saw the two-by-two coming down from behind the stack of pallets beside Chumboy, but it happened way too quick to do anything about it.

"Christ," Chumboy yelled, jumping back and away as the board swung down a second time. He could see the stocking feet as he grabbed behind, thinking he couldn't believe the empty boots fooled him, and he reached and caught the edge of a parka. Then the glint of a knife, cutting into his hand, and where the hell was Larose anyway, and the knife fell to the floor as he whacked it with his free hand but then the parka was at him, punching and kicking. Christ, even screaming.

"Larose! What the fuck? Now would be a good time…" but he could see Larose standing there, looking a little stupid, maybe surprised.

"Fuck this," Chumboy said, thinking of the door that this bastard couldn't even kick in, and the fact that he must be a good foot taller than the squirming sonofabitch. He reached up over his shoulder, making contact with what felt like the back of the neck and pulled, but hands came up and dug into his eye. Chumboy yelped and dropped her, "Holy shit, you little witch."

"Screw you," she yelled, slamming her shoulder into his knee as he cradled his eye.

"What are you trying do, blind me?" Chumboy cried, trying to shield his face and grab onto to her coat, and then to Larose yelled, "Ever crazy girl her, get her the Christ off of me."

"I can see it's a crazy girl, Chum, " Larose said, edging forward, but the two were so tangled up now it was hard to get in at them, Chumboy holding onto her snowsuit and her flailing away at him.

"Calm down," Larose barked, "we're not going to hurt you. Just stand still for a goddam minute."

She was yelling too. "Tell him to let go."

"Chum, let her go, just get away from her."

Chumboy flinched as he released her, expecting another round of abuse, and sort of ducked away, but she lost her balance and tipped over, catching herself against the truck. Chumboy turned to face her, rubbing the back of his head. "Jesus," was all he could manage.

She straightened herself and backed up along the truck, asked, "Who are you guys?"

Chumboy was rubbing his shoulder, said, "It's not really you who should be asking the questions here lady, I think maybe you should be saying who you are."

"Susun Latour."

She was slender, probably more like scrawny, dark hair long, blue eyes that were showing fear. Chumboy figured she'd been here a while from the looks of her.

"Chumboy," he said, nodding, "and my paralytic friend over there is Harvey Larose."

Larose was sort of laughing, shaking his head. "That scrawny bastard almost kicked your ass Chumboy."

Chumboy grimaced and ran his hand across his neck. "That hurt man," he said, sounding wounded, turned his attention to Susun, asked, "This your home?"

She said, "My home? Does it look like a home to you?"

"Calm down, it was just a question. It does seem kind of strange you out here in the middle of nowhere, this must the old town works building maybe? Hasn't been open in, oh, a couple of years? So don't try and tell me you were temping here."

"I'm not alone here."

Chumboy said, "So who else is here?"

"Never mind. Why don't you just go now, okay? Leave us alone. We have nothing you want here."

"Might be interested in those generators there," Chumboy said.

"Take them, take them and get out of here, okay?"

"You sure are in a hurry to get rid of me and my good buddy here. Hope that isn't because you beat your last visitor into a bloody pulp with that two-by-two of yours."

"You security?" she asked, sounding unsure, moving back a little along the edge of the truck.

Chumboy snorted in disgust. "Don't think so."

"If you aren't security what are you doing up here."

"There hasn't been security up here in many months lady, and, we could be asking the same of you."

She hesitated. "Are you part of a community?"

"You're asking a lot of questions missy, why not just take us to our buddy, okay? We know he came in here, we saw his tracks."

"Buddy?"

"Yeah, buddy. Lady look …"

"Johnny Slaught's your buddy?" she asked.

"You know Johnny?" Chumboy asked, thinking things were getting a little weird.

She just stared. Chumboy wondered if she was having some sort of breakdown. What were they going to do with her, bring her back with them if she was all psycho? Didn't think they couldn't leave her here though, not out here. Chumboy waved his hand at her, "Uh, hello in there, uh, Susie, still home?"

She didn't say anything, just sort of moved away from him further along the truck towards the cab, breathing hard. Larose asked, "Do you have a man here with you? I mean, other than Johnny."

"He's not a man," she was almost spitting, "he's a coward, a damn pig…"

"Whoa Nellie, what is your problem?" Chumboy said. "Unless you dated the guy back in high school you've only known him for, what? a few hours? That's a lot of abuse for a few hours worth of contact. So just take a deep breath, show me where he is, and since you loathe him so much, I'll be happy to get him outta your hair, okay?"

"Screw off," she said.

"What is your problem lady?" Chumboy threw up his arms. "We gotta get going, it's going to be dark soon. We'll leave you here if we have to…"

"Fine with me, she said, "though I'm surprised you haven't just raped and murdered me already."

"Well, Susie Q, I guess I'm going to have to turn you down on that one, " Chumboy said, then moved forward quick and grabbed her arm, "for now," then quietly, tightening his grip on her arm, "you're going to take me to Johnny."

"No. I won't."

Chumboy looked at her, her staring past him, breathing fast but her face tight, and he said, "Oh screw this," letting her go, picking up the two-by-two, saying to Larose, "let's just look around ourselves, these head games are making me cranky."

"Fine," Larose answered, just as Chumboy saw Susun reach in and grab a 30-06 out of the back of the truck, the woman holding it like she was used it. She had damn big hands.

"Steady now, honey," he said, "no need to get excited. Don't want anyone to get hurt here."

"Yeah right, tell that to the people on the bus."

Chumboy said, "Lady, I've never seen that bus before."

"How stupid do you think I am, I know you killed those people."

"Killed them? I don't think so."

58

"I know all about you guys. You and your buddy Slaught there, you're the Wintermen."

Chumboy said he'd heard that some people called them that but he wasn't sure what that had to do with anything. He was watching her, she was pale, looked like she could hardly breath, hands holding onto the rifle like she was being pulled up out of the ice with it.

"Just take it easy, okay?"

"You think I should take it easy? I think I should kill you both, right now."

"Listen Susun, you have the wrong idea about us."

"I was here before. In this very place, that's how I know."

Chumboy figured it must've been some time ago, maybe during the evacuations.

"Know what? When were you here?"

"I came down with Operation Clean Sweep, was one of the last ones out because I had some nursing training. We were loaded onto a bus with lots of older people, most of them sick. We were headed to North Bay, but had to pull in here because our driver was sick too. It was already dark, big moon up in the sky, and it was weird, there was nobody around. There was smoke coming out of the chimney, but no one around. The driver was sort of peering out the window, trying to see, and then all hell broke loose, these big dark snowmachines were everywhere, their lights shining into the bus, blinding us, we couldn't see anything, and then the doors popped open, some guy jumps in and grabs the keys out of the ignition, shoots the driver, jams the door. Then they were gone. It took like, what, five minutes? Well, by the time anyone got there late the next day, they were surprised to find some of us alive. They told us that it had been the Wintermen, that you'd come through, stole all the sleds and gasoline, left us to freeze to death. Real tough guys aren't you?"

"Okay, Susun, I don't know who told you that, but it's bullshit, that whole Wintermen thing isn't real, it's just, like one of those urban legend things."

"That right? It looked real to me."

"No, I'm telling you," Larose said, "it's made up. We're a community, you know, just trying to make a go of it. Trying to start over up here."

"Just shut up, okay?"

"You gotta listen to me, we have a place, a big place, with families and old folks too, just up the road, in Cobalt. After the government pulled out, well, some of us decided to stay. Johnny was the one who pulled it all together, who stood up for us. We've been hanging on ever since. You could come with us. Be honest, if you were going to shoot us, you would've done it by now."

"You know, I'm getting tired of you. I've had a long day and I got more important things to deal with than you two. I'm done with you guys."

Larose said, "Whoa there, hang on a minute, don't be doing anything crazy."

"Hey Susun, where you from?" Chumboy asked, suddenly conversational.

"What?"

"You're a Latour right? You one of those Latours from Marter Township?"

"Maybe."

"You know Tiny Latour?

She frowned, holding tight to the gun.

"What?"

"Tiny, you know him?"

"Yeah, I know him, he's my cousin."

"Wanna have dinner with him tonight? He's cooking."

Chapter Four

Tiny was holding court in the kitchen, bare-chested under the white apron, the only way he could cook. "I cook the way I cook, got a problem with that?" was his reply when questioned about it.

"Hot as a mother in here when I get going," he said, more of an announcement than an invitation to converse. "I think we need to get some sort of fan over this rig," he said to Chumboy. He was at the far end of the kitchen, turning a full pig on a spit.

"Ever scrawny, that pig," Chumboy said, pulling up a chair across from Susun.

Tiny said, "What d'ya expect, thing's been rooting around eating birch bark and moss."

"Hope it doesn't end up tasting like birch bark Tiny."

"Fuck you Chum, I can make anything taste sublime."

Chumboy looked at Susun. "Your cousin is one touchy fellow.

He should consider himself lucky to be cooking in this kitchen. This place used be one fine hotel, was a classy joint back in the day, the old Fraser Hotel."

She managed a smile but didn't say anything, just looking at him with those navy blue eyes.

He tried, "So Susie, how'd you sleep? Seems to me you must've been at it for a good fourteen hours or so. "

She said she slept okay.

"Well then," said Chumboy, "now that you're all rested up, why don't you tell us your story?"

"Maybe some other time. It's a long story."

Chumboy shrugged, "Time is one thing we got here."

He watched her nod slowly, looking around. She'd said she didn't remember too much about what had happened, so he'd told her that she'd passed out, told her it was because she'd been eating all that canned boy-are-dee shit for so long. Told her a big slab of roast pig was just what she was needing and she'd lucked out cause that's just what was on the menu.

"Where'd you get that thing," she asked, nodding her head towards the pig.

Tiny laughed.

"You wouldn't believe the things they bring me in here to cook. Christ almighty, the first week here, they dragged in a goddam horse!"

Susun winced but Chumboy said, "Hey, a man's gotta do what he's gotta do, but as it turns out, the horse had other ideas. He's running the logging crew now, sleeps in the back of our workbay."

"I've served some fine meals in this joint," Tiny told her. "But unfortunately, I gotta rely on these morons. That Slaught bastard, he was supposed to bring me a cow."

"Hey, come on Tiny, he brought you a family reunion instead."

"Big fucking deal, can't eat a family reunion."

Chumboy refilled her cup with a dark looking tea, nudging her in the back as he passed. "Hey girl, look lively, this is some kind of swell place you've landed yourself in. Lot better than that pigsty you came from. Your other ladies seem to like it, settling in just fine."

"Grace is just happy to be some place safe with her baby and Mary just wanted a real bed."

"Ah, come on now," Chumboy persisted, "so how about this joint, ain't it special?"

The joint looked like maybe it had seen better days. The kitchen itself was impressive enough, huge stove, lots of stainless steel counter space, but the paint was peeling off the walls and the metal railings along the ramp down into the kitchen were nicked and going from the pale green towards rust. Along the railing, laundry hung drying. Had the feel of some sort of decrepit ship.

"Nice enough set-up," she said.

"Retrofitted for revolution," Chumboy responded.

"Revolution? All I see is a bunch of wet long johns and an industrial strength kitchen."

"Yeah, well get any of us boys in those long johns, then you'll see industrial strength."

Susun asked what they all did with their industrial strength, because from the stream of people in and out of the kitchen, it seemed to her that tea drinking was the number one occupation.

"Nice talk from the new guest." It was Slaught, coming into the kitchen, limping a bit. There were a few welts along the side of his face.

"Guest? More like prisoner," she said.

"You are one ungrateful lady."

"Don't mind her 'Winterman,'" Chumboy said, winking at Susun, "she's just grumpy. Needs some serious beauty sleep, her."

"Ungrateful?" Susun asked, but Slaught just ignored her, pulled up a chair beside her and said, "Grumpy or not, everyone pulls their weight around here," starting in on her right away, "and you should think over what it is you want to contribute to our little community. Mary, who I might add has a far better attitude than you, says she is going to fix up the infirmary. The new mother said she's willing to pitch in as soon as she gets her baby settled. Now you got some skills in that department, so maybe you should get down there and lend a hand."

She looked across at him, sitting there laughing at her because at first he'd thought maybe she was a doctor, and she'd said, no, she was a midwife. Like a nurse, then? No, a midwife, and he said she better get her certificate up on the wall then because people weren't going think she was official, and she told him she didn't have a license to practice midwifery and he said "for fuck's sake." She told him that it was the way it used to be, before the government took over and started making rules and restrictions. She was going back to the old ways. Women used to just train each other, told him she'd learned from the daughter of a back to the land type called Mae Mullins. He said that figured, with a name like Susun. She asked what the hell that was supposed to mean, and he said, "I pegged you for some messed up hippie the minute I saw you."

Now he was sitting there, looking at her expectantly, like he was saying, yeah so what can you do, and it was making her flustered. She figured it was all about her putting the boots to him.

"Are all you revolutionaries celibate?"

Slaught cocked his head, catching Chumboy's eye. Chumboy just shrugged. Tiny said, "For fuck's sake Susie, don't be so goddam belligerent."

Slaught said, "I was looking for more of a 'I can clean the toilet' kind of offer."

"Listen," Susun said, "just because it's the end times doesn't mean that your ladies can't get pregnant. You'll be needing me soon enough, what with all that industrial strength in your long johns and all."

Ricky had slept through the alarm clock again and had to rush into work. He'd wanted to get up and see the team off, wanted to really badly, but he'd gone and slept in. Figures he could mess up just about anything, least that's what the Captain was always telling him. Right now, though, the Captain was telling him what a lousy job he'd done in the storage sheds, telling him he was being reassigned to office duty.

"In my office," he said, like it was a threat. Ricky thought the Captain had a pretty nice office, it had a big couch and everything, but he liked being down in the storage area. People left him alone and he could listen to the radio.

"Is it 'cause of her?"

The Captain, sounding annoyed, asked, "Her? Who?"

"That Miss Black. She hated me."

Muspar looked at Ricky and said, "No bloody wonder, now move your ass and get upstairs Skinner, before I really lose my patience with you. Police Services cooperates with work support only when you can actually do the work. We're not a goddam charity."

When they were on the way up, with Ricky huffing to keep up with the Captain, the Captain turned on the stairs and told Ricky that he was going to have to do some filing for him this afternoon and Ricky said, "Captain, that's girls' work," which made the Captain get mad again and say, "Yeah, well that's why you're doing it Skinner."

Ricky didn't say anything after that until they got up to the office and the Captain showed him a stack of brown files and Ricky asked, "How do I file these? Haven't ever done it before."

"You don't have to Skinner, I'm keeping it nice and simple for you, just check to make sure every file in this pile has a match on the computer. See, the names are written on them, I'm backing everything up and want to make sure I've got everything covered, know what I'm saying?"

Ricky said, "Uh, yeah, I got it."

"Sure you do, you'll probably screw it up as soon as I leave." With that the Captain slammed his big hand down on the biggest pile of folders. "These ones. Right here. Match them to the list right there in the computer. They go by name and number, it's simple. And when you're done that, put on a fresh pot of coffee."

"But doesn't Miss Saxon do that?"

The Captain stopped in the doorway and turned. Ricky involuntarily took a step back.

"Stop with the damn questions, okay Skinner?"

"Sure thing, Captain."

Ricky decided to put the coffee on first because there were so many files he thought it would take him all day, and then the Captain would be mad that there was no coffee. He thought that was a good decision and the Captain had told him he couldn't make a good goddam decision to save his soul. Well, maybe now the Captain would see that he could. Then maybe he'd get to go out on a mission. Or even get posted to one of the border stations, as a watchman or patrol guy or something. That would be the perfect thing, sitting up there at the edge of the City, with a walkie-talkie and those big, heavy flashlights. Then he'd be able to see his Uncle Delbert.

Ricky sure missed his Uncle Delbert. Delbert had moved into their house after Ricky's dad had run off to Florida with a woman who had rented a cabin down the road where all the fancy cottagers stayed. The woman had a silver motor home and an orange tan. Ricky hadn't liked her and Uncle Delbert had once called her a whore and told Ricky that word was from the Bible. He had also called his dad a bad seed.

He wondered if he could sit on the couch while he sorted through the files but then decided that was a bad idea. He moved all the files to the extra desk beside the computer and stood as he placed a file down and then checked the list on the computer, making a little check mark on the list like the Captain had shown him when he'd said, "Better show you how to do this or you'll screw it all up royally."

Ricky had been at it for over an hour, double-checking everything just to be sure, when he noticed a big file box on the desk beside where he was working. It was labeled "Zone 6." That was the Territories. That's where the mission was going, way up to the Territories, up where his Uncle Delbert lived. Where the Wintermen lived.

Chapter Five

Susun had decided to check in on Melinda. She found Melinda and Mary both up and busy with the baby. Mary seemed very happy, whispering to Susun, 'There's some hot looking fellas here," and then saying the new mama and baby seemed to be doing fine.

The young mother was cuddled up with her baby, said it was funny to be staying in a hotel, said her man Will would think it was funny too if he were there, said she couldn't wait to get a message to him, telling him to come find her in Room 25 at the Fraser Hotel.

She was down a long hallway of rooms at the very end, a big window looking out on the street below. She'd told Susun maybe when she was feeling better the three of them could open up across the street, pointing to the solid looking storefront with a worn sign announcing it as a Gem Shop, snow drifted up over the bottom of the big windows. She said they could have something like a healing centre, and maybe she could start sewing diapers, things like that, said right now she was having to use pieces of old bed sheets for baby Grace and they weren't working out too good. Maybe put a little potbelly stove in the store, could be cute, she said.

Susun checked Melinda's stitches. They seemed to be healing up okay, but still looked a bit sore. Susun said she'd go see what she could find to help with the healing process, heading back downstairs to find Tiny.

He was in the kitchen, complaining to Chumboy that the last batch of flour was so stale it was probably from back in the day when Cobalt was a fucking boomtown. Susun said she hoped he had something a little fresher in the way of some healing herbs, did he have any comfrey kicking around? Tiny asked what she was talking about, comfrey, what the crap was that? She half smiled. It was good to hear Tiny, been years since she'd seen him. But it was also almost too normal all of a sudden, after things had been so messed up for so long.

Tiny said, "Don't have nothing called comfrey here. You were always into that witchy stuff."

She sighed, and seeing Slaught walking into the kitchen said, "You really got to start growing some medicinal plants here," and Slaught said, "That right? Well feel free to get right to it. That's how things get done here, you do it yourself."

"It could help a lot of people, you have a lot of old folks, we could start growing some plants for teas and medicines, you're going to run out of drug stores to rip-off soon enough, and then what are you going to do?"

He was about to answer but then paused, thinking about it, thought she was probably right, said, "Never really thought about that. I think Chum's Auntie knows about that stuff, we could ask her." She said anytime he was ready, just to let her know and she'd sit down and give him a list. He said he was sure she would, but he was a little more interested in how she was going to help out now.

She said not to worry, she was headed outside soon, going to get some cedar for tea.

"Outside for some cedar?" Slaught asked.

"If you're going to be out here depending on the land, you might as well be using it properly."

"Amen Susie," Chumboy said, turning to Slaught. "Johnny, I think this lady is going to teach you a thing or two."

Slaught could see her watching him, she had a habit of rubbing the back of her neck, and she was doing it now, maybe still tired, maybe still pretty shook up. He wondered if he was being too hard on her. "No doubt you're going to try," Slaught said to her, "but for now school's out, got work to do."

She said, "I think maybe you're too angry to learn anything. Anger blocks your positive energy, shuts your mind down."

"That right?"

"Yeah," she said, "that's right."

He asked, "So what am I so angry about?"

She smiled, he realized he hadn't seen her smile yet, and it was nice, standing close enough to her to see the lines around her eyes, and she said, "That I kicked your ass yesterday."

He heard the guys beside him laugh, felt a little pissed off as soon as she said it, but she was looking at him and still smiling. It was a no win. He said, "You might be on to something there, think I might try to get my positive energy going as I work on those generators. Give my wounded a ego a chance to recover."

"You do that Winterman," she said, and he could feel her watching him go. Well, maybe he handled that okay after all.

Susun turned and looked over at the bunch of guys still sitting around one of the big tables. "Is that all you guys do, sit around, waiting for your revolution?"

"Revolution's waiting on us Susie," Chumboy said.

Larose asked if she needed anything. She said menstrual pads and diapers and he said, "Uh, well, I'll see Johnny about that."

She shrugged, said, "See whoever you like, but I could use some curtains too, something for some privacy."

Larose told her in the spring they were thinking of taking over a few of the nearby houses, fixing them up again and moving some of the families into them. Like the suburbs, Chumboy offered. Tiny said he wasn't moving to no goddam suburbs, was going to keep sleeping in his kitchen. Guarding his stash.

"So you don't have any herbal teas in that stash of yours Tiny?"

"Herbal teas? You gotta be kidding."

"I'll ask my Auntie, she'll have some of that brew around," Chumboy said.

"Mr. Winterman mentioned your Auntie, she a healer?"

"My Auntie Verla, she knows it all, more than a healer, you want to talk industrial strength, she's one industrial strength spiritual woman."

"Well, I'd love to meet her if she's around."

"Every now and again she shows up. When she's ready. But in the meantime Susie, why don't you tell us how you and your female tribe ended up back at your bus stop, figure it wasn't nostalgia brought you there."

Susun said there wasn't much to tell. Said she'd been down working in the Talos greenzone, said it was called that because of all the greenhouses they were running there. "During the evacuation, anyone with any kind of nursing training was kept back at the border to help out, a lot of really stressed out people were coming through, as you can imagine. Half of the people were saying they hadn't wanted to leave, but there they were, bus after bus, medications left behind, people halfway through medical treatments, it was chaos. So I stayed, but by the time the evacuations had slowed down, there weren't any places down in the City. I was just as glad, it sounded like a madhouse down there, so I took work at the greenhouse and stayed. They put us all up in motels, dorms, whatever they could find. It was crap, but everything was crappy, so what difference did it make?"

"Something made a difference or you'd still be there."

"Well, yeah, I met Melinda. She was working at the greenhouse, so was Mary. I found out Mary had been apprenticing as a midwife when Melinda told us she was having a baby. Said she'd become separated from her man during the evacuations. They'd wanted to stay, told Talos they were fine, we're going to give it a go with some other folks. Talos wasn't having it. Talos orderd her guy Will to help with the evacuations and she had a choice of the greenzone or the City. She opted for the greenzone."

She stopped, thinking something over, rubbing the back of her neck and frowning.

Chumboy asked her if she was okay, but she was just staring, like she was playing something over in her head. "Susie?"

"I just can't believe I was so stupid, never thinking it was Talos who had ambushed our bus."

"Some things are pretty hard to believe though, Susie."

"It doesn't make any sense though, why would some big corporation bother killing a bunch of old people. It's crazy."

Chumboy went over and took her by the arm, pulled out a chair, said, "Susie, think you better sit down, you don't look so good."

"I remember him, the guy on the bus, his body bent over the steering wheel, I wasn't going to look when we got back in there the other day, but I couldn't help it. Part of me wasn't really even sure it had actually happened, that we'd been shut up in that bus like that. But then there he was, the driver, slumped over, just like the day they killed him."

Chumboy said, "Probably thought the bunch of you were just dead weight, more of a strain on the resources."

Susun nodded slowly, said, "We came back because Melinda was looking for Will, her boyfriend, Gracie's dad. When Will left to help with the evacuations, Melinda told us they'd agreed that if something went wrong, if he had trouble getting back to the green-zone, that they'd head back to her family farm, meet up there. She was sure he was waiting there for her. She wanted to have her baby up here and was making plans to get out, been saving her money. She was getting pretty desperate. Mary and I figured she might try to leave on her own to find him. Seemed wrong to let her take that chance on her own, so we pooled our money, the three of us, and headed back up here. The trip sent her into early labour, so I went to the one place I knew there was a big wood boiler and probably some supplies left behind. And so that's where you found us."

"Pooled your money for what, you couldn't exactly pick up a bus ticket home?"

"No, of course not, got a couple of sleds on the black market. You can find them, especially if you're up in the border zone, you get to know people, hear things. I figure you guys are using black market gas, right?"

"We steal some, but yeah, mostly black market."

She just nodded, looking tired of talking.

Chumboy asked, "Quite the risk, your mom and her fella, deciding to make a go of it farming now, with the snow. Did they have a plan?"

"She just wanted to get out of there. Guess they were willing to take their chances."

"And you, were you planning on going back?"

Susun shook her head, said she hadn't even thought about what she was going to do, said she couldn't think, not then and not now. Said she didn't understand anything anymore.

"Look Susie, you've been through a lot, maybe it's time for some more shut eye. Things will look better in the morning."

"I just got up."

There was that awful flat voice again, Chumboy could almost watch the energy draining out of her face and the hardness creeping in. He said, "If you need to sleep, you need to sleep. Probably making up for a month's worth of sleep deprivation."

She nodded, said maybe he was right, started out of the room moving slow, like it took effort to lift each foot. Chumboy, watching her go, said, "I'm worried about that girl Tiny."

"Don't be. Tough as nails, all the Latour women are."

"I thought you said your mother was all sweetness and light."

"She fucking had me didn't she?"

"This sucks."

Turner was bellyaching again, said they were wasting their time. Laskin was feeling generous, though, so he was ignoring him, just glad to be out on the trail. It was reminding him of the time he had been in Alaska back in the day, before everything went to shit and snow wasn't exotic anymore. He'd been there racing dog teams for some lame-ass charity thing. What a rush though. And he scored some not so bad northern tush too.

"Turner, it's just part of an overall strategy. You're getting all messed up by the details, just do your job and trust in the big picture, okay?"

They'd headed out early that morning, driving up through the security corridor with their snowmachines and gear loaded on the back of the truck. It wasn't the first time Laskin had made the trip up to the border, but it never failed to freak him out, bombing up the single highway edged by giant snow banks, no real traffic except for Talos vehicles, not like the old days when it could take you two hours just to get onto the main highway leaving the city. Even though the amalgamated City was now four times the size it had been before the crisis, it took no time at all to clear the final edge of it and be on the lonesome highway headed north. Miller had asked him if he thought the summers would ever come back and Laskin said who the fuck cared, he couldn't even remember what summer was like. Miller said he loved summers and Laskin had said he guessed that was too fucking bad for Miller then.

Once at the border of the territories, they did a quick equipment check and then sent Solanski and the Talos boys up ahead towards Temiskaming to break trail. The rest of the team had left a couple hours later, Laskin saying they were lucky to have a hard cold day. They'd met the others up at an old hydro dam not far from the targeted area, crossing over the top of the dam to where Solanski had already set up camp in the shelter of the pumphouse. Turner had asked why they were camping outside when there was a whole fucking town sitting right there for the picking, and Solanski had said it had creeped him out when he went to a couple of houses and the doors were locked, like the people thought they would be coming back, said it wasn't that much warmer inside the buildngs anyway.

Laskin was now in his tent, thinking about having Mitch in soon, maybe she'd be into warming him up some before they hunkered down for the night. Turner was still fussing with his tent, pouting and cursing way too much. Laskin figured it had been a while since the big boy had been camping. The Talos guys, as usual, had checked their gear, got their tents up, and were now getting ready to turn in. They were like fucking robots if you asked him. He could see Miller and Solanski up at the fire, had it going good, maybe he'd go out for a while and warm up there. Bond with the boys, then see what kind of a mood Mitch was in.

He got bored pretty quick making small talk with Miller so he headed up the trail, finding Mitch in one of her 'am I the only one doing any work around here' moods. Bent over her machine, she didn't even look at him when he gave her bottom a friendly tap.

"Do you mind, I'm working."

He liked that, her being all official in front of the boys.

"Sorry ma'am."

She straightened up to look at him. He was standing too close, so she pushed him back a bit. All she said was, "You should be."

Laskin, trying again, "Nice handiwork," nodding towards the machines, "pretty convincing looking."

She looked at the machine too, all outfitted with the brand new decals, a big yellow circle with a happy face and "Park Warden" written in hunter green along the outside. "That's us, keeping the tree and bees safe. I got Miller to stitch the badges onto our parkas and I switched all the gear so it's standard issue."

"You've been busy babe," Grier said, now wanting her to warm up to him badly, seeing her there, all kind of pissed off, those long legs now straddling the machine as she slapped the decal on the far side of the hood.

She finished smoothing the decal on and turned back to face him, crossing her arms, smiling now, whispered, "You know the rules boss, no fraternizing when we're on a job." Smiling more, "It's bad for the other boys' morale."

"But I don't really give a shit about their morale."

"It's your job to care Grier." And then showing him she was being playful, said, "We could take a quick recon. I've never done it in the snow."

By the time Mitch and Grier got back, the sky was going from violet to dark blue and the three men were hunkered down around the fire. Grier figured the Talos boys were tucked in for the night. Seemed like Turner had been doing more bitching because the sound of his big voice died off quick when they walked up to the fire.

"Boys." Grier said, pulling off his mitts and rubbing his hands by the fire.

"So? See anything out there? Tracks?" asked Solanski, the other two just staring into the fire.

"Snowmachine tracks everywhere, they definitely aren't in stealth mode. Nothing too recent though, so we still have the element of surprise."

"We gonna need it?" It was Turner asking, all big and leaning into the fire, face red from the heat. He added, "What's with all this cat and mouse bullshit anyway, we're just going to go in and blow the guy away, right?"

"You always need the element of surprise," Laskin said, "plus we need a cover story, we're in deep ops guys, we need to have a legit reason for being here, you never know what kind of questions are going to get asked and by who. So just stick to the script Turner, and stop thinking so much, it isn't good for you."

Mitch interrupted. "Okay boys, let's shut it down, we got an early morning."

The men got up, tending to the fire and tidying up the area, checking things over one last time. Laskin grabbed a lantern and headed towards his tent. He was bending through the flap his tent when he heard her say, "Lights out muchachos. I'll see you all at 5:00 a.m. sharp."

He thought about her back in the snow, him pushing her up against a big birch tree, her saying the snowsuits weren't going to work out for what he had in mind. He'd seen her expression, said, yeah, it's awkward, but you could do me, that'd be nice. He was starting on his zipper, but she'd grabbed his hand, said "Don't think so sweetie, but first chance we get, I think it's my turn." Man, was she keeping score? She better not be, he thought, she was lucky to even be in the game.

Susun woke up with a start, sitting right up in her bed, disoriented. She pried open her eyes, dried and gummy. The light coming through her small window was soft and grey, she figured it must be morning. Another entire day gone, she couldn't believe how much she was sleeping. She thought immediately of Melinda, but then relaxed, Mary was around, she'd make sure the mom and baby were doing fine.

She dragged herself out of bed. The jeans lying at the end of her bed were stained, the bottoms coated with a rim of mud. She dressed anyway and headed downstairs.

Chumboy was just leaving the kitchen when she came in, said he was glad to see her, hoped she was feeling a bit better and that Tiny had made a great breakfast for a change. Tiny told him he was a bastard and that all of his breakfasts were great, then asked Susun if she wanted to start with a hot cuppa.

Susun said, "How about a shower instead? Is that possible?"

Chumboy said, "Sure thing, right at the very back of the building, we took some old boiler room or something, knocked out a wall or so, planning on putting in a multiple shower and laundry room at some point but for now we have to share the one, use it for more storage too. Anyway, we got a schedule for it but nobody follows it. Just don't climb in with that bastard Larose, last girl who did that went blind."

She managed a smile but it wasn't convincing. "Yeah, just still feeling a little grungy from that place, know what I mean?"

"Sure, no worries girl, Tiny, toss your cuz a towel. Should find the other stuff you need already there."

"Rights, thanks."

She found the maintenance room easily enough—the lime green cardboard sign announcing 'shower' tacked to the door. She knocked, heard nothing and peeked in. Looked empty, a very large room with one of those big tubs, a workbench stacked with soap, toilet paper, and shampoo. Part of their booty she guessed. She locked the door behind her and checked out the shower, baffled at first by the set up but desperate enough to try anything. And it was narrow, must have been rigged up over the janitor's washout area. She climbed in, wondering how a big guy like that Slaught could fit in here, thinking it might not be so bad to see him try. Then thinking she had better get her brain under control, the guy was a jerk.

The first surge of hot water hit her. She soaped herself up then stuck her face up into the water, just standing, eyes closed, trying not to think, feeling the water pour over her. The water was warm, almost hot. Pouring down over her shoulders, down her back, Christ, could anything feel so good?

"Hey, lady, you going to be in there all morning? You know it takes some time to get the next tub of water heated."

The voice startled her. Shit, it was him. She wondered if she had fallen asleep on her feet, feeling out of it, like she'd lost all track of time. All track of herself.

"Lady, hey, I'm talking to you." He knocked on the door again.

"Well, my name is Susun, okay?" She was shouting, not sure if he could hear her over the water.

"Okay, fine, Su-sun, get outta there, you're draining the goddam lake."

She reached up and shut off the hose. That had sure felt good. She hadn't had a real shower in ages. And it had almost been a real shower, better than the lake, but not quite the Travelodge. She wondered if there still were Travelodges. It was freezing in the room now though, and she was immediately shivering.

"Give me a minute, okay? Believe it or not this is my first taste of civilization. I haven't even been in here that long."

"It's been over thirty minutes."

"I don't think so." There was no way it was more than five or ten minutes, at the most.

"I timed you. 36 minutes."

She padded over to grab a towel, leaving wet marks on the floor. Over a half hour? Was that possible? She rubbed her head. It still hurt, ached all over. And she was so cold.

"You timed me?"

There was a silence, then he said, "Well, listen, I'll be back later, since you need more time."

"What else would you do, just stand out there?"

She didn't listen for an answer, rushing to dry herself off as best she could. She was rushing, hopping on one foot as she tried to pull on her jeans. She stopped, staring down at the ragged bottoms of the jeans, muddied and stuck half way up her still damp legs. Then she crumpled down on the wet concrete floor and started to cry.

"How long has she been in there?"

There was a small group gathered outside the door. Slaught was leaning his forehead against the metal door. It was nice and cool. He checked his watch and said, "About forty minutes. After the shower."

Larose asked Slaught, "Can you hear anything in there?"

Slaught looked over at Larose and just shook his head.

"So, are we worried yet?"

Chumboy said, "Nah, I once had a girlfriend shut herself up in the can for five hours."

Larose asked, "Yeah?"

"Yeah. I mean I tried for the first while but, come on, it just gets silly."

"So how'd you get her out?"

"I didn't. After the five hours I just packed up my stuff and moved out. Could still be in there for all I know."

"Thanks for that Chumboy," said Slaught, moving away from the door and rubbing his forehead. Christ, his head was still hurting. And his goddam ribs were aching from the way she'd whaled on him. "But that's not really an option right now. Maybe somebody should get one of the ladies to help us get her out. Maybe get Mary."

Larose pressed his ear up against the door. "Can't hear anything. Did you try calling to her?"

"Of course, feel free to try if you want."

"We didn't store any of our booze in there did we?" asked

Chumboy, sounding panicked. That was the hardest thing to find, and the homemade stuff just did not cut it come Friday nights.

"No Chum, we didn't. Nuthin' in there but except soap and asswipe," offered Max coming down the hall, "and it's asswipe I need for the toilets up front."

Chumboy said, "I just put toilet paper up there, man, those kids, they go through the stuff like it was gummy worms."

Slaught could feel the stiffness in his neck. What the fuck? Break down the door? He guessed so.

"Max, go get the gooseneck, we're gonna bust in. I mean she could have fainted right?"

Max looked skeptical. "That's what we're going tell her, we thought she fainted?"

"Unless you have a better plan, then yeah, that'll have to do."

It took a good six attempts prying with the gooseneck and them taking turns booting the door to bust the latch on the inside. Slaught cursed Larose who had put the goddam thing on in the first place, asking him if he'd been expecting a fucking invasion. "Not doing a job if it isn't done right. Don't like it, ask somebody else next time," he'd sniffed.

So when the door finally flew open at the count of three, Larose was still sulking and Slaught was wondering about checking all the latches in case another 'situation' developed, so it took a few seconds for them to realize the room was empty. Not a trace of her.

"Goddam me, that is the second time that woman has messed with my head."

Chumboy looked over at Larose, eyebrows raised. "Me, I think that sounds like love in Johnny's voice."

Slaught was staring up at the open vent on the wall. "No, its madness Chumboy, fucking madness."

"Not much difference Johnny."

Larose said, "I can't believe she did this, is it even possible to get anywhere through those vents? Are they even big enough?"

Chumboy peered up into the vent, said, "Worked for those guys getting out of Alcatraz. Also, this is a serious mother of a building, vents are nice and roomy, plus it is a short, straight run from inside to the hallway by the doors."

"You guys take a look around here, I'll check the kitchen," Slaught said, "maybe she pulled a Houdini then went to see Tiny. Chum, her room and the new mom's. Larose, could you fix the goddam door? And it's a fucking shower, not a fort."

They met up in the kitchen, Slaught was already there, asking Tiny if knew what a pain in the ass his cousin was. Tiny said his mom has always talked well of Susun's family and weren't all women a pain in the ass anyway.

"Is there a chance of getting any tea in here?" asked Chumboy, coming in with news that she was not in her room, but her few belongings still were.

Slaught was wondering if maybe they should have been more careful with her. She could cause a lot of trouble if she wanted to. He asked, "Anything in her room to help explain this bullshit?"

"Death by herbal tinctures is what awaits us gentlemen," Chumboy scooping two big loads of sugar into his cup.

"Any ideas of where she might be?"

"Melinda said maybe she just needed a 'time out' to get her head together. Said she held it together all through the shit that went down, maybe she just unraveled a bit."

Slaught thought about that. "Climbing into a vent? I don't know, most people just go for a walk. Maybe we could send Sylvester up into the vent to see if he can tell where she went?"

"Think he's too heavy," Chumboy said.

"Maybe one of the kids?"

"Can't do that—the mother would kill us."

"But what if she does something crazy? Like sets a fire in there?"

"Why would she do something like that? She's just upset," Tiny snapped, slopping coffee on the table as he refilled their cups.

Slaught thought the coffee smelled good. Raising his cup he said, "Not your usual crap Tiny."

"That bastard Laurent brought some of the real stuff in the other day. So, yeah thanks, guess I'll take that as a compliment."

"You do that Tiny, and while you're at it, why don't you give some thought to what your nutjob cousin might be up to?"

Tiny was looking at Slaught now a bit differently, noticing the tone of his voice. "Hey Johnny, I don't think it means anything, you know, I think she's just flipped out. Think of what she's been through. She just did what she had to do, know what I mean, she's kind of like that."

"Kinda like what exactly?"

"Well you know, headstrong. Always has been, you know, come to think of it, I think she ran a way a few times when we were kids, I remember once we had to go down and look along the Blanche River there, her mom thought she might have thrown herself in or something. We all had to go, all of us kids, me, Jimmy, Louie, my Dad's uncle's son Cliff, yeah that's right, even my Grandpa came down to help look. We looked till it was too dark to see. Christ, I remember the bugs were bad that night."

"So?" prompted Chumboy.

"So? She showed up the next afternoon. Had six walleye, nice sized ones too. Had a good fish fry that night."

"It always come back to food with you Tiny."

"Chumboy, it always comes back to food or women, and food is just easier."

Slaught was thinking that Tiny was right about that. He could still see her, face just stony, eyes almost black, putting that boot into him, and then winding up and doing it again. She'd been pissed, that was for sure.

Chumboy said, "You know guys, she could get herself into trouble."

Chumboy was wondering why they didn't hear her moving in the vents. She must have popped down somewhere pretty close by, could even be stuck. Maybe they should go figure out where that vent came out. "Hey Johnny, I know you're still smarting over her getting the drop on you, but she may not be thinking too clearly. Could head off…"

"How? Walk out of here, there's nowhere to go guys. I say maybe we ignore her, forget about it, she'll get tired of pouting up in the vent right around suppertime when that pig is hitting the plates."

"I don't think she's going to be joining us for supper boys, sad to say," announced Larose as he rounded the back corner of the kitchen.

"Why's that?" Slaught was already up on his feet. Thinking the worst. Maybe she'd fallen, suffocated, Christ, they hadn't had a death yet, he wasn't sure how'd they handle it. Have a funeral?

"Looks like the little witch took off by sled. Took the vent just over to the next room, kicked out the cover, it was just sitting in there anyway, then down the hall, outside and off she went. I give her about at least a twenty minute head start by now."

Slaught grabbed his coat from the back of the chair. "I'm going to grab my gear. Chumboy, get your skates on, if we take my sled and Tiny's we might be able to catch her. She can't know too much about the lay of the land here, there is nothing but trouble waiting for that girl. Larose, mind making sure my tank is filled up, it's close to empty after yesterday."

"Don't worry about it, Johnny," Larose said with a wink, "I'm sure she filled it up nice and full before she rode out on it. You can borrow mine. Oh, and grab a coat, she took your parka too."

—

"Hey Larose, you ready yet?"

Slaught was wanting to get going, couldn't understand why it was taking Larose so long to get it together. Chumboy was still drinking his coffee, not too wound up either.

"You know Johnny, you gotta learn to relax."

"That so?" Slaught was feeling anything but relaxed. The girl had taken off on his snowmachine. That, he figured, was a goddam haywire thing to do. Climbed into the vent? He couldn't even picture it, trying, but it ended up looking like some sort of action movie, instead of a limp-haired, scrawny broad shimmying along ten feet of vent soaking wet. Christ almighty, she could freeze out there. And him leaning on the door, telling her to hurry up. Jesus.

"Yes, that's so," answered Chumboy. "You're going to have blood pressure issues."

"Why don't you stop dishing out the medical advice and get your ass in gear."

Chumboy looked at Slaught over the rim of his mug.

"Not feeling the love Johnny. Not feeling the love."

Larose said the sled was ready. Then he told Chumboy to drive careful and not let Johnny wreck his machine. "Just because he's all pissed off doesn't mean he can abuse this baby. I don't see much point in chasing this crazy broad all over hell's half acre anyway. I think his judgments off, " Larose said, patting the hood of the machine as he moved out of the way for Slaught, adding, "Remember Chum, he's wrecked machines before."

Slaught sliding on his helmet, "Can we just get going?" but Chumboy looked over at Larose, nodded, "I'll keep an eye on him."

"Fuck youse both," Slaught said.

"Hey, wait up, buddy, the love doctor's coming," yelled Chumboy, seeing Slaught finally revving up and moving out of the bay. Chumboy looked into his cup, still a few good mouthfuls, Johnny could wait. He got on his machine, still holding his mug, pulled out onto the street then stopped. Above Slaught's disappearing sled the sky was all slate coloured, clouds folded up way to the north, bruised and cold looking.

Larose followed Chumboy out, said, "Quit sight-seeing and get going, you'll never catch up."

"Buddy, he's riding your sled, I could start tomorrow morning and catch up. A wise man gets the lay of the land before he goes rushing into things."

"So what are the skies telling you, wise one?"

Chumboy expression changed, frowning now. "Storm's coming."

"It doesn't look that bad to me," Larose peering up into the sky, trying to see what Chumboy saw. He'd told Chumboy once that it always pissed him off, that they'd both be looking at the same place but Chumboy would always be seeing things first, the moose tracks or the goddam geese way off in the distance. Larose swore the guy had a different kind of eyes. Chumboy told him they were Indian eyes. Now Chumboy was taking off his helmet. Larose said, "Hey buddy, it doesn't look that bad, you gotta go with Johnny."

He pointed, said "The storm's coming to us," and Larose could see two sleds coming around the corner at the top of the road, tearing down the main street towards the workbay. It was Slaught bringing up the rear. On the front machine was the girl. And she had somebody with her on the sled.

CHAPTER SIX

WHEN THEY PULLED INTO THE WORKBAY and parked the machines, Larose pointed at the small, old woman that had ridden in on the back of Susun's snowmachine and asked, "Who's that?"

Chumboy didn't say much, just went over and waited as she got off the machine, then started to help her off with her long, dark parka, big mitts and a bright-coloured toque in different shades of blue and green. She looked like she was at least eighty.

"When I first saw her," Susun answered. "I didn't think she was real."

Slaught, now looking over at her, barely able to speak he was so pissed, asked, "What?"

"Well, I don't know, she was just standing there on the trail, by some big cedar trees, not moving, just standing, staring down the trail as I came around the corner." Then Susun added, "Like she was waiting for me."

Larose rolled his eyes and said 'for chrissake' under his breath, but Susun gave him a dirty look and said she meant it, Larose then turning to Slaught said, "Well, who is she?"

Slaught shook his head and said, "Didn't really have time to ask," wondering why they were all talking about her as if she wasn't there, maybe she wasn't real, then Chumboy said, "You guys don't know her?"

"I think we've established that Chum, got something to contribute?"

"This is my Auntie, my Auntie Verla," Chumboy said, "Auntie, these are the guys. And Susun. Now what brings you to town today?"

"I'd like some tea." The woman had a harsh, flat voice. "And Darla says hello."

Larose glanced over at Chumboy. "Darla?"

"My wife."

"Your what?"

"My wife. Darla. I've mentioned her."

Slaught shaking his head, "No way, you have never, ever mentioned a wife Chum."

Chumboy asked them where they thought he went when he headed out on his own, said he'd been over there just last week to see her.

Larose said, "Thought you just went to party at the rez."

"It ain't the rez anymore good buddy, it's just our territory, like it always shoulda been."

"Well, wherever you go, I don't think it's to see your wife, it's to go hunting, you always bring something back."

"That's from Darla, sometimes some of the boys load me up. Know I've been sort of taking credit for all those partridge, but folks out on the territory, they got your back. I told them you guys couldn't hunt worth shit. "

Larose persisted, "Still, you've never mentioned a wife. That's a bit of an oversight."

Chumboy shrugged and said she was a great girl, then said they should get a good strong cup of tea into his Auntie. Slaught nodded his head towards Susun saying, "Maybe we should lock her up first until we get some answers."

"No incarceration without tea, Johnny," Chumboy answered, "and it sure looks like your felon could use a cup. All things will be revealed in the kitchen I'm sure."

Slaught noticed Chumboy was looking a little worried now about his Auntie turning up, said, "Fine, we'll get something hot into these two, but I want an explanation about what the hell you were thinking, bolting out of here like that," pointing his finger at Susun, seeing her eyes looking straight back at him, same colour as the darkening sky behind her, then her saying "I'll explain what I can."

—

"What does this look like, a fucking refugee station?" Tiny barked as they came trailing into the dining room, him sitting just outside the kitchen door. Slaught asked Tiny to put on the kettle and Tiny barking again, "And doesn't anyone say fucking please anymore?"

Chumboy dragged a few tables together then pulled out a chair for the old woman. "Hey, Tiny, don't talk that way in front of my Auntie, and would you please make some tea."

Slaught was standing with his arms folded, staring at Susun, but she was busying herself setting out cups and spoons. He wasn't going for it. "As much as we all want to know how Chum's Auntie is doing and let you polish up your domestic skills there, I think you owe us an explanation."

She was mad right away, slamming down the spoon, saying she wasn't a schoolgirl in the principal's office. "Hey, Susie, you stole the guy's sled," Tiny said quietly, sort of shrugging at her as he passed her a pot of tea, giving her a look like stop acting like such a goddam loose cannon, "Come on, there's got to be a story here."

She stopped scowling, asking Chum's Auntie if she'd like a cup of tea. "Yes, I'll have double double, me."

Susun dropped two big spoonfuls of sugar into Auntie Verla's tea, sighed as she passed it over and said, "Sorry, okay? I lost it. I just felt like I had to get out of here. I suddenly just felt panicked, really panicked, you wouldn't understand, but I think now I panicked about the wrong thing." Then she looked at Slaught, like it was his turn to say something. He shook his head and avoided looking back, saying that wasn't good enough and did she think stealing someone's sled was okay?

"I wasn't stealing it."

"I don't believe this," Slaught muttering under his breath, then said, "You climbed up into a vent and took off into the great unknown, that isn't exactly taking a walk around the block." It bugged him that she said he wouldn't understand. Understand what? Panic? Yeah, he knew all about that. Feeling the Remington in his hand, it pushing hard into his ribcage when he fired, that guy falling onto the snow. Then trying to get him into the body bag that had been waiting for Darren Cooper, Chumboy asking at the time, "What, do they carry these things around with them just in case?" And then they finally shoved the guy into the bag, but it was so fucking cold and the guy's boots were big and heavy and hard to get in, but no one wanted to take them off his feet. They finally got him on the truck and sent it off down the road. Then they were all off into the great fucking unknown.

"Listen, it's a good thing I went, otherwise Chumboy's Auntie would still be standing out there, or worse, maybe she'd have given up and gone home, after waiting too long."

Slaught looked to Chumboy, "What is she talking about?"

"I guess my Auntie went to meet her, I don't know, it's women stuff you know. Guess we'll find out soon enough."

"So how far exactly did you get before you ran in to Chum's Auntie?"

"Not very far. But what difference does it make? There is something important going on here and you're too busy being pissed off."

Ignoring her, feeling madder than he wanted to be, he asked. "You were gone a while, what were you doing out there?"

"I stopped part way to think things over."

"And then you went on?" Slaught couldn't believe her, sitting out there in the snow, on his sled, taking the time to think it over, and then still bombing off further down the trail.

"She was coming to meet me." Chum's Auntie saying it like it was a fact, slurping a bit of her tea.

"Well, she may have run into you on the trail," Slaught said, "but she was actually running away from the only people who have done her a good turn in some time."

But Auntie Verla said, "No, she was coming to see me, 'cause of the things I saw."

Chumboy decided to step in. "Yeah, Auntie, let's get to that. Maybe you could tell us what you told Susun."

"I told her that I saw seven shiny new black snowmobiles."

"That's it?"

Auntie Verla shrugged and took another loud sip from her mug.

"Well, what did Susun say?" asked Slaught.

"Why don't you ask me, I'm right here?"

"Because I was trying to get a straight answer."

"I came back didn't I? To warn you."

"Would you two stop your bickering for a minute?" Chumboy said. "I'm getting a bad feeling here. Auntie, what's on your mind?"

But his Auntie just took another mouthful, so Susun said, "I was going down the trail and I saw Verla standing there, in a big clump of cedars. Like she was waiting for me, because she wasn't surprised to see me. So I slowed down and drove over to her, killed the machine and she said: "I thought you might have come earlier, so you better hurry back now. There are seven shiny dark snowmachines camped not too far from here. Coming your way."

Slaught said, "Then what?" Paying attention now, getting a bad feeling himself.

Susun said, "I've seen those snowmachines before. That's why I got scared and came back with Verla."

"Meaning?"

"Verla said the ones she saw had those stupid happy faces on the them. Meaning they're Talos security, that's who is sitting just south of here."

Slaught stared. He'd seen those happy faces too, on the shoulders of those fucking security guards that day on the loading dock. He could see Reitman, lying in the snow, flat out, almost like he had passed out or was going to make a snow angel or something, except for the blood in the snow beside him. Good Christ, what would Talos be doing up here, after all this time?

Susun said, "I think they are coming to get you." As if she was answering his question, as if she knew what he was thinking.

Slaught frowned. "That's a bit of a leap."

"That's what I think, and I'm right."

Chumboy poured more tea into his Auntie's cup and she blew across the top of it. He asked, "That what you think Auntie Verla?"

"Me, I think Susan's right."

Slaught was thinking it didn't make any sense. Hadn't seen anybody except stragglers up this way in over a year. Why would Talos be up here? If they'd wanted him, they were two years too late.

These women were spooking him out. "You think it has something to do with me?"

"Yes."

"Come on Susun, I need a little more here."

"Call it women's intuition."

"Well, I need more than that."

"What does that mean?" Chumboy's Auntie was looking up at him now like she was sort of sizing him up, taking his measure. Slaught felt suddenly uncomfortable.

"Well, you know, maybe they'll be gone by tomorrow. Maybe we keep an eye on them, just wait and see. Don't push the panic button."

The woman shrugged and turned her attention back to her tea saying, "I'm going to go rest now," but Slaught could tell she didn't think too much of that idea. He threw Chumboy a look.

Chumboy said, "Before you go Auntie, anything else we should know about these guys?"

"They had lots of gear, big boxes of it, on four of the sleds."

"And?" he prompted.

"Six men and a woman."

"Really? That's good to know," Slaught said, feeling unsettled, then asked, "Anything else?"

"Me, I think they'll be here by tomorrow night, being careful. They are ready to come in but they aren't, taking their time like."

Slaught asked, "Why would they be taking their time?"

She looked at him like she was about to scold him but then turned to Chumboy, like she'd clocked Slaught as a non-believer so wasn't about to waste her breath on him. "I saw them Chumboy, there in the clearing with their dark small tents. They're coming to do the devil's work. You should get ready, maybe push that panic button."

Chapter Seven

"I THINK SUN TZU MIGHT HAVE SOME HELPFUL ADVICE on this matter."

They were sitting now in Chumboy's room up on the top floor, talking things over. When they'd crowded into the room to try and come up with a plan, Chumboy had told Susun that when they had gotten set up in the hotel, he had insisted on a room on the top floor, telling Susun he'd always wanted a penthouse suite.

Slaught glanced over at Chumboy. "Who has advice?"

"Sun Tzu. You know, the general that kicked ass all over China, worked for some king, around the 6th century BC."

"Okay, cut to the chase."

"Sun Tzu said all war is deception."

Slaught said, "Did this Sun Zoo guy have anything to say about fighting the 'devil's work'? What does that even mean?"

"It's 'Tzu,' and me, I think the approach speaks for itself. Look, these guys are doing their whole stealth thing out there, going all ninja in the northland, let's just ride out and meet up with them. Find out what they got. Invite them back. Get them on our turf. Country mouse advantage."

Susun, shaking her head, asked, "Are you crazy?", saying it more as a statement than a question. Susun didn't wait for an answer, saying that if it was Talos who had ambushed their bus, then they had no idea what they were up against. They hadn't seen these guys in action, how they had just up and shot the driver of the bus she'd been on. And then there'd been the sound of the driver hitting the glass window, making that thwapping sound, and then everybody yelling, and they didn't care, just jammed the doors shut from the outside. Just like that. Then smacking the side of the bus, like they were closing up camp for the winter. She said, "If they're that close maybe we should be getting ready to get out of here."

Slaught shook his head. "This is our home now, we aren't going anywhere."

"But go out and invite them in? That's insane."

Chumboy said, "That is exactly what Sun Tzu would recommend, that you lead your enemy into thinking you were nuts, when in fact you really have things under control."

Slaught was nodding. "Then I guess before we roll out the welcome mat we better get things under control. Maybe we should call a community meeting?"

Larose looked surprised. "Community meeting? Have we had one of those before Johnny?"

"Not yet. First time for everything."

"But won't it get people stirred up over what might be nothing?"

"You heard Chum's Auntie, these guys look serious. People should be told."

"Clarification, she didn't say 'serious,' she said the devil's work." Susun was scared now, thinking they were taking this way too lightly. She looked right at Slaught, said, "Don't mess with these guys."

Slaught started to make for the door but Susun said, "Hang on a minute. What? That's it? What if you ride up to those bastards and they just pull out their guns and that's that?"

"We'll burn that bridge when we get to it, for now we got to tell everyone, so they can make up their own minds."

"This is serious," she was insisting now, her hand on his arm, stopping him from leaving, "you gotta believe me, these guys are coming here to do us harm, serious, bad harm." She was meaning it, letting him know she'd seen it up close and he was reading things wrong. He liked the feel of her hand on his arm, she had a strong grip, and she was staring right into him, now saying, "Seriously. This can only be bad." She looked so sure, almost looking like she was going to cry, her eyes vivid and blue, and him wondering if he would regret not listening to her, she said, "I can tell, everyone looks up to you guys, they'd listen to you."

"It isn't my job to tell them what to do. Now let's put it to them and see what happens, okay? You want to take the infirmary and rooms along the east end of the building, ask everybody you find to meet in the dining room. You guys do the workbay. I'll hit the dining room and basement."

Susun protested, saying it was a bad idea, thinking people might not respond so well to her, after all she was a newcomer and they probably all knew by now that she had locked herself in the bathroom and stole Slaught's sled. She told him she didn't know her way around. Slaught told her to follow the vents, that she should do just fine.

"So you liked Sun Tzu's approach, eh?" Chumboy said to Slaught.

"Yeah, but I think I'm going a little Clint Eastwood on this too."

Chumboy said, "Dirty Harry?" looking worried, but Slaught shook his head, saying, "Might stick in your craw Chum, but I've always preferred the western."

Susun was surprised at how many people actually lived in the hotel, wondering what they did all day that she hadn't seen them. She knocked on a few doors, some still with room numbers, thinking of it way back in the day, with chambermaids and a lobby full of rich mining men coming in from out of town. Must have been something. But that was a long time ago, before the silver was gone, before the town died, and way before the winter decided it was staying.

She'd rounded up over a dozen people, and now there had to be over fifty crammed into the dining room. She said to Tiny that she couldn't believe how many were there but he said, "You kidding me, I feed these people, I thought there was more."

Chumboy said there were more but some were out on scrounge patrol.

"Scrounge patrol?" asked Susun.

"Everyday, whether we need to or not," Chumboy answered. "Gotta get our grub and gear some way. These days, we are having to travel too far afield to get it though." Chumboy explained they kept a big list down in the workbay and the team would look it over before heading out, going through the region, quadrant by quadrant, hoping to find what they needed. Sometimes bringing back stuff they thought might be helpful. "Johnny tells them though, you bring shit into my yard and you'll never get on patrol again."

"Seriously? It doesn't seem like that big of a deal."

"Remember how your digs looked? That was not right. A civilized person could not live with that amount of crap and chaos."

"Hey, that wasn't my choice, trust me."

"I'm just saying you've gotta have some order. Like what would happen if one of our scroungers brought back a fancy blouse or something for his girlfriend but forgot the beer? Know what I'm saying here?

"And so Slaught just lays down the law?"

Larose got into it now, joining them against the wall. "Well, basically yeah, you gotta have rules and a leader. Johnny's the man. What do you think we are, a bunch of anarchists?"

"Yeah, as a matter of fact I do. You are definitely anarchists. You live in a commune and spend your time stealing from the government. What do you call that?"

"Justice and the redistribution of wealth," Slaught answered, leaning into her a bit as he passed by them, heading up to the front. She watched him turn and sort of settle himself into the role of head honcho, getting comfortable with it, sort of squaring himself off to look tough but at the same time raising his eyebrows at the number of people crowding in front of him. Some of them were sitting at the round tables, like they were out for a drink together, more leaning along the paneled walls, a few kids sitting cross-legged up along what used to be the bar. She thought Slaught was maybe surprised at how many people there were, a bit unsure about what was coming, but then he started to talk.

"Okay, folks. This is our first community meeting, and by the looks of it, we're going to have to start having some more, there's getting to be a fair number of us here. I'm Johnny Slaught, case some of you haven't met me yet, and I'm sort of the unofficial spokesman for this group of reprobates and outlaws."

"And anarchists," Chumboy offered from the back.

"Them too," Johnny said. "Now, we have our first serious decision to make so I want everyone to listen up while I lay out the situation, think on it a minute, and then throw your ideas at me. Sound like a plan?"

No one really said anything, people looking a little unsure, having no idea what was coming—food shortage, maybe some kind of sickness?

A kid around eight, sitting cross-legged in the front with his mom and dad, said, "We don't have to go back to school do we?"

"Uh, well, it's not a bad issue to talk over, and maybe we'll get to that in some other meeting but not this one," Slaught said, smiling as the kid did some weird little victory squirm from his spot, then adding, "This is a bit more serious than that. We got some trouble headed our way, some serious trouble."

Slaught waited, letting it sink in a minute, getting people's attention. "There is a small squad of government types in the neighbourhood. Sounds like they are probably from Talos. Most of you probably ran into Talos during the evacuations, they were running the show. I think probably by now they run pretty much everything, jails, border security, transportation, the whole nine yards."

"So what the hell does the government do now?" It was an old guy sitting at the back. Slaught thought his name was McLaren.

"Write cheques to Talos?"

"Goddamit," the old guy almost spitting, Slaught thinking it didn't take him long to get ramped right up, "those corporations were already taking over everything before things went to hell in a handbasket, and now they're poking their noses around up here. Christ, we just wanted to left in peace after all that turmoil a couple years back, rounding everybody up. And now you tell me they're back for more?"

"Looks to be the case, yeah," Slaught answered.

"How do we know its them?" McLaren asked. "There's been other fellas running around out there." Then nodding towards Melinda and her baby, added, "Few of them showed up here after all."

"Well, that's true, but from the description we got, sounds like Talos, new sleds, not old beaters like most of us are using. Plus, they're traveling in a group. Now we've had a few stragglers ourselves, but there are seven adults, that just seems unusual. And why'd they be up here is the other question. We'd heard rumours a year or so back of some final clean outs south of here, people down around the border but still inside the Territories. Talos guys come in to an area, sometimes with a military back-up, find any hold-outs and give them twenty-four hours to get out. Guess most of 'em go because otherwise their places are torched, everything, vehicles, homes. Might be hard to believe but that's what we've heard."

Someone scoffed, muttered, "The government can't do that."

"You wouldn't think so, but that's what we're hearing. And technically, it's Talos doing it. Then Talos goes in and claims that the chunk of real estate belongs to the government, and so any houses are there illegally. Get the picture—just a way to keep people out. So refusing to leave equals resisting arrest." He shrugged, "That's what people told us anyhow."

"So what else do we know about these fellas heading our way?" McLaren asked.

"Sound like they're probably armed to the teeth," Slaught said.

Someone's hand shot up. "Are we well armed?" It was Larose's young fella Shaun, eighteen years old and a good six feet of testosterone. Wasn't really the direction Slaught wanted to take the conversation, not yet anyway. Before Slaught could answer though a woman stood up, her dark hair a bit graying, pulled back in a tight ponytail.

"What kind of question is that?" She didn't wait for an answer, even though the young lad looked like he had one for her. "I mean, we should be getting ready, right, they are probably here to take us to the City. To rescue us. It wouldn't take me twenty-four hours to get ready."

The place erupted at that. Some people shouting, one guy saying he couldn't believe she'd say that, and others turning to their neighbours to say stuff.

Slaught held up his hands. "Okay, whoa." Heads turned back to him. "Look, first off, everyone can speak their mind here without getting shouted down. I guess if we are gonna have rules, that's the first one. Now, let's just back up to what this lady here had to say, what's your name ma'am?"

The woman said "I'm Sheila Merrill, from Henwood Township, just up the highway from here."

Johnny nodded, remembering the place, maybe a dozen houses and a store that was also a post office and liquor store. "Okay, Mrs. Merrill, I have to be straight up with you and tell you I don't think they are here to save us. They don't seem to have a way to take anyone out, they sound armed to the teeth, and they are sitting up there by the old dam on the highway just checking things out. Way too cautious to be a rescue squad. Now I don't know what kind of experience you had back in the evacuation period, but some of us got the impression that those Talos fellows would just as soon leave us by the side of the road to die. I'm thinking we gotta handle this one right."

"That's ridiculous. You don't have a spit's worth of sense. You people wouldn't leave," she was pointing her finger at Slaught, her voice rising a bit each time she finished a sentence. "They tried to help you, but you were all too stubborn, and now you're stuck here, in the middle of nowhere, with no police and no doctors, living day to day. That's no way for children to live. You have elderly people here, sick people, this is a ridiculous situation."

"Hey lady, you're here too you know." It was Larose's lad again.

"Her name's Mrs. Merrill," Larose barked over at his son.

She turned on Shaun. "I'm here because my husband wouldn't leave the house that had been his father's house. It was insanity, thinking we could hold out until things changed. Well, I'll tell you what happened, the government walked away on him, on us, finally, fed up with him. Three weeks after they pulled out, he had a stroke. Died right there in the living room."

"Where he wanted to die. Better dying in your own home than as a slave down in the City."

Slaught shot Larose a look saying 'can't you get your young'un to shut the fuck up' and said, calm like, "Listen Che, the lady is just telling us her story, okay, no need for freedom or die right yet. I know some people had a rough time of it, my only point, right here and now, is that I'm not sure the Talos folks touring around our neighbourhood are friendly."

"Well I think if you feel that way Mr. Slaught than perhaps you are not fit to be our so-called unofficial spokesman. We need someone impartial and skilled at negotiating."

"Well, you might have a point Mrs. Merrill. I certainly didn't go looking for this job, just sort of fell in my lap. And you're right, I'm not much of a negotiator. So if we want to stop things here and settle that first, if a bunch of you are feeling that way..."

"Wait a minute, I have to say something." It was Susun, standing away from the wall so people could see her, hands dug into her jean pockets. "You know Mrs. Merrill, I thought the same way you do. When the final eviction orders came, I was working as a midwife, and Talos kept me busy nursing folks till the very last bus out of Englehart was ready to go. At the last minute, our driver got sick and we had to stop, just up the road a ways."

Slaught was thinking it was taking her a long time to get to the punch line, but still, people were listening. She had a nice, quiet way of talking.

"When they came, those government men, Talos or whoever they were, on their skidoos, it was night time and it was damn cold. It was hard to see, there were only the lights from the skidoos, shining into the bus, making it hard to see and they were revving their motors, circling around, and then one guy came on, said, all sort of formal like, ladies and gentlemen, my name is John Slaught. Then he shot the driver, jammed the door and left us stranded there in the cold. Most of the people on that bus died from the cold."

Everybody shot a glance over at Johnny, standing there now, arms crossed, frowning as the story went along, wondering why she hadn't told him that. That seemed like a fucking important detail to leave out.

Nobody was saying anything though, just looking at her. Slaught was thinking her delivery was pretty good, but with kind of an abrupt ending, guess that's how it felt though. Maybe she should have cleared up the fact that it wasn't really him, some people looking back and forth between him and her, unsure. Mrs. Merrill wasn't too sure what to say and looked over at Slaught. He shrugged.

"Not sure what that is about, though I have heard that there are some rumours out there. I always figured they were tied to the original incident, but maybe they are hanging all kinds of things on me now, I don't know. I know this whole Wintermen bullshit has kinda got out of control over time. But that isn't the issue here. What's important, really important folks, is that Susun here says that these guys that are in our neighbourhood right now sound like they have the same sleds as the guys who killed all those folks on the bus."

"Look Johnny," said McLaren "this is a hell of a thing you and your boys have pulled together here, and we really appreciate it. I'm one hundred percent behind you, and I'm sure I'm not the only one. Just tell us what to do, I assume you have some sort of plan don't you?"

But Mrs. Merrill wasn't finished. "Why are we asking him what his plan is? Asking him what we should do like he was our elected leader. I never voted for this man. And I think, in light of what we've just been told, those government men are probably coming to get him. He's a wanted man for god's sake."

"Look Mrs. Merrill, you might have a point about the whole election thing, but it hasn't really been an issue until now. Up until now there weren't too many of us and we just sort of settled into this way of doing things. And as far as them coming for me, you may be right again. That's why I'm going to go see them first."

Mrs. Merrill tried to respond, but the old guy turned to her, cutting her off. "Enough from you," he said, "we got a crisis here so we better deal with it now. Go ahead, let's hear this plan of yours."

"Well, it's going to take all of us. My part is easy, a few of us guys are going to go out and meet up with this crew and bring them in. The rest is up to you guys." He scanned the crowd, looking for a couple of faces, not seeing them. "Don't we have a few theatre types here?"

Someone pointed over their shoulder at two guys in their early twenties slouched against the back wall. Jordan Barzman and Jeff Millen. They'd shown up soon after the guys had the hotel up and running, Jordan telling everyone they'd been out at their A-frame south of Cobalt, keeping an eye on the modest grow-op they'd been nurturing along, when the last sweep of the Talos recon crews found them. The officer in charge had told them to "Get their shit together" because they were being charged with using too much hydro, the fine was five grand and since it was pretty clear two assholes like them didn't have the money, they were heading for a tidy little prison term. Jeff, the dark haired one, had said "Hate to break it to you smiley, but we aren't going anywhere," and then the officer had said to his buddy "I don't have time to waste on this shit, I'm out of here," but the other guy had said, no, they were supposed to bring everybody back to Central, even pieces of shit, and so then Jordan said, "But what about the magic word dude?" Jordan explained that at that point the Talos guys beat the crap out of them, set fire to their house and then just left them there.

"Yeah," Jeff answered, standing up and looking around as if he'd been caught sleeping, "we were in a theatre troupe, The Acid House Players. But it was, like, well, a hobby."

"Doesn't matter," Slaught said, "cause you boys are going to take charge and implement our plan."

It was Jordan now, looking nervous. "Uh, like, what plan would that be exactly?"

"We're going to be putting on a play."

"A play? What kind of play?"

"It's called The Welcome Party. I sort of got the idea from a Clint Eastwood movie."

Chumboy asked, "Which one?"

"*High Plains Drifter.*"

"The welcome to hell one?"

"Well, it's the devil out there isn't it?"

Chapter Eight

Mitch was surprised.

They had spent yesterday doing some recon in the area, making some wide sweeps, checking for activity. It didn't take them long to identify a few heavily used tracks, all leading right into a town only fifteen minutes up the road from where they were camped. Miller had said it used to be a mining town way back, that he'd been through there on training exercises several years ago when he'd been in the armed forces. Said there hadn't been much to the place, a barber shop maybe, one restaurant or so, not even a grocery store.

When they had circled on the far side of the lake, keeping to the shelter of the trees, Laskin had said that Miller sure wasn't exaggerating. All they could see was a straggle of houses along the main street, some more up on a hill behind, but clearly the big hotel on the corner was the centre of activity. Grier said they'd spend the day watching the place then hit it after dark. Mitch and the Talos guys were to take the lightly used trail, sit tight on the ridge of houses up behind the place, keeping an eye on things for a while, then come down the hill from behind the hotel. Grier would come riding right into the centre of town. He said he wanted to head down the main street, just like in the westerns. He was such an asshole.

They had just been getting ready to roll out when she'd heard the machines coming. She tried to pin point the direction of the sound, staring though the thick bunches of cedar and spruce surrounding the clearing for any movement, but by then the three snowmachines just came riding into their camp, like they were out for a Sunday drive. Nobody even had a chance to go for a weapon.

Mitch didn't like surprises.

The riders pulled up alongside Grier who was the closest to the edge of the clearing. Thank Christ they'd finished loading up the weapons, five minutes ago the clearing had looked like an arms bazaar. Mitch could see the one guy raising his helmet shield and then yelling something over the noise of the machine.

"What?" she heard Grier yell back.

She was figuring there was no way these guys weren't Slaught's crew, there was nobody else up here. But why would they just turn up, be so casual? This was something different. She hoped it didn't get too fucking different, though she was curious about this Slaught guy. Most of her gigs lately had been civilian snatch and grabs, going in to remove potential security threats. Drug dealers, black market sharks honing in on Talos turf, boring stuff. Every now and again they'd get a bigger fish, a judge maybe, and she liked seeing him in his nice office, the look of disorientation, him saying "Who me, you can't do this to me." Well, actually I can, asshole. That felt good. Those ones she didn't mind. The rest just pissed her off.

She moved up beside Grier and the new guy on the snowmachine nodded a hello at her then leaned towards Grier.

"I said do you folks need any help?"

Just like that. Mitch saw Grier shoot a look over at her then shake his head, drawing his fingers across his neck, yelling "Cut your engines," wanting to be sure he heard right.

The guy obliged, turning and shouting at the two sleds behind him to do likewise. "Yeah, sorry about that, just stopped to see if you folks need some help."

"And who are you?"

She thought the guy looked offended as he answered, "I'm Chumboy," pulling off his glove and putting out his hand to shake Grier's. Grier took the hand, saying, "But 'who' are you, I mean we're kind of in a no-go zone."

"I was just thinking the same thing about you, but from your tracks out there, criss-crossing and doubling back, well, we thought maybe you were a little lost so we figured we'd take a chance and come on down and see. Now if you don't want our help that's fine, we'll just head on home…"

"And where is home?" Grier asked, and Mitch thought he sounded like a real hard ass, so she stepped in, deciding to play to this guy's country mouse ego, lifting her shield and holding out her hand, making it up as she went along. "Hey there, Mitch Black, with Parks and Natural Resources. I have to apologize for my partner's manners, we were just under the impression that this area had already been cleared. We camped here last night, taking some time to check over one of our machines that's giving us a bit of trouble. And to be honest, yeah we could use some help. We're supposed to be marking a new border for the Territories, one further north. But our maps don't seem to be all that accurate and, well, it's a damn sight colder than we thought it was going to be."

Chumboy said, "Well, we'd be happy to lend a hand, and you're all welcome to head back with us and sort yourselves out if you like. We have a place just up the trail, oh, about 20 minutes or so. Could fix youse all up with a hot cup of tea anyway."

"That sounds great." Mitch smiling, wondering why the guy was talking like some dumbass hillbilly, and then saying, "And where are we heading?"

"A place we're all pretty proud of Miss Black," Chumboy said, "a little place we call Lazarus."

"Lazarus?"

"That's right, now just follow along then. Come on boys," he yelled, "we're heading home." And with that they were gunning their engines and heading back down the trail. Soon enough their machines were swallowed up in the bush that rimmed the clearing.

Grier said, "Do you think that's him?" saying it like it would be a big let down if it was.

"I don't think so, nothing in the file about the Slaught being aboriginal. But there's only one way to find out."

"That was way too goddam easy," Grier said.

Mitch just shrugged, not so sure.

She fell in behind the string of machines, bringing up the rear. She'd tried to check out the three drivers but it was hard to get a bead on them. Big enough guys, no weapons on them as far as she could see, driving crappy machines too.

It took over twenty minutes before 'home' came in sight, the machines leading them right down the main street of the town that they'd been scoping out the day before. Surrounding the three-story brick building on the far corner of the street was a chain link fence, the gate left wide open for the guys to drive through and park their machines along the side. There were trails leading away from the building in a few directions. Mitch noticed one heading off down a slight incline into a large sized metal clad building, wood smoke chugging out the top of it. Although there were some tracks coming and going, few of the other buildings seemed to be in use.

She watched from her sled as the lead guy pulled off his helmet and loosened the top buttons on his parka. He had a long black braid down his back, was a good six foot two, maybe a bit taller. She pegged him at around 35. Big enough too, had to be 200 pounds.

He swung off his machine and nodded to the fence, "Keeps the wolves out, these days they're highly motivated scavengers." He was smiling, moving towards Grier and extending his hand, as if now it was going to be official, welcoming them to his home.

"Chumboy Commando, at your service," he said, grabbing Grier's hand and pumping it a few times.

Mitch saw Grier try to match the grip. "Grier Laskin, good to meet you." And then sort of eyeing him said, "You Cree? Look like the boys I rode with some years ago way up the coast?" Letting Chumboy know that he was cool with his First Nations brothers.

"That right?" Chumboy asked, shaking his head affably. "Well, no sir, I'm Algonquin actually. Common mistake," he said with a reassuring wink.

"Algonquin? Cool. Well, this is my team, we're under Parks and Natural Resources" he said, pointing down the chain of snow-machines, "Turner, Miller, Solanski, Burke, Leclerc, and of course, Ms. Mitch Black. She's really the boss," saying it like he was joking, the big guy smiling, playing along. Mitch thinking it wasn't so funny, starting to get an uneasy feeling. They'd better be careful how they played this thing.

Slaught was crowded with the rest of them trying to find a spot to hang up his gear. He'd backed up around the corner a bit but was still able to see Mitch Black checking out the place, looking like she wasn't sure what was going on. Chumboy had ushered them through the side door of the hotel into a foyer area where wall hooks were loaded with parkas and scarves and there were piles of boots lying stacked against the wall. He was watching her now as she zipped out of her snowmobile suit, standing there now in some sleek black get-up, fitting like a second skin with two thin white racing stripes running from her shoulder down to her ankles. It was hard not to stare, but then he caught the Laskin guy out of the corner of his eye and it kind of put a damper on the whole thing. The guy was now also free of his bulky snowmobile suit, standing there in an outfit identical to Mitch's, it also fitting like a second skin. He was sort of preening as he sauntered over to Chumboy saying, "I can almost taste that tea."

Good Christ.

Chumboy said, "Right this way folks."

The woman turned to one of the men with her, telling him to stay put and watch the gear, check over the machine that seemed to be losing fuel, she'd send something back for him, but Chumboy threw his arms up expansively. "No way little missy, I'm not going to hear of that. We got a lad who can do that, kid's pretty handy in the garage. I'll send him back tout suite. Just hand over those keys and you all come on in and relax."

Slaught could see she was torn, seeing Chumboy's hand out for the keys, not wanting to leave their gear behind. Laskin interrupted, said, "You guys are life savers, come on Leclerc, gather up our keys and pass them over to Chumboy." Slaught figured he was letting her know that he had things under control, that he was cool.

Chumboy was smiling, moving them down a long hallway, pointing now to his right, "Over there are the stairs to the second and third floor where most of our living quarters are, and this, right here, is our dining room, kitchen's there in the back. Nice set up, eh?"

Chumboy led them over to a row of tables where a few guys were already sitting. "Make room, boys, we got visitors."

There was a scraping of chairs and some friendly, maybe expectant, smiles. Chumboy said, "These folks are the, what was it again?"

"Parks and Natural Resources. We're up here doing some
boundary surveying."

A younger guy stood up, extending his hand and said, "Shaun
Larose. Nice to meet youse."

Chumboy said, "These folks need you to take a look at one of
their machines, might be leaking. Think it was the second last one
in the row.""

"I'm on it," he said, emptying his mug and tipping it towards
Laskin. "I'll have that fixed up in no time." Chumboy passed over
the keys, said, "You might as well move them down to the workbay
Shaun, and let us know what you come up with."

Slaught was still standing so he reached out to shake Laskin's
hand, "Pleased to meet you Mr. Laskin, I'm John Slaught. Welcome
to Lazarus," feeling sort of stupid as he said it, wishing they'd
come up with a cooler name for their faux community. He'd asked
Chumboy if he was joking when he'd first heard it, but Chumboy
just shook his head, "Jeff said resurrection was a perennial theme,
couldn't go wrong with it."

Laskin didn't miss a beat, leaning in to take his hand. "Laskin,
Grier Laskin, I'm team leader. And my team, Ms. Black, Brad
Turner, Pete Solanski Kyle Miller, Dan Leclerc and Drew Burke."

"Well, let me do introductions," Slaught offered. "This here
is Harv Larose, you met his young lad Shaun, and Chumboy, and
right here is Jordan and his buddy Jeff, these two young fellas sort
of run the place. I guess you could say they're our team leaders,
we got lucky, Jeff was a junior preacher back in the day when we
actually had seasons. "

"Pretty impressive operation boys." Mitch moved along the
length of the table, coming up behind and resting her hand on

113

Jeff's shoulder, him trying to peer up at her by twisting his head to look over his shoulder. "Must keep you busy taking care of an operation like this. It's amazing, out here in the middle of nowhere, that you could get all this together."

She left her hand resting there, smiling, and Jeff said, "Yes, ma'am, it is amazing. And we wouldn't be able to do it without the Lord."

Slaught could see a small frown flit across Mitch's face, like that wasn't what she expected to hear. But then she was turning her attention to Slaught. "And what is your role here, Mr. Slaught?"

"Call me Johnny ma'am," thinking as he said it he was maybe over-playing his hand. He'd asked Jeff how he was supposed to play some Jesus freak when he hadn't been to church since he was eight. Jeff had said, "Pretend you're stoned."

Smiling at Slaught, turning it on, her tawny eyes locking onto his, Mitch said, "You don't have to call me ma'am. You make me feel like your grade school teacher."

"Fair enough Ms. Black," Slaught thinking he'd never had a grade school teacher like her. She was something all right, but unnerving too, letting her eyes wander up and down him, like she was picking out her next fur coat. He almost expected her to reach out and stroke him.

"It's Mitch."

"Mitch? Well, that's different. Alright then, Mitch it is."

"You were going to tell me what you do here Johnny."

"Well, we all do different things, but I mostly help in the kitchen, whatever the cook needs," he said, gesturing over to Tiny who was now coming to fill their mugs. "That's my boss."

"Really? You don't strike me as kitchen boy material," she said, staring again at him, still smiling but maybe letting him know she wasn't buying it but she'd still play along. He was hoping she'd play nice, but he had a feeling she didn't really know how.

"That's probably because you haven't seen me in the kitchen yet. Force to be reckoned with."

"That so?"

Slaught was glad when Jeff interrupted. "So, Chumboy tells me you folks are up here scoping out a new border?"

Laskin said, "That's right. Now that everything is stabilizing down south the government thought it was time to open up some of the Territories, make sure everyone was doing okay up here and get the services flowing again." Saying it like he believed it.

"No kidding?" was all Jeff could manage.

"Things are getting much better," Laskin said reassuringly.

"Last time I heard, oh, this goes back a ways," Slaught was saying, "the City was totally closed off. Weren't letting people in or out. Still the case?"

Laskin stretched back in his chair. "Not to worry, pretty soon you'll be able to hit the big city streets anytime you feel like it. Take the Missus down shopping and the kids to The Wonderland Complex. The bright lights are just waiting for you. And there'll be even more bright lights once we get up here and start up some of these dams, might even be jobs for some of you."

Jeff said "Well, we sort of like our simple life up here, but it would be nice to visit the City, some of us have relatives there we've haven't seen in a while, you know how it is."

"Sure, sure we do. Maybe once this border is adjusted, you might be able to head on down there, maybe even relocate."

"Well, right now we are just making the best of it, getting by and taking care of each other. That's the Lazarus way. And speaking of which, is there anything else we can do for you folks?"

"I should probably try and contact Parks headquarters from here, let them know about our delay. What do you have in the way of communications out here?"

"I gotta tell you," Jeff said, " and I'm sorry about this, but that's one of our problems, we don't really have the capacity to communicate much beyond our compound, just don't have anything except a few walkie-talkies for our own use, just sort of here in the building. Not even great range on them."

"Really?" said Laskin, not being able to help sounding like a smart ass, clearly not believing him.

"Yeah, Shaun has a set, got it for his sixteenth birthday, they're pretty good ones, and then we got a few sets that aren't so great. But to be honest, we don't really have much need for them. Everything we need is right here."

"That right?" said Laskin, now sounding annoyed.

Jeff shrugged good-naturedly, "That's right for sure. Of course, it wasn't long after the evacuations that the maintenance just up and stopped on all the fibre optics lines, cable lines, you name it, every outfit that was servicing the area just up and left us high and dry. Truth be told, this area's connectivity was somewhat challenged before the long winter came, but afterward? Nothing. We tried at first, tried satellite but all the dishes were plugged up with snow, signals were all messed up, and we had so little power, relying on some windmills, weak solar collectors, couldn't get batteries, so finally we just acknowledged our limitations, tried to turn them into strengths. Embraced the simplicity. Know where I'm going with this? That's right, prayer is the ultimate wireless connection."

There was something about the way Jeff delivered the lines like some low rent street preacher that just wasn't convincing. And if Slaught wasn't buying it, Laskin sure wasn't.

"Simple is all well and good Jeff my boy, but how do you eat?" Laskin asked, sounding more combative, sitting there now with his arms crossed, trying for a look of bemusement but just looked pissed.

Slaught watched Jeff nodding as if he understood where Laskin was coming from—of course, how did they get their food, reasonable question. Slaught thought Jeff was doing a not so bad job on the whole acting thing, now saying, "You might not be aware, Mr. Laskin, working as you do in Parks, but Talos Humanitarian Services does do food drops for the Territories once a month. You have to go down to the border to pick it up, but we do go and get the basics we can't get off the land, like coffee, tea, sugar, flour. Not a lot, but enough for our needs up here. We get by."

Jeff was talking absolute bullshit, there wasn't even a Humanitarian Services any more, that lasted only for a few months in the very beginning. Coffee for sure was one of the things they missed the most, usually they were stuck drinking Chumboy's homemade tea blends. Every now and again though, going through someone's house, hallejulah, coffee in the cupboard. It was usually the first thing they looked for after gasoline and booze.

Slaught watched Laskin thinking it over, sorting out what he was going to say, after all he was standing there pretending to be a Park Ranger. "Well, Talos sure provides, doesn't it?"

"It sure does," Jeff answered, then said, "Hey, I'm sure you are in a hurry but how about I give you all a quick tour, that way you can rest assured that we are doing okay up here when you report back. Then we can stop by the map room and see if we can find you a quick way back to wherever you're headed."

"Map room?" asked Laskin, wondering what the hell they'd be doing with enough maps to fill a room.

"The map room is great, but let's start with our Chapel, okay? It's our pride and joy."

Laskin told Mitch to stay behind, saying maybe she could help clean up, thinking it was funny he was treating her like the team secretary or something. He figured it would piss her off a bit, but he also knew she wanted to check this Slaught guy out so she wouldn't complain too loudly. He'd worked with her enough times to know she loved the cat and mouse shit. He'd rather just go get his Glock, walk back into the kitchen and, bang-bang, you're dead, picturing their faces as he dragged Slaught through to the back, then maybe popping the big Indian guy too, saying something like, "You know my biggest problem? Over-efficiency."

For now, though, the deal with Mitch was that there'd be no decisive action until they decided together. He'd heard through the grapevine she'd been working with another Talos operative when he jumped the gun, literally, getting skittish and firing off a few rounds that almost took out Leclerc. After that Mitch was pretty hard-assed about the 'coordinated effort' shit. He said, "We're off to the map room Mitch, back in a while."

"Later." She didn't even look at him, already sliding around the table to position herself across from Slaught, Laskin now wishing he could stay and watch.

"I guess I get left here all alone with you boys?" Mitch said.

"Guess so," Slaught said, thinking her cropped hair was way too much like the bullshit king's there, Laskin's, all blonde and sticking up. But hers was shaved up at the back, showing her long, slender neck.

"Well, why don't you show me around the kitchen," she said, walking into Tiny's domain and pulling herself up lightly to sit on top of the counter, "not having had too much experience myself."

Slaught said, "I'd be surprised a woman like you wouldn't know her way around a kitchen."

"Well let's find out," piped in Tiny, tightening the strings on his apron, "Johnny, get started on those spuds. Miss Black, if you please, chop me up those onions there."

From her expression, Slaught figured she was thinking 'not

fucking likely,' but she kept her voice sweet, saying instead, "Oh, I can't cut onions, they make me cry."

"Johnny, pass me over that carver," Tiny asked, taking the knife and starting to drag it over the sharpening stone. Mitch looked over, and by her expression, Slaught figured she had just noticed that Tiny was standing there with his apron over his bare chest, a gold chain around his neck, hairy arms working away at the knife.

"Uh, isn't that somewhat unorthodox, you know, cooking without a shirt on?"

"Can't cook wearing a shirt. Never could."

Trying another tact she said, "Most men with a belly like that would be covering it up Tiny," delivering the insult like she was sort of teasing.

Tiny patted his gut with the knife.

"Are you kidding, it took me a lot of work to get this baby the size it is, I'm not going to hide it from the world."

She seemed barely able to look at Tiny, Slaught thinking there were days he had a hard time too. Mitch asking, "You don't find it a bit unsanitary?"

"I find it where I can, honey," Tiny sliding the knife through a fat slab of ham on the table in front of him, the meat falling onto the cutting board. "Mitch darling, this ain't the Royal York Hotel, it's Tiny's kitchen and in Tiny's kitchen, Tiny rules. And the rules say, no shirts."

"Got it," she responded dryly, "but if it's alright, I'll keep mine on."

"Good thinking, you can use it to wipe up your tears," Tiny said, shoving the bowl of onions towards her. "Glad to have you helping out Ms. Black, its nice to have a woman in the kitchen for a change."

CHAPTER NINE

THE FILES HADN'T BEEN MOVED AT ALL. Ricky thought maybe the cleaning lady might have pushed them to the side or something, but they were right where he'd left them. The Captain had told him if he wasn't done by today he was going back to the 'retard ranch.' That was what all the guys called the Workplace Halfway House where Ricky had been living. Ricky'd been there for three months. That was how long his sentence was after he had been caught trying to leave the City.

Ricky hadn't really thought about not being able to go back home when he decided to move down to the City. Never should have done it. He hadn't realized they wouldn't let him leave to go back. Next time, this time, he'd know better. He would plan things out better. Last time, he just hadn't thought it through.

It hadn't been all that hard to get on one of the big trucks leaving the City's central terminal. One of the guys at the Halfway

House had told him there was hardly any security to control the greenhouse workers heading up north to the border zone, said if Ricky was thinking of going he should go soon since Talos was planning on cracking down because of all the smuggling that was going on, everything from booze and drugs to gasoline. Ricky had asked him why they hadn't been checking people trying to go up there and the guy had laughed, said you'd have to be fucking crazy to head up there, that it was a shithole of epic proportions, guys working fourteen hour shifts and eating shit out of cans.

So Ricky had just lined up, said he was going to the greenhouses for work, got put on one of the big trucks headed to the border zone. When he got there no one really noticed him so he'd just hopped off the truck and started walking down the narrow road towards the big gates, not really sure what to do next. The snow was ploughed and piled up high along the edges of the road, must have been seven or eight feet high, the snow loud and crunching under foot. Ricky knew then that there was no way he was sneaking out anywhere, he was the only person around, he couldn't get up over the snowbanks without being seen and even if he did, then what? The snow'd be so deep he wouldn't be able to move. He could see a big green sign over the gates at the end of the road, "Property of Talos—Trespassers will be Prosecuted." He stood thinking about what to do, knowing his Uncle's cabin wasn't far but also knowing too it might as well be a million miles away, thinking maybe he'd go back to the City and make a better plan, but it was already too late because two men in dark green uniforms were running toward him, yelling.

Ricky couldn't make out what they were saying, both of them yelling at the same time, so he wasn't sure if he should put up his hands because they had guns or if he should get down on the ground. He just stood there staring until one of them moved into him and slammed him down, the hard ice scraping his cheek as he hit the ground. It had hurt more than when he'd skinned both his knees tripping and skidding down the gravel road when he was running to get the school bus on his first day of junior kindergarten. He'd stood up and the kids were looking from the bus window. One girl with brown hair was crying in the window, and the bus driver was staring at him, and Ricky turned and ran back up the long lane to his house with his knees bleeding and the taste of blood in his mouth. He didn't go back to school until Grade One.

"Skinner! Get to work or you can take your tooth brush and head on back to the ranch."

Muspar's shouting dragged Ricky from his thoughts, his mind full of pictures of the yellow school bus all mixed up with the guards in green uniforms from the border. He shook his head as if trying to dislodge the images and said, "Yes sir, I'm going to finish it up real soon."

"And Skinner," Muspar was saying, heading now towards the door, "I'm out for the day and won't be back until very late this afternoon. I want you done and gone by then. Do not be here when I get back, understand?"

Ricky mumbled "Yes sir," then felt relieved, glad to have the Captain gone so he could work without worrying if the Captain was reading his thoughts. That was bothering him, that the Captain might know what he was thinking, especially since he was about to do something wrong.

How wrong he wasn't real sure. His Uncle Delbert had once said, "Well Ricky, there's wrong, and then there's wrong," but Ricky was never sure about the difference. He didn't think what he was about to do was very wrong. Nobody was going to get hurt after all. He just wanted to know if his Uncle's name was in the file, because he lived in the Territories and so did the Wintermen. He was worried about his Uncle, thinking maybe he could find out about things and then go and tell his Uncle, not leaving through the main exit like last time but going cross country, because he knew there wasn't much security in the bush and he'd heard other guys say they were planning on going over the snow walls, said all you needed was some sort of climbing hook to help pull you over. If you were fast they'd never see you. He'd also heard other guys say they got over the snow wall but then had turned back, it was too spooky, there was just snow and trees and darkness, nothing out there. But Ricky knew his Uncle was out there, so he figured he wouldn't get spooked.

Ricky sorted through all the other files first, saving the one he needed for last in case the Captain came back. Ricky worked his way through the stack and was done. It was only lunchtime.

His stomach was growling and he thought about going down to the stockroom and having his lunch. Just thinking about it was making him hungry. But he decided to wait. He sat down and took the big file marked "Zone 6" and opened it up. Inside were smaller folders and along the top of each one were typed different cities or townships.

Ricky looked for the township his Uncle's hunt camp was in and he flipped through the papers until he saw his Uncle's name, "Skinner, Delbert" and beside it was stamped the letter "E" and another number.

The letter "E" was beside his Uncle's name. He just stood for a minute, trying to think, feeling nervous but wanting to know what "E" meant.

Excellent.

Elephant.

Envelope.

Ricky had no idea. He flipped through the pages, noticing

that there were different kinds of papers in the back half of the file folder. There was also a photo, a picture of his Uncle's hunt camp, the main building pushed over on its side and partially burnt. Then another photo of the building, burnt to the ground, the woodstove coated in ash, stranded in a pile of charred rubble.

Ricky stared at the picture for a long time.

He dragged his eyes past the photo to the paper where it said "Skinner, Delbert." Below that someone had typed "Refusal to Comply—Talos Order #2435" and then it had a list of what read like some sort of charges, like resisting arrest, unlawful and dangerous use of a firearm, assault with intent. It was dated a month ago.

There were other pieces of paper stapled to the sheet and Ricky flipped the front sheet over and there was one that said Certification of Death for Delbert Skinner. Ricky couldn't read anymore. He put the file away, stacked the files and then left to get his lunch.

Laskin couldn't believe it. An hour later and Jeff was still dragging him through every last broom closet to meet every last hillbilly on the planet. Laskin was ready to just bag Slaught and get out the hell out, but he was a little uneasy, not sure what was really going on. He wasn't even sure if it was Slaught back in the kitchen peeling potatoes, or if that shitbird Muspar had all his Intel wrong. If any of it was right, these guys were supposed to be a fairly efficient criminal operation, not Jesus freaks. And they were fucking convincing Jesus freaks. The people seemed glad to see them. A couple had given him and Turner a little Bible tract to read, saying

"It'll clear your head and your heart Mr. Laskin, so you can focus on the Lord." And then they apologized to Solanski and Miller, saying they were running low on the little books and maybe they could borrow Mr. Laskin's sometime.

"So here we are Mr. Laskin, right back where we started," Jeff said.

Laskin saw Mitch over in the far end of the kitchen, her back to him.

"Thanks Jeff," he said, " that was great. And the maps did the trick, I think I got my bearings now. Gotta say you've got quite the operation here."

"Hate to put a damper on things but I got some bad news for Mr. Laskin." It was Jordan, coming in with Shaun Larose. " I think I also have some good news for you too though, I guess that's the way it goes here at Lazarus. I was out helping Shaun here take a look at your machine and you were right, it's leaking like a sieve. Shaun says it's going to take him overnight to get it fixed up, maybe even into tomorrow."

Laskin looked over at Leclerc, but he just looked confused.

"Oh, and fellas," Shaun added, "you must've been driving in some rough country, see, I got to thinking maybe I should just take a quick look at the other machines, you know, didn't want to send you back out there if the sleds weren't 100%, know what I mean? So I checked yours, Mr. Laskin, and one other, and boy, you guys are hard on your sleds. I figure I can scrounge up the parts but it's going to take us, well, at least a day or so to get them trail worthy. Looks like you might have a throttle problem. We're just checking around for the parts now."

Laskin didn't say anything. He'd checked all the machines that morning himself and everything looked fine, but that kid standing there, all smudged up with grease, just looked so dumb, could he really be bullshitting? So Laskin tried, "That's the bad news, what's the good news?"

Shaun smiled at Laskin, and Jordan was smiling too, saying, "It was Shaun's idea and I think it is a good one. Since you're stuck here, as it were, overnight, and that seems to us like a pretty special occasion, we were thinking about having a party. What d'ya think?"

"A what?"

"A party. A welcome party. It is a special occasion for us, that's for sure, to have visitors, especially an interesting group such as yourselves. Everyone, I know, would be real excited to get more news about the City, and Tiny's still got lots of that great ham, so I think we're all set. What do you say?"

"Uh, yeah, well, why not," Laskin said, stumbling a bit because he really couldn't tell what the hell was going on. Were these guys for real? Maybe just as dumb as they sounded. "Sounds like a good time, one way of making the best out of a bad situation." Then Laskin added maybe he could just head out and take a look at the sled himself, you know, just to be sure.

Jordan said no way, Shaun was really the best, and Laskin shouldn't trouble himself, the kid just loved it anyway, up to his elbows in parts. "Dude, don't you worry about any of it, just grab your gear from the hallway there, a couple of the boys brought it up for you."

"Alright," Jeff said, "let's get this party started. Jordan, why don't you rustle up an emergency party committee and I'll see what I can do about finding these folks some accommodations for the night. The Lazarus Hotel. I like the sound of that."

"Yeah, me too, its sounds great, eh Mitch?" said Laskin, watching her finally turn from the counter to look over at him, her eyes hard even as they were rimmed with tears from the onions. Man, that woman could throw out the bitchbite when she wanted to.

Jordan left them in what Miller figured had once been some sort of apartment or very large hotel room, Jordan explaining they had knocked a wall out to make a bigger storage space, said the rooms in the old hotel tended to be pretty small. He said they were planning on getting the basement up and running to move all their gear and goods down there in order to make room for more people. In the meantine, though, they'd just have to make do with the set up, the space crowded now with cots and at the far end he'd rigged up a blanket as a sort of curtain, Jordan saying that the lady should have some privacy since there wasn't another room to be had.

Miller found the whole set up weird, all these random people in this old, rambling hotel. Hardly felt like the headquarters of some terrorist outfit. He'd thought the Wintermen would be armed and dangerous, but he was beginning to wonder. He was keeping his thoughts to himself though for now, but it was pretty obvious that Turner wasn't. He'd been complaining for the last ten minutes about the mission, saying he'd had just about had enough of all the bullshit.

"Sir, I have to go on record as saying I'm finding this playing dumb routine hard to take. Those assholes are really getting under my skin."

Laskin glanced over. "You eat shit now 'cause that's the plan, okay? It's my call when we stop playing nice, got that gentlemen?"

"So in the eating shit department, Grier," Mitch started in, "do you really think we've fooled them? Are they really fooling us? I don't believe for a minute that our Snow Pirate is really Betty Crocker, do you?"

"I don't know. They all strike me as dumb fucks. I mean walk-ie-talkies, Christ almighty."

Miller let out a loud sigh. "I gotta go with the boss on this one, I was doing some recon during that tour of the place, and I didn't see any sign of communications, no weapons, nothing. Looks like they have some solar heating for their water, they have that row of wind turbines up on the ridge behind here, couple of wood stoves cranking out heat, other than that this is hippie homesteading 101. Not overly sophisticated. A third of the people here have to be well over fifty, and there's kids here too. I mean these guys are talking to each other with kids' walkie-talkies? And that chapel," shaking his head, like he couldn't believe it, "that was something else."

"No shit," agreed Laskin, grinning now, "It was really trippy. You should've seen it Mitch, I mean it was the only real room in the joint, had these dark blue curtains up everywhere, and all this religious shit on the walls, and god, the candles. There must have been a hundred candles, and that Jeff guy telling us they keep one lit for every member of the community…"

"So, how many people are here?" asked Mitch.

"Well, I didn't fucking count them."

"There were forty-four candles Ms. Black," Miller offered, Laskin shooting him a dirty look.

Mitch said, "Muspar did say it was between twenty and two hundred. We could have a real mess on our hands though, taking these guys out with all these civvies everywhere."

Mitch crossed over to sit on the edge of the cot, rubbing her eyes. She looked at Miller. "Forty-four? That's a lot of people to manage." She was quiet for a few seconds, staring up at the ceiling, thinking, then said, "Okay boys, go find out more, number of families, what kind of structure exists, any secret stashes. Be subtle though. And check in on our machines too, don't want them to be stripping them for parts."

The guys left the room, Turner taking the opportunity once they were down the hall to start bitching that all Laskin and Black ever do is screw, they could have done that without dragging everyone out here. They should be paying attention to getting Slaught and then getting the hell out. Then as the two guys from Talos drifted off to check out the dining room area, Turner said they were fucking creepy spooks. Miller told Turner he should watch what he said around those spooks. Turner said he didn't care anymore, he just wanted to get the fuck back to civilization.

—

They were already in bed, him having pulled her over to his cot, undressing her quickly.

"What's your read Mitch?" Laskin asked, his hand lingering over her breast then running slowly down along the length of her stomach, now playing between her legs.

"I'm not sure, but I'm not buying that Jesus crap," she managed to say before his mouth covered hers and he was on top of her. She had her hands on his back, sinewy, it felt strong, feeling him pushing his weight all along her body, nice and heavy. She figured Slaught had twenty pounds on Grier, wondering what that felt like, thinking maybe he had a woman here, thinking maybe he was sleeping with all the women.

Then Laskin was in a hurry, burying his face in her neck, immediately inside her, not wasting any time. Laskin was saying something in her ear, his breath hot on her neck, his body suddenly rigid, and then he was done. She pushed him off and he stretched out on his back beside her, tucking his arms behind his head, crowding her towards the edge of the cot. "This welcome to dullsville tonight will give us a chance to maybe look around a bit. And maybe you can get Johnny boy to loosen up a bit. If I'm not mistaken, the pleasure of a female companion who isn't old enough to be his mother or doesn't sport a mullet might just cause him to let down his guard."

"Sounds to me like you're letting me off my leash," she said playfully, running her hand over his chest but still thinking about Slaught. "Just how far are you suggesting I go?"

"Baby, if you can get us out of this dump sooner than later, you can go as far as you want."

She was wondering if he really meant it, and thinking too about how Slaught checked her out when she walked into the kitchen, and she felt that aching feeling between her legs come back. She got up and crossed over to her own cot, lying down on her belly, said, "I think I'm going to get my beauty rest so I'm ready to party with the locals."

A couple hours or so later she was up, dressed and ready to go.

Seeing that Laskin was still wearing just his thermals made Mitch say, "Forget to get dressed?"

Laskin grinned, "It's part of the plan Mitch, letting Slaught know I'm relaxed, totally chill, not expecting anything, making him think he's got nothing to worry about."

"And does he?"

Laskin whistled slowly at her, looking at the long legs ending under the short stretch of a black spandex miniskirt. The big boot liners she was wearing just made the skirt look shorter and the legs longer. "I think he's got plenty to worry about. Where'd you get that little number?"

Mitch smiled, letting Laskin pull her towards him, running his hands over her back and sliding them to the bottom edge of her skirt. She said, "A girl always needs wardrobe choices Grier."

He ran his hands playfully along the hem of her skirt, saying, "Tomorrow baby, you and me, we're outta here. Then it'll be easy sailing , maybe we'll go some place far away."

"I'm game, let's just keep our eye on the prize for now."

"It's in your hands, get him drunk, get him horny, whatever, just get him off alone, and we can do the rest. I take out Tonto, the boys grab Tweedledee and Tweedledum, and the rest of this mess is Talos's problem. Turner is going to wait 'till he gets the word and head outside to hit the workbay and grab our weapons. You got yours some place close by?"

"Under my pillow."

Laskin raised an eyebrow. "You think you'll need to get him in here?"

"If I'm lucky," Mitch answered, then added when she saw Laskin starting to scowl a bit, like he wasn't sure if she was joking or not, "Only in his dreams, Grier."

Slaught was telling Chumboy and Larose about his recent encounter with Mitch the Bitch. Jordan had given her the name after she snapped at one of toddlers who was having a hard time resisting the racing stripes up the length of her leg. Jordan had said, "Don't mind Josh, he's just a curious little guy," and Mitch had said, "That's what killed the cat."

Chumboy said the woman's maternal instincts were like those of a komodo dragon. "I saw this show once, how the mother dragons eat their young, the babies have to go hide in the trees all the time."

Slaught downed the shot of scotch, tipping it towards Chumboy to refill it, having just told them that he had finished showering and was stepping out into the hall still doing up his belt when he nearly ran right into Mitch and Laskin. Her skirt couldn't have been shorter or her shirt tighter. Her eyes were all over him, and then she'd cocked her head to one side and had said, "Hope you're undoing that belt and not the other way around?"

Larose drained his glass, "So what did you say to her?"

"What was I going to say? I said something lame ass about being sorry for nearly knocking her over but I was, as a matter of fact, rushing to get things ready for the party. I'll be glad when this is over."

Chumboy was laughing, "No more for you buddy," screwing the cap back on the bottle. "I know you're suffering trauma here but this stuff is too precious. Me, what I want to know, is whether the Ice Queen is going to be able to melt your heart or not?"

Slaught said, "She's not after my heart."

Chumboy raised his glass. "To our very own Casanova."

Larose said, "Hey, enjoy it man, there isn't a guy here wouldn't trade places with you. Call her bluff, maybe you'll get something out of it, know what I mean?"

"Harv, she's with another guy and still sending it out like that? No, its just part of their game, though I gotta admit, I just can't see where it's going."

"Johnny, come on, I can't believe you, go for it, what harm can it do? So what if it's part of their plan, the woman is almost ripping off your clothes every time she lays eyes on you."

"Do you feel threatened by her aggressive sexuality?" Chumboy asked.

"No," Slaught answered, wondering if he was sounding way too defensive, "that's not it at all."

Chumboy nodded sagely. "Vagina with teeth."

"What?" Larose asked.

"Vagina with teeth, Larose, the reoccurring belief throughout history that somehow the female parts are in fact a trap for the unthinking man, that a woman's vagina is a deadly weapon. It's all about castration anxiety."

"What are you talking about?" Larose asked, sounding mad. Slaught figured it really pissed Larose off when Chumboy started in on the bullshit. He was with Larose on this one.

"Johnny does not want to engage Ms. Black in sexual relations because he is afraid, on a deep, psychological level, that her vagina will sever off his weenie."

Larose shot a confused look at Slaught, asking, "You're worried she's going to cut off your dick?"

Slaught sighed. "Not quite, Harv, I'm actually worried that she already has one of her own. "

"You serious?"

"No Harv, I'm not serious, not literally anyway."

"Well, I don't know what the fuck everyone is talking about anymore, but it seems to me we'll be better off once they're gone, they're upsetting things around here. I think they're making us crazy."

"Steady Harv, we just gotta play this things out." Then taking a deep breath, Slaught added, "it's time to face our public."

Larose, shaking his head, said, "Maybe we should just forget the whole plan, let's just load 'em onto their machines and drop them off at the border."

The plan was to get them relaxing and distracted in order to get the jump on them, get them under lock and key, and away from any weapons or communications. After that no one was really sure what to do with them, but at least they wouldn't be calling the shots. Slaught could hear the worry in Larose's voice, said, "Nah, its okay Harv, in fact, its going just the way we want. No point hitting the panic button."

"But isn't that what Chumboy's Auntie wants us to do?"

"Yeah, well, that's on my mind too."

CHAPTER TEN

"JOHNNY, ARE YOU LOOKING UP MY SKIRT?"

Slaught had just pulled up a chair, flipping it around and straddling it so he could face Mitch. She was sitting up on the bar, her long legs crossed, the skirt riding up to her hips. Slaught wondered how he could do anything but look up her skirt. He said, "Good Lord, no," trying to stay in character but feeling moronic.

She smiled down at him. "Are you blushing?"

Slaught shook his head, taking a quick look around to see if Chumboy was moving in on Grier yet. Where the Christ was everybody? The plan was to break up the team, try and move them off into different parts of the room. Once Shaun had finished up going through their gear he'd show up and they'd be pretty much ready to pull the plug. Slaught was watching the door for him, but the night seemed to be dragging on forever and no Shaun.

They'd already eaten, Slaught sitting next to Laskin watching him choke down a piece of ham after Tiny had delivered a thick slice onto his plate. Mitch had said no thanks, she was vegetarian, and Tiny had answered, "Right on, then you're gonna love the ham, did it up with some very nice lima beans," and slapped it down. She'd looked at it for a second then grabbed the plate, stood up slowly and walked over to a garbage bin to scrape the ham off her plate, then paused and just tossed the whole plate into the trash.

Soon after that, he'd been helping Tiny clear things away when he saw Mitch and Susun talking and figured he'd better get over there. Mitch was perched up on the bar, Susun standing, both staring at the big dining hall that had been transformed, coloured streamers hanging off the string of lights that had been hung along the wall and around the windows, kid's drawings stuck up along the blonde paneled wall. Jordan had gathered up a batch of old green wine bottles and stuck white candles in them, placing them randomly on the bright red tables, the three colours making Slaught think of Christmas, thinking too that the old Fraser House didn't dress up so badly.

When he got closer he could see that Susun, arms crossed, had a strained look on her face. Mitch had her legs crossed, doing her best to look bored. Slaught couldn't imagine two more different looking women. Beside Mitch, looking pale and toned, Susan was small and dark, wearing her long hair pulled back in a sky coloured kerchief. When Jordan had passed her the scarf, saying, "Put it on," she'd protested, "Really? Kerchiefs?" but Jordon had insisted, "You want to look like a bunch of religious extremists, the women gotta wear kerchiefs. It's, like, a non-negotiable." And so she'd put it on. Standing beside Mitch, she'd looked like an extra from Jesus Christ Superstar stumbling onto the set of Blade Runner.

Slaught had heard Susun say, "Things look pretty, eh?" and Mitch smirked, asked, "Your handiwork?"

Susun, using what Slaught figured was all her restraint, had answered, "The kids did them," then she asked Mitch, "No children of your own?" Mitch had given her the look, said, "Don't think so. I suppose you have a dozen or so." Johnny liked the way Susun answered her, saying, "Not yet. Soon I hope." Then Susun said it'd been nice meeting her but she had to go, drifting off to join Jeff in keeping on eye on Solanski. Johnny was sorry to see her go, worried about having only a plastic chair between him and Mitch as she swung her legs, staring down at him playfully, giving him goose bumps.

Mitch was content to just watch him for now, his big shoulders sort of leaning back, arms the size of friggin' pylons resting on the chair back. Either he'd been living as a monk for the past few years or something was up, because the man was definitely squirming, couldn't even make eye contact with her. She was just watching him, biding her time a little bit longer until Grier was able to get that big fucking Indian alone somewhere. Might as well have some fun while she was at it, hopping down off the counter, leaning back on it and putting her foot up on Johnny's chair. He stood up fast, then backing up, suddenly looking relieved as he said, "Hey there Kirstie."

Mitch turned, hoping to Christ it wasn't that hippie broad that'd been hanging around before, and saw a girl around sixteen, a roll of pudge sitting along the top of her too tight jeans.

Slaught said, "Mitch, this is Kirstie. She's running our daycare now."

Mitch, letting Johnny know she was getting fed up with the Jesus Freak routine, said, "I guess you figured Karen here was perfect for the job? You make all the decisions around here Johnny?"

Flushing, picking away at the chipped pink nail polish on her thumb, Kirstie didn't look up when she said, "My name is Kirstie, and actually Jeff put me in charge of all that, he's like our preacher."

Mitch stared at her, thinking the girl was a shit liar. "Your preacher?"

"Yeah," Kirstie said, suddenly looking up. "He let me choreograph the little kids in our production of Splish, Splash Bible Bath for the Christmas concert." She smiled and added, "It was awesome."

Mitch said, "You can't be serious?" but Kirstie just smiled and Mitch thought what a dumb cow she was but could anyone really make shit like that up? Mitch said, "Sure nice meeting you, but I'm sure I can hear someone calling you over there. You better go."

Mitch saw Kirstie shoot a look at Slaught, sounding flustered when she said, "Well, I just came to tell you Shaun's almost done."

"That's great Kirstie, thanks, maybe you can go round him up, tell him to get a move on? Almost time to shut her down and clean up."

Mitch watched the girl leave then pushed the chair off to the side, stepping in closer to Slaught. "We've still got some business to finish Johnny?"

"That right?"

She could tell she surprised him when she asked, "You married Johnny?"

Slaught told her he was once but not anymore. So she asked what was stopping him, adding, "I know you want to."

"Stopping me from what?"

"Taking me to bed."

She'd decided to throw it out there, finding herself excited around the guy. Maybe because she knew what was coming, feeling some preemptive adrenaline, maybe too because she could tell, even though he was panicking as her hand was slowly tracing his collarbone, that he wasn't really afraid of her. She said, "Let's go to my room."

He said, "But you and Grier, I thought…"

"Mr. Laskin? He's my boss Johnny, I'm free and single."

"Hard to believe."

She said, "Johnny, maybe it's been awhile for you and you're nervous, but I promise, I'll make it worth your while. Let's just go."

She was looking at him when he looked right back at her. She felt a slight tingle along the curve of her neck where his eyes strayed for a second, and he said, "Yeah, it's been awhile." But he just kept looking at her, his eyes moving to her mouth, up along her sharp cheekbones, and she hesitated, enjoying the blood moving under her skin, but then she moved her face close to his, slipping her finger over his belt, eyes on his, whispering, "Let's just go."

Slaught was having a hard time concentrating, her hand hooked onto his belt, standing way too close. Where the fuck was Shaun? Feeling her leg move against him, he knew he was getting in trouble, but he couldn't stop himself looking at her, and she said, "I can feel your heart pounding Johnny," and so could he, pounding like an oncoming train wreck.

Thank Christ the lights came on, taking her face from the shadows and hitting it in hard relief, the sharp cheekbones, hard eyes, but she just stood there, right up against him, like she was locked on her prey and couldn't disengage. He could feel people maybe looking over at them, saw the sky-blue kerchief and Susun's dark eyes stray from him as Shaun and Max came in the room saying," I wish I had some decent news for you folks," and Slaught took hold of Mitch by her arms and moved her back a bit, said, "You'll probably want to hear this." He finally felt himself breathe, realized he'd been holding his breath.

"Yeah, and its too bad, you know," Shaun continued, standing there in his parka and stocking feet, folks now all turning to hear what he had to say, "you guys could have saved yourself a heap of trouble too."

Laskin, from across the room, said "Oh?"

Slaught could see the uncertainty on Laskin's face as he watched the hint of a shit-eating grin flicker across Shaun's face. "How's that?" Laskin asked.

"Well, I guess you get used to hauling lots of equipment around and maybe you don't need it so you just don't check. But you can give us our old maps back for sure, you guys got a good half dozen state of the art GPS trackers out there in your gear."

Slaught could feel Mitch staring hard at him, he met Mitch's glare. "GPS, eh? I guess that would be standard for Parks guys. Nothing unusual about that."

Mitch, leaning back on the counter, coming across as pretty relaxed, said, "We're a pretty new team, guess we were relying on Turner to tell us what we had," but Slaught saw her face tighten as Max stepped over towards them, passing Slaught one of the rifles and Slaught said, "Guess poor old Turner forgot to mention these babies too, though they don't seem too standard for Parks now do they? What are they? M4s? Not bad for Smokey the Bear."

A good half dozen of the weapons were now scattered through the crowd and pointed at Laskin and his team. Slaught said, "Guess the party is over folks, time to go think over your lame-ass story. Folks here are wanting the truth, and nothing but."

Laskin tried going on the offensive, saying, "Come on, what's going on here?" but Slaught just said, "Enough bullshit."

Laskin sat down on the table slowly, stalling maybe, buying himself time to come up with some plausible explanation. Finally he said, "The honest answer is that we are a government team sent in to expand the park boundaries. As you know, people are not allowed to reside in the park, so it was our job to clear the park of people."

"And you needed these to do it?" Slaught asked, brandishing the weapon.

"Well Mr. Slaught, I'm sure you must be aware that you have a heavy rap sheet—robbery, assault, murder even—and right now, by doing this, you're just making that rap sheet a lot longer and a lot more serious, beside getting all these good people here in trouble too. "

"You work on your story over night, see what you can come up with. Chumboy and the fellas will see you to your room," Slaught said, then turned to the people crowded around, said, "So guess the show is over folks and you did great, we can give ourselves a real party sometime to celebrate but for now, let's get our guests tucked in and hopefully it'll be back to usual sooner than later."

Chumboy nodded and, with Larose, started to march them out. Mitch hung back, passing close to Slaught and saying, "You were looking up my skirt though, weren't you?"

"Yeah, I couldn't quite see the For Sale sign up there until I took a closer look."

"Fuck you."

"I don't think that's going to happen any time soon, and for chrissakes, tell your boyfriend to wear some pants next time, he's embarrassing himself."

CHAPTER ELEVEN

"MOVE IT, WOULD YOU SKINNER?"

Muspar started the day already pissed, and now here he was getting hauled over to the Neighbourhood Surveillance wing of Talos operations to meet Bob Scott. He glanced at the back of Skinner's neck, the kid driving like he was somebody's granny. "Skinner, if you don't get me there in five minutes, I'm going to have you doing duty at the kennel."

"Wouldn't mind that sir, I like dogs."

"Skinner, you being a wise ass?"

"No sir, I really do like dogs, my Uncle Delbert raises dogs, had a real nice Springer spaniel, and man, every fall that dog would just go crazy," Ricky grinning, remembering the damp sludge of leaves underfoot, and the dog racing and yapping around the yard as they got ready to head out. "One time sir, there was this partridge, and the dog, his name was Bo, well he..."

"Shut up and drive."

Ricky looked through the rearview mirror at the man, but he was already back to reading his pile of papers.

He dropped the Captain off at the bottom of the range of office towers that formed the home of Talos Enterprises Inc. It had taken him a few turns around the block to find the proper entranceway to the Civilian Security building that was the linchpin of Talos's domestic operations. Muspar wasn't paying attention at first, then looked up and saw them drive past the bright yellow symbol of the little house with the big eye in the centre and the stick family holding hands beneath it. Over top, like a rainbow, was written KEEPING AN EYE ON US. "What the hell Skinner!" bellowed Muspar, startling Ricky who slammed on the brakes, "Let me out here, I'm already late and I don't want to ride around the goddam city sightseeing with you. Park the car, find Suite 500, and be waiting there for me."

With that the door slammed and Ricky could see the Captain rushing up the sidewalk towards the Rainbow archway, half walking and half running. Ricky didn't think there'd be much to go sightseeing for in the city, he'd been there for just over two years now and hadn't seen anything interesting. Just grey streets wet with snow and slush, and rows and rows of people always waiting for the buses or for groceries or for fuel. His family had told him not to go the City, but at the time everyone else had been going. His two cousins had already left and they had said there was lots of work and he should come down before the big evacuation when there'd be no jobs left.

Two more times around and he found a parking spot, got his yellow ticket and headed up the elevator to the fifth floor of the building. Every so often along the grey walls were the posters saying different things, like WATCHING OVER YOU with a big yellow sun peering down on the stick family, mom and dad and a little boy. Ricky could see the cameras in all the corners of the hallway and wondered if those were the same cameras that you saw on the street, and then wondered about the men who sat and watched the images from the cameras everyday. Thought of them sitting in their booths, just watching.

That's what the guy Miller had told him. He asked Miller about the cameras when the guy had come down to get his requisition filled for the mission up into the territories. Miller had said that there were cameras everywhere, not just in some public spaces, but even inside people's homes, and there were guys who sat all day watching to make sure nothing bad happened. Ricky didn't really believe that, saying you could see if someone put a camera in your home. And then Miller had said no, it wasn't like they were sneaking them in there, people wanted it, you know, to be part of I-TIME, to film themselves doing things. Like what? Ricky asked. I don't know, said Miller, everything, eating, fighting, screwing, whatever they wanted. Miller explained that people liked that shit, though he found it boring, except when there was crime and stuff, or a couple got into the fighting. Or to see some titties, that was okay too.

The way Miller explained it, I-TIME had started off just as entertainment, but then one night some guy had busted into a home with I-TIME and everyone saw this punk pound on this old guy to get his prescription drugs until finally one of the neighbours had realized it was just next door and called the cops. Ricky asked what happened to the old man and Miller said "Well, by the time the cops got there the guy was flatlining, the perp had used a rolling pin on his head." Then Miller added, grinning, "It went totally viral, watched it a few times myself." Miller told Ricky that I-TIME was now tied into the security network in order to protect people. Protect them from what, asked Ricky. Bad guys you moron,

I just told you. Miller had grabbed a gun off the rack and pointing it at Ricky, said, guys like home invaders, they're everywhere, tie you up, rape the women, torture the husband right in front of the whole family, it was happening all over the place. Miller said there'd been big problems with roving gangs, especially along the edges of the City. Ricky didn't know what else to say so he had dropped it, feeling suddenly uncomfortable, thinking about the man and the woman tied up in their living room, the men in the booths watching and the gun Miller was pointing at him.

"Can I help you?"

Ricky looked at the young woman sitting behind the grey desk. She had soft brown hair. Ricky said. "I'm looking for Room 500."

The young woman frowned a little, looking very official, asked, "And what business do you have here?"

"I'm picking up Captain Muspar. He's in an important meeting."

Ricky looked around. There was a pair of blue chairs right along the wall, a nice little table between them. The woman had a coffee maker behind her desk and there was a cup of coffee on the little table.

"500 is straight down the hall, see?" She pointed. "You can go wait there."

Ricky looked down the hall and could see the row of spare grey chairs near the end of the hall.

"Could I wait here," asked Ricky, gesturing to the empty chair "maybe get one of those coffees?" Smiling, all friendly, thinking the woman was pretty even though she wore those small black glasses that made her look like a librarian.

"No, you can't. Down the hall, please."

Ricky smiled again, not sure why he was smiling because he suddenly wasn't feeling very happy, but it was just a nervous reaction he guessed, and he was sort of embarrassed. Ricky turned and shuffled off down the hall, wondering how she decided who got to sit in the blue chairs.

It was impossible to get comfortable on the grey chairs so Ricky kept getting up and walking the short length of the hall to the window, would look down below at the adjoining roof and stare for awhile, and then walk back, sit for another few minutes until his legs got too cramped, and then he'd walk back to the window. The meeting was taking a long time.

Sometimes he could hear the men talking loud, like maybe they were arguing. That didn't surprise him much, seemed to him that the Captain liked to argue.

Ricky wasn't really sure what they were talking about, but he started to listen harder when he heard "Raven Uplands" because he knew that was the new name for where he had grown up. They had renamed it just before he'd left, a huge area that Talos had said they were going to turn into a park. They came in with big green signs that had said "Welcome to The Raven Uplands: Talos's Vision of our Future" but that was before things got real bad and everyone had to leave, even the park officials. Ricky liked the signs though because there were lots of ravens in the area, and sometimes they even sat, hunched over and squawking, along the top edge of the signs.

Once, one of his neighbours had sat up all through the early morning and shot every raven he saw, then walked along the road to the next bush and did the same thing, shooting them and tossing them into his wheelbarrow. He killed a huge pile of them then pushed them back to his place while Ricky and his mother had stood at the end of their road to watch him go by. Ricky followed along beside him, saying nothing, watching the black tangle of feathers, the flat eyes looking back at him.

The old guy put them in a big mound in his backyard and covered them with dried up grass and then poured gasoline all over

145

them and set the whole pile on fire. It stunk up the whole road. The old man was mad because the ravens had pecked the eyes out of one of his newborn lambs. Ricky's mom had said to him that it was a good thing it hadn't been one of the neighbourhood dogs that'd gotten his sheep or he would've started World War Three on the road. Ricky supposed that was true.

The Captain's voice came through the door but it was too muffled to hear, then the voice was clear because the door opened. From where Ricky was standing he could see the Captain's hand on the doorknob and that Mr. Scott guy was telling the Captain it wasn't smart to be walking out at this point.

"Smart is the last thing I'm worried about."

Scott said, "Well, a smart man would be thinking of his career right now, would be thinking about what is good for himself and for the City."

Captain was saying, "You threatening me?"

"Hardly, you are the one threatening things here, and the biggest thing you're threatening is the success of this mission."

"No. I wasn't aware of the exact nature of this mission when I released my men to you. It's risky and it's wrong. That's not how we do things. I want to be on record as opposing this..."

"You're missing the point Captain, there is no record."

"Well I keep records Scott, and I'll go up the chain of command if I have to."

"Listen to me and listen closely, because this comes from up the chain of command. You know who is at the top of the heap here? Our shareholders. And right now, all of Talos's services are overstretched. We're maxed out, my correctional facilities are beyond capacity, and there are hundreds of assholes lining up every night for a bed in one of our work shelters. And we aren't making any money off them, we've got as many as we can working, but right now some of them are costing more than we can make off them. So what I don't need are any more yokels down here, especially not troublesome ones, and I also don't need any negative publicity on this. You understand what I'm saying? No more warm bodies down here and no one knowing there are warm bodies up there. That simple."

"I don't know what your corporate culture is, but at Police Services, we do not execute people. Understand? This isn't a dictatorship where you can just eliminate people. My god Scott, we're public servants."

"That's where you are wrong, very wrong. At Talos we don't work for the public, we work for our shareholders. Our corporate mission is, however, to ensure the best interests of the public are identified and accommodated. You may not have noticed, but we are operating under extreme conditions, we need to maintain order or this whole place could explode into chaos. That is not in the best interests of the public, now is it? And get your head out of the goddam sand Muspar and get real. How do you think Talos has been getting things done?"

"I thought it was by the book."

"It is, Muspar, but by Talos's book."

"This wasn't how it was supposed to go down."

"I am going to tell you how it is going to go down," Scott said, and Muspar's hand came away from the door but the door stayed ajar and Ricky could still hear. The Scott guy talked for awhile longer, talking about Laskin and the mission and that the only ones coming south would be the Wintermen in body bags, and then some other things Ricky didn't understand.

Then the door came wide open, Muspar turning to face Scott, said, "If this thing goes south, Police Services will not wear it, not this time."

"Have a good day Captain."

Ricky straightened himself out, but the Captain walked right past him, not even really noticing, making some sort of gesture that Ricky figured meant for him to follow along. It was a long ride back to headquarters. Ricky was thinking back to the files, wondering if there was a mistake, but then thinking back too about what that Mr. Scott had said about killing people. Something inside Ricky's stomach was starting to feel bad and he was pretty sure his Uncle Delbert was dead.

He needed to know for sure though, so he'd been thinking more about his trip up north, heading up to see if his Uncle really was dead, then maybe going to see his mom. He just felt too bad to stay in the City anymore, but he was hoping the Captain couldn't tell what he was planning because he would probably try to stop him. He knew it wasn't really possible for the Captain to read his mind, but one time the Captain had yelled at him, saying, "Skinner, I catch you looking at Miss Saxon again, you're out of here. I know exactly what you are thinking, once more and you're gone. I won't have that in my office."

He'd been thinking about the black lace he could see through Miss Saxon's white blouse and he turned red and the Captain had sworn at him and Ricky could feel his face going even redder, and he tried to explain that he hadn't meant to stare but the Captain said, "I told Community Services, no retards and no perverts. Christ almighty, you're both."

Since then, Ricky tried not to think about much when the Captain was around. That was why he liked to be down in the storage room, because he could work without anyone noticing him. He could think all he wanted about the black lace that covered Miss Saxon's breasts. And how he was going to get out of the City.

Laskin figured she'd probably been up all night. A slice of dark blue sky through the window, almost dawn, and there she was, sitting on the edge of her cot. Laskin stretched and then patted the space beside him.

"Come on Mitch, you gotta sleep. Come to poppa."

She crossed over quietly and sat down on his cot with her back towards him. The rest of the team was asleep, Turner snoring loudly. They were back in their cramped room, Jeff and Larose having locked them in there, saying they'd see them in the morning.

Mitch said, "My head hurts."

"Too bad baby, you shouldn't stayed up all night fretting, come on, lie down."

She rubbed her temples. "What went wrong Grier? We've never had problems like this before?" and then she asked, "Do you know how many ops we've done together?

Laskin said no but he figured it'd be quite a few.

"Twenty-eight, not counting the recreational shit."

"Yeah?" He was surprised there were that many. Surprised too that she was keeping count. He'd always had the feeling that it wouldn't take Mitch much to cut him loose, a job promotion, a bigger alpha male—though that would be unlikely. He figured he was about as alpha as any guy was going to get. And he was going to prove it too, once he got it all worked out.

"And out of that twenty-eight not one has gone wrong till now."

Laskin sighed. "We've run into some rough spots before, come on Mitch."

"But we sorted them out."

"Well maybe this is just another rough spot. It's not over yet."

"What? The hillbillies toss us out, shaking their fists at us, send us packing back back to the City with our tails between our legs? It was supposed to be a simple gig, we bag 'em and tag 'em. And now this shitshow? We might never work again."

Slipping his arm around her waist, he said there might be better ways to spend their time in the room besides whining.

"I'm not whining, I just want a plan."

"Time for some hardball Mitch. That's the plan. I mean look at it, they only have maybe ten able-bodied men. I think we could take them out pretty easily. We need to teach them a lesson for punching above their weight class."

"No, this thing is all fucked up. We got an entire population that's compromised. We can't go in with guns blazing, not with the kids and seniors, not with the orders we're operating under now. Talos would be pissed and we definitely would not work again. Especially not with Police Services involved like they are."

"Since when do you do things by the book?"

"Since always Grier. We're going to have to go back."

"Okay, then we go back. But we can't go back without our shit. We'd look like dickheads. Gotta salvage something from this crapass mission."

"Grier, do you like my hair like this, maybe I should've kept it long?"

Where the Christ did that come from? He looked up the curve of her back, running his hand down along her spine and letting it rest against her rump. He hadn't known her when she had long hair, imagining it all pale golden, way down her back. That'd be okay, but he liked her this way. "You know honey, if I didn't know any better, I'd say you were more pissed off that your Snow Pirate kept his chastity belt buckled up than the fact that we're being held prisoner along with a year's worth of toilet paper."

She looked over her shoulder, him figuring she could hear in his voice that he was annoyed. She said, "Look at it this way Grier, it might just work for us. After all, hell hath no fury like a woman scorned."

"Have something in mind?"

"I got a gun under my pillow and a hard-on for some payback, my mind's got nothing to do with it."

———

"So now what?"

A few of them had gathered in the kitchen. It was another cold one, Tiny's thermometer saying it was minus 25.

"Good question, Harv. No way of keeping them here, we just don't have the facilities. And who would want to? Imagine looking after that bunch day in and day out. I think we didn't count on them being so loaded for bear—these guys are the real deal."

"I say we kill them," Tiny said.

Slaught looked over at Tiny to make sure he was joking but it was hard to tell. "Kill them? Then what?"

"Stack 'em outside. It's cold enough."

"So," Slaught moving to change the direction of conversation, "Do you think they really came to move us out?"

"What? Park Rangers?" Chumboy skeptical, raising his eyebrows.

"Well, maybe not Park Rangers. But maybe one of those evacuation teams, everyone knows there was some serious shit going down in some places during the evacuations. Not that it really matters, I mean one of those Talos departments is the same as the other, but I guess I'd like to know why the hell they're bothering with us. That was the whole point of this party charade, to find out just what the hell they wanted, and we're still not really clear on anything."

"Me, I go with the big trouble option. Stealth Barbie doesn't look like any of the Park Rangers I've ever run into and trust me, I ran into a fair number back in the day. I say we let 'em stew for awhile, maybe a day or so, go through all their shit again to see if we can turn up anything, and just go about our business. We could send 'em packing without their gear, maybe just a GPS so they don't end up back here by mistake. We can't really tangle with them too much longer, already lost a day of hunting. Christ almighty, we'll be down to pigtail soup pretty soon."

True enough, Slaught thought. "Guess we don't have the luxury of sitting here worrying too much on it, we need food for sure. And the list of supplies is growing by the minute, it's going to be a full time job keeping this place supplied. And now having to deal with these clowns."

"Well, like I say, we let them sweat a bit, send them down the trail without their gear. Don't see as we have much choice."

"I don't know, Chum."

"That's not like you big guy. That chick's got you rattled."

"What chick?" Susun asked as she pulled up a chair. Her hair was loose this morning, Slaught thinking he hadn't realized how long it was, thinking 'what chick' was a good question.

"Just pondering our prisoners."

Susun said. "I say kill 'em."

"What's that, the Latour solution to everything? Kill 'em?"

Susun looked over at Tiny and nodded. Tiny nodded back, said, "Fucking A," then asked Susun if she wanted some pancakes. "They're hot."

"Load 'em up, I'm a hungry girl. Starting to feel myself again."

"That's a good thing," Slaught said, "you'll need the fuel, I was thinking of sending you out on a scavenge today. We're sort of short handed with our guests, plus we got a ton of stuff we need. Thought maybe you and Jeff could go out."

Susun asked, "Looking for some alone time with Mitch?"

Slaught looked at her, not sure what he saw in her face, was she just playing or maybe she was actually pissed. She sure did have a sarcastic disposition. But he liked her almost too long face, eyebrows raised now, looking straight at him waiting for an answer. He couldn't think of anything to say so he just looked back, and she said, "I just think maybe you're out of your league with that one."

"You think so, eh?"

"Well, come on, she had you up against the wall like she was stealing your school lunch."

"I think I can handle Ms. Black."

Susun took the maple syrup from Tiny, him saying to her, "It's the real thing, don't waste it." Susun said thanks, then turned to Slaught, suddenly serious, "I'm not so sure you can handle her, I have a bad feeling about this."

Johnny had a bad feeling himself but he was doing his best to ignore it. Seeing the sled full of weapons? Man, it was some heavy-duty firepower. But they'd started this chain of events, and now they had to see it through. Didn't need her stirring up doubts either. "That's all you got, bad feelings. Christ, for someone named after the sun, you're just goddam gloomy."

Susun shrugged, "Okay, sorry, just thought I should say something. If you listened to what your gut was telling you, you'd agree, but you're just too stubborn to admit it."

"So now you know everything about me."

"I know enough, yeah."

Slaught suggested maybe she could figure out the rest when she was out on the trail, was she going to go or not?

"Yeah, I'll go."

"Good, 'cause we're running low on everything. You could check the maps and see if there are any places we haven't already hit six times. Jeff's just getting things together now."

"Okay, but maybe you should start thinking about what happens when you've picked your cupboard bare out there. Time to start thinking about the long term, putting down some roots here, figuring out how to grow some food maybe. You'll be looking down starvation alley if you don't get your shit together."

"Look, our unwanted guests are already giving me more than enough grief, so no more of your doom and gloom routine, it's hard on my nerves."

Susun shrugged and got up to leave, then put her hand on his shoulder and leaned around to look into his face. She was smiling, said, "Well, Winterman, your secret's safe with me, that barracuda doesn't need to know that you're just a bundle of raw nerves."

She told him to watch his back while she was gone. He said he'd do his best.

The first thing Mitch shouted through the door when they knocked was that she wasn't dressed yet but they could come on in anyways.

"Now what?" Chumboy whispered.

"She's bluffing," Slaught said, turning the key and then pushing open the door.

Solanski and Turner were still tucked in, Tuner snoring loudly. Laskin was stretched out in the bed across the room, his head propped up on his elbow, smiling. Miller was playing cards with the other two guys in the far corner. Mitch stood in the centre of the room facing the door, back to Laskin and the boys, dressed only in a small pair of black briefs.

"And I took you for upstanding Christian gentlemen. You surprise me, walking in on a lady like that," she said, just standing there.

All Slaught could see was Laskin's smug self-satisfied jerk-off grin. Had to admit, though, she had a near perfect rack. He grabbed a shirt off the end of Miller's bed and tossed it at her.

"You're no lady. Now put this on and keep it on or you'll be wearing your skivvies out in the snow. And you, Laskin, wipe that piece of shit smirk off your face. You may not realize it, but you people are not in a very good situation here."

Mitch looked a little thrown off but pulled on the shirt, slowly buttoning it up. Chumboy said later he didn't know how a girl doing up her shirt could still look like she was stripping. Slaught waited till she was finished then told her to go sit down on the bed with Laskin.

"Okay Laskin, you got one minute to explain what you people are doing with two sleds worth of shit that would've made Al-Qaeda horny, or else we're dumping all of you out in the bush and your girlfriend here can perform her floor show for the wolves. Understand?"

"Like I already told you Mr. Slaught, we are an advance team from Parks, basically recon, you know, here to find out what's in the way of the new boundaries, and if there are going to be any problems. That's what we do."

"You're outta time Laskin."

Laskin sighed, "You know guys, I'd be willing to overlook all of this, I could even leave the hostage-taking and threats out of my official report. But you aren't coming across right now as very reasonable. The government needs to know you are up here so that they can facilitate your evacuation. Simple as that."

Chumboy said, "Facilitate our evacuation? Whoa up there, General Custer, you white guys already tried that with us once, and as you can see, my Algonquin brothers and sisters are still here and planning on staying." He looked at Slaught. "Me? I say these guys are full of the same old shit."

Laskin said maybe they shouldn't be so quick. "We got a few carrots to throw your way boys, might want to have a listen. Safe transportation for your entire community out of here and government sponsored food and accommodation for the first six months of residency in the City. Also job placement support and any necessary counseling will be provided."

Slaught said to him, "That's all you got?"

Laskin was looking a little too self satisfied as he said, "Well, I also have the authority to offer full pardons if that is of any interest to you."

"Pardons? For what?"

Mitch spoke up, crossing her legs, elbow on knee and leaning forward to rest her chin on her hand. "You know it's against the law to live within the Territories right now."

"Hey man," Chumboy said, "enough of your bullshit, this happens to be Algonquin territory, always has been, and right now, you're the ones trespassing.'

Mitch barely glanced at Chumboy, saying to Slaught, "And it is also against the law to threaten and forcibly confine Talos employees. Not to mention those murder charges from a few years back. You're not a very nice boy Johnny."

"Is that right?"

"Yes, it is, and pretty soon you and all your friends will be hauled off to correctional facilities. We're talking serious prison time. Is that what you want for your little community? For your friends? I don't think so."

"Well, that's a good point, maybe I'll go ask them."

Mitch said, looking straight at him, "Why don't you do that Johnny, and at the same time, ask yourself if you really have the stomach to see this thing through?"

Slaught saw her eyes, the colour of hard toffee, like the candy bars he had as a kid, needing to smash them to get smaller pieces, and thought she was asking a damn good question.

CHAPTER TWELVE

A DOZEN PEOPLE HAD DRIFTED INTO THE DINING AREA after dinner to hear the latest. Slaught gave the update, saying they really weren't sure what to do next because they weren't getting any straight answers. A couple of the young guys offered to 'handle' things for him, if he knew what they meant, but Slaught just thanked them and said he'd get back to them on that. Maybe for now they could head on over to the workbay and help Shaun finish stacking that twenty cord of firewood lying out in the snow.

Mrs. Merrill said they should lock up that Jezebel and throw away the key. Slaught, assuming she meant Mitch Black, explained that they just didn't have the means to hold anybody prisoners and she said, "Mr. Slaught, I've seen that woman, she has the evil eye. Don't turn your back on her."

Slaught agreed and then to get Mrs. Merrill to shut up because she was starting to freak him out, asked her if she would mind going and helping out Mary because they were trying to figure out how much extra bedding might be around and it was time to get that organized. Mrs. Merrill looked put out, saying she was busy working on her needlepoint and she held it up to show Slaught, the little blue house surrounded by red and green flowers with neat, tight little stitches that said "God Bless This Home." Slaught nodded appreciatively, wondering if she was being ironic, but then said in a confidential tone, "She could really use your help Mrs. Merrill, she's well meaning, you know, but not the most organized, if you know what I mean."

"Oh, I certainly do Mr. Slaught, we had some of them come up back in the day, when I was still in school, back to the land types, you know, hippies. Couldn't keep house to save their souls."

"Yes, you're right again Mrs. Merrill, but I gotta say, they deliver a mean baby."

Once Mrs. Merrill was on her way, Slaught told everyone he'd let them know if anything exciting happened, then headed down to the workbay.

Chumboy was going through all of the gear, saying as Slaught came in, "Man, this is like Christmas."

Slaught said, "Yeah, I guess we're going to have to start thinking about that, having a real Christmas, now that we got all these kids."

"Yeah, well I don't think this stuff is really going to cut it for under the tree, it isn't exactly little toy train material. But we got ourselves some great toys for big boys."

"Anything we can use?

"Most of it. It's pretty slick shit though so I guess it depends what we get up to, I mean its not moose hunting gear, eh? Scored some fine battery power though."

"Don't suppose there's any paper work in there is there? Orders you know, any mission impossible shit?"

"You know Johnny, you're very old school. No paperwork, but buddy there had a laptop with him, I passed it over to Jeff and Jordan, see if they can find their way around the thing."

"Well, that's something I guess, but what we need right now is to get those rambo types the hell outta here."

"No kidding. No one wants to even bring them their meals. I asked for volunteers and no takers."

"Well, we can't keep 'em forever, but I think we're stuck for another night at least—send 'em out first thing in the morning, I can go down tonight to feed 'em if no one else will go."

"Not to worry, I told Jordan he had to, but he is some terrified of your Mitch Black."

"Mrs. Merrill called her Jezebel."

"Jezebel? I don't know about that, all Jezebel did was try to stop folks from worshipping Yahweh and slaughter a few prophets. And for that, her servants tossed her out a window so a pack of dogs could divvy her up. No, I was thinking more along the lines of someone like Sekmet or even Artemis."

"Never heard of Sekmet."

"Some Egyptian type, apparently had eyes that shone like fire."

"Yeah, that sounds about right—what about Artemis, that Greek?"

"Greek indeed. Goddess of the hunt. Reputed to wear a necklace of bull scrotums around her neck. Some poor sap came along and saw her in the buff, she turned him into a stag and then his own hounds ripped him to shreds. So keep your peepers to yourself buddy until Ms. Black is long down the trail."

"Just glad I don't have any dogs."

"Well, that Sekmet chick wouldn't be any easier. She got it in her head to destroy the whole human race."

"I think you're making this shit up Chum."

"No way man, honest truth."

"Then how come I've never heard of this Sekmet, then?"

"Come on Johnny, think of the all the things you've never heard of. That's why you need me around."

Slaught was just staring at him, thinking he was a pain in the ass sometimes. "If you're so fucking smart, how do we deal with a hellcat like the one sitting in our storage room?"

"Beer."

"Beer?"

"That's what they used to distract Skemet from her path of destruction."

"So she's all ready to rip some poor slob to shreds and someone yells Miller Time and that's it?"

"Not quite that easy, it took seven thousand jars of beer dyed the colour of blood."

"Thanks Chum, I'll get right on that."

"Anytime buddy."

Slaught told Chumboy that most of his information was as useless as shit but he did think it might be a good time for a beer. Maybe they could find Susun and Jeff, see how the scavenging went. Chumboy said he'd go get Jeff, would leave Susun to Slaught since he was such a lady-killer.

Susun was just shutting her door when Slaught came climbing up the stairs. She stopped when she saw him, asked, "Looking for me?"

"Matter of fact I was, thought I'd see how you were feeling after your first day as an outlaw."

She smiled, said, "Rifling through some lady's kitchen with Jeff didn't exactly make me feel like Bonnie and Clyde, but we did find some useful stuff. Got a large batch of beeswax."

"Beeswax?"

"Planning for the future, thinking of setting myself up as an herbalist, could use the beeswax for ointments."

"Did you find anything that we can use now? The future is kind of a crap shoot."

"That's your problem right there, the future is already starting. You have people coming here all the time, families, old folks, a young couple the other day. You think you're hiding out at your hunt camp when in fact you're smack dab in the middle of a community."

"Guess I should of holed up in my ice shack instead of a goddam hotel, eh?"

"Okay, I have to ask. Why a hotel? Not exactly a classic hideout, know what I mean?"

"Well, the Fraser isn't just any hotel, it's one made to measure for any end times scenario."

"Yeah? How's that?"

"Well, you might not know this, but back in the day, this town was a textbook case of a firetrap, burnt down as often as they could rebuild. Finally, they built this place, fire proof to the max—it isn't going anywhere."

Susun smiled, said, "Well, Winterman, you're right, I didn't know that, and know what else I don't know? Where to get a beer in this lousy joint. Tiny said I was the best scavenger he'd met so far so I think I deserve one."

Slaught asked her what she'd snagged to earn that praise and she said two sealed bottles of Napoleon Brandy.

"God almighty, you gave that to Tiny?"

"Said he could use it for Christmas cakes. Figured you guys would just polish it off, it seemed special, so, yeah, I gave it to Tiny."

Slaught couldn't believe it, but decided to drop it, said, "So did you enjoy your first scavenger trip?"

She was leaning against the door, arms crossed, hair scraggly, a bit like the first day he saw her. She smiled, saying it was a little weird going into people's houses, seeing things like toasters and pillows coated with ice, seeing where animals had gotten in, caught a raccoon sleeping on a turquoise sofa, paw prints all over the coffee table, but said yeah, the ride was great, and that it felt good to be doing something instead of hiding. "You get a little crazy when you're hiding all the time, waiting for someone to come and pick on you."

"I noticed."

She gave him a dirty look, but could tell he was joking, and then he said, "Not so bad being one of those anarchists is it?"

"No, guess not. "

He sort of stared at her, unsure of what to say. She just looked back, so he said, "Well, why not come down for that beer then, rite of passage."

"Even though I gave away the brandy?"

"Yeah, but it's your loss. If you'd thought about it for a minute before turning it over to Tiny, you could be drinking it right now. As it is, you're stuck with Chumboy's homemade hooch."

Jordan had groaned when Chumboy said he'd have to be the one to go check on the prisoners before bed, toss some food through the door and make sure they were tucked in for the night. Shaun had slapped him on the back, tossed him the keys and told him to man up. Jordan had steeled himself, finding Mitch Black to be one terrifying broad, expecting his dinner delivery to be rough but not expecting to end up with a gun to his head and being frog marched back down the hallway towards the back door of the hotel. At this very moment, his life totally sucked.

She moved fast, you had to give her that. He'd found them all sitting around when he knocked, he sort of stopped part way into the room because there was something funny in the way they were looking at him, and Mitch had said, "Jason, nice to see you," and he said "It's Jordan" and then she was right beside him with a gun to his temple saying, "I don't really give a fuck what your name is, in fact I think I'll call you Janice."

And then the big tray of food was all over the floor and they were all up, dressed in their snow gear, and he was moving down the hall, wondering what the hell to do now, wondering too if they were just going to pull the trigger, it must feel so easy when you're holding the gun to just pull the trigger. He had never pulled a trigger. Never even shot a partridge.

"Get a move on, Janice," Mitch said, twisting the gun barrel against his head.

In what seemed like a matters of seconds they were down the hall and Laskin was booting open the door, the cold air blasting into Jordan's face as Mitch shoved him in front of her through the snow. The sky was navy, the hard diamond stars flung up here and there across the horizon, the snow hard packed but Jordan still tripping in it, Mitch yanking him back and tightening the grip on his shirt. It smarted a bit and Jordan asked, "You going to kill me?"

"I'd love to, so just shut the fuck up or I will."

Jordan figured he'd better do as he was told because this wasn't really his kind of situation, and by the look on Shaun's face as they all came ploughing through the door of the workbay, it wasn't really his either. Kirstie was there, sitting on the workbench, and Shaun had just straightened up from laying down another armful of firewood. Shaun made eye contact with Jordan but it wasn't helpful, more like what the fuck is going on. Kirstie looked scared, eyeing the gun in Mitch's hand. Shaun moved over beside Kirstie, saying, "We got a problem here?" Jordan thinking it was obvious there was a problem, but Mitch said, "I think you have the problem asshole, and if you don't do exactly as I say, your problem is going to get a lot worse."

The two guys that never talked went straight over to get the machines ready. One of them said it looked like most of their extra fuel was gone but Laskin said it'd be fine, they'd fuelled up just before coming in here. Then the big loud mouth was checking the bins saying, "There's nothing fucking here," and Mitch turned to Shaun, "Our guns?"

"They're in lock-up."

"Where's that?"

"Back inside."

Jordan heard Mitch curse under her breath then she looked to Laskin. "So?"

Jordan could see him thinking, someone needed to get the guns but there was just one weapon between them. Laskin asked if the machines were ready to go, and Leclerc said everything seemed fine. Laskin said, "Turner, behind you, the drill, give it." Laskin sounding impatient, waving his hand as Turner passed him the drill, then saying, "Get the big doors open and the machines ready to go. And now, which of you puppies has the keys to the lock-up?"

Nobody said anything. Laskin made a 'tsking' sound and revved the drill a bit to make sure it was working, and moved over to the workbench where Shaun was standing. "Ever see that movie, what was it, *Saw*, maybe *Saw II*?"

Jordan figured Shaun was trying to put on a brave face in front of Kirstie, her clinging to Shaun's arm as he said, "If you wanted to crash our party you should've just said so. Sorry, no movies, but there's more beer outside in the snow."

"This isn't a party, jerkoff, its is a fucking home invasion. Now if you don't get down to the lock up and come back with our stuff I'm going to take this drill to your honey's face. I'll make *Saw II* look like *Mary* fucking *Poppins*."

Jordan said, "Okay, okay. I have the keys."

Mitch barked at Jordan, "Get over here. And you, you little bitch, I want you to tape your boyfriend here up nice and tight, okay?"

Jordan said, "Alright, just calm down, I'm going, but I'll need a bag or something."

"Get back here quick," Laskin said, telling Leclerc to toss him a bag from the sled. "No complications and these two will still be able to pucker up, understand?" Jordan glanced back at Kirstie, her trying to get the tape started, dropping it, swearing, then hearing the tear of the tape as she got started on Shaun's ankles.

Jordan didn't want to run, more because it made him feel panicked rather than worried he might attract attention. Where the fuck was everybody anyway? He wasn't sure if he wanted to see anyone, might make a mess of everything, but then maybe he did. He didn't know what he wanted and he sure didn't know what to do. Man, this was messed up, this was like a 'no fucking way out' situation. He pictured it, positioning the gun in the bag, coming into the room, swinging up the bag and shooting Laskin, but then what? There were too many of them, five other guys plus the psycho bitch. He didn't stand a chance.

He got to the lock up, hands shaking as he tried the key, sliding open the door and stepping in, scanning the shelves, seeing the guns sticking out of a big box marked For Elves Eyes Only. Chumboy's handwriting. He grabbed them, shoved them in the hockey bag then dumped in several clips. Grabbing a few GPS he headed for the door, stopping first to listen, then heading back down to the bay, the bag bumping against his leg awkwardly.

When Turner let him in through the door he leaned into him, said, "You're a lucky little shit you delivered the goods," sounding tough but smelling too much like the sickly aftershave you wear in Grade Ten. Jordan didn't say anything, but walked over to where Laskin was waiting and dropped the bag. "A few guns, several clips, GPS. Okay?"

Laskin unzipped the bag and had a look, saying he was indeed fucking lucky but they still owed him some hardware and he'd be back for it.

Jordan said, "Yeah, well, I don't feel so lucky."

Both Laskin and Mitch laughed, and Mitch said he sounded like he was pouting and Kirstie said, "Never mind Jordan, come on over here."

Jordan couldn't hear what Laskin said to Mitch as he reached out and she passed him her gun, but when he turned around he said, "Okay fellas, mount up, time to ride out of shitsville."

Jordan was wondering why he wasn't feeling relieved at this point, but it was probably the look in Laskin's face as he shoved the gun into his belt, something just not quite right, and then Mitch said to Laskin he should get a move on with whatever was going down because they didn't want anyone surprising them at this point, so Laskin said, "Hey, Kirstie, I want you to do me a favour."

Shaun said, "Leave her alone."

Laskin was taking the drill off the bench saying, "Shut the fuck up and listen, because you have an important message to deliver to Slaught, understand?"

Kirstie just stared at Laskin, Jordan figuring she wouldn't want to be looking at the drill.

"Kirstie, you focused here?" he asked again, giving the drill a shake in her direction.

"Leave her alone," Shaun said again, moving forward to try and get in front of her, but his ankles were taped now and he moved awkwardly, leaning too far forward, and Laskin brought the drill up and slammed it hard across Shaun's face, throwing him into Kirstie and opening a thick gash of red angled along his temple.

"I said shut the fuck up, okay? Now, Kirstie, listen, I am going to take this drill to your boyfriend here. Don't worry, I'm not going to kill him or anything, I just really liked that movie, know what I mean? And then you're going to tell Slaught that I'm coming back real soon with a bunch of my guys to do the same thing to every last one of you. Got that?"

The sound of the drill started up and Jordan could hear Kirstie crying and swearing as she bent over Shaun, but Jordan couldn't feel anything, felt like he was paralyzed, watching Kirstie trying to stop the blood but it was sticky and getting on everything and then he could see Laskin holding up the drill, readying it to bring down on Shaun, and Kirstie letting go of Shaun and taking the edge of the work bench and tipping it up, shoving it into Laskin. It knocked Laskin off balance, the drill flying backwards, him yelling "You little bitch," and then he steadied himself, reaching across and slamming his fist into Kirstie, sending her crumpling up against Jordan, Shaun falling forward across the bench.

"For Christ's sake," Mitch said, sounding more exasperated than anything, but Laskin's face was hard as he slammed the drill down again against the side of Shaun's head, letting go of it then and whipping the gun from his belt. He aimed it first at Shaun. Shaun was wiping at the blood on his face, trying to see, yelling, and Jordan was trying to think but everything was moving way too fast, and he was tangled up with Kirstie and she was moaning and then he saw Laskin swing the gun down towards them and Jordan tried to pull himself up but couldn't get his hands to move where he wanted. Laskin said, "The little girlfriend will have to give Slaught the message another way I guess," and he shot her twice. One shot seemed to clip her elbow that was sticking out as she was squirming to find a way of pulling herself up, and then the other bullet plunged into her side, sort of grabbing her in the gut, making her sort of bend up then fall back into Jordan who was yelling her name, and then both of them losing their balance and pitching sideways into a stack of milk crates. Then everything went black.

Chapter Thirteen

Shaun standing in the doorway smeared with blood sobered Slaught up quick. The kid was yelling, Slaught thinking maybe a machine fell on him. Susun was already up and moving towards him but Shaun was just screaming, "The bay, gotta come to the bay," and she yelled okay and ran after him, Slaught and the rest right behind her.

He couldn't see Shaun as he'd rounded the corner up the hall, the walls now marked with a few bloody smears where he must have grabbed at the wall for balance, and then they were running across the snow in the dark, hearing Shaun up ahead sort of sobbing and gasping for breath in the cold, his old man calling his name, then Shaun hitting the edge of the big doors as he ran inside, the metal clanking harsh in the night air. Slaught figuring there'd been an accident, but when he stepped into the bay it was fucking obvious that something way worse had happened.

Shaun was hunched over Kirstie, yelling, "Christ, look, look what they did, he was going for me, look what they did," and Larose now was trying to pry Shaun away from the tangle of bodies, saying, "We got to check you son, see what's wrong."

Chumboy was pulling the crates away from Jordan's head and shoulders. "Susun, get over here and help me move Kirstie off of Jordan," saying it like he already knew she was dead.

Susun rolled Kirstie to the side, Chumboy then moving around and pulling back the workbench to make more room, the blood leaking from Kirstie's stomach seeping into the sawdust and making it gooey underfoot. Chumboy slipped a bit, and Slaught thought he was about to lose it, but he looked over at Susun and said, "We're going to need a blanket or something to move her," so Susun squeezed out along the wall, stepping carefully past the bent figures of Shaun and his dad.

Slaught was having trouble taking it all in, the blood coating the strip of Kirstie's pale gut that showed beneath her baby blue t-shirt, the blood over Shaun's face, streaked with tears and looking gummy and stiff in his hair. Jordan was propped up against some milk crates, ashen, blood from Kirstie over his arms and chest. Slaught was moving the mess of tools and snowmachine parts away from Jordan, straightening out his legs and talking quietly to him when Susun came back with an armful of blankets. She passed them to Chumboy and they rolled Kirstie onto the blanket, and when they went to lift her the body shifted and Susun recoiled, dropping her end, and Slaught moved in behind her and said "I got it," and took the other end, and he and Chumboy carried her out, Slaught saying to Susun, "Find some plastic sheets and meet us in that room we'd set up as a chapel. Guess we'll be needing it after all."

It took a few hours to get Shaun and Jordan settled in the infirmary. Larose said he'd stay with Susun and the boys overnight, just in case. Shaun's head had been stitched up while Jordan sat stiffly in a chair, Chumboy feeding him scotch, Jordan telling them what had happened, and who said what, and how there really wasn't anything any of them could've done, and then Susun had said, "Lay off the booze, you just don't know with head injuries, we'll have to keep waking you up through the night."

Shaun just sat stooped over, head resting in his hands, not moving, just staring down at the floor. As he sat there Susun cleaned up his hands and got most of the bloody gunk out of his hair. He didn't even seem to notice as she washed him off, turning the warm water in the shallow plastic bowl a bright red.

Slaught was watching Susun, watching as she stroked Shaun's hair with the cloth, pulling sometimes at stuck bits of blood with her fingers, wiping them carefully on the cloth then rinsing it and wringing it out and starting over. There were some steady nerves there he thought. His weren't feeling so steady right now. "I'll go get us some tea. I'll let Tiny know."

—

Slaught was standing in the doorway of the workbay, staring at the stain of blood and the chaos of sled parts strewn across the cement. Some were stranded in the sticky pool of red. His tea had gone cold. He was remembering Darren Cooper, the same blood, the same fucking cement. He heard Jeff saying behind him, "Uh, Johnny, got a minute?"

Johnny turned, Jeff looking like he had just rolled out of bed, hair sticking up, wearing just a t-shirt under his parka, track pants stuck inside his boots. "Just talked to Jordan."

Johnny just nodded, "He gonna be okay?"

"Yeah, I think so, he is pretty shaken up though. Not really prepared for anything like this, I mean, like, this is seriously demented."

Again Slaught just nodded, seeing the drill on the ground,

thinking of Kirstie, smiling as she'd walked by him after the party. Man, he really fucked this one up.

Jeff said, "I just wanted to let you know something, well, something a little, well, potentially helpful but definitely weird. Like bad weird, know what I mean?"

"Not really, Jeff."

"Well, it is sort of like awful, and bad, but maybe it could help, but I thought I should say something either way, okay?"

The guy sure had a hard time getting to the fucking point.

"What's on your mind, Jeff?"

"Well, I actually meant to mention this to you sooner, but I'd set up a surveillance camera, nothing fancy, just to see if it would work. I know I should have asked you guys and all, but basically I was just at the stage of screwing around with it, seeing about the range and all of that…"

"Jeff," Slaught interrupted, sounding to himself like he was shouting, having a hard time focusing on Jeff, seeing the drill there, still bloodied, "what's this about?"

"I'm pretty sure I got it all, Johnny."

"Got what?"

"Well, Jordan and me, we had it set up to capture you guys at the workbench, see what I mean? We thought maybe we'd patch together one of those funniest home videos with a three stooges thing of you guys working on the sleds, you know, for a laugh. And we left it on yesterday by mistake, forgot you know, what with all the shit going on, probably drained that generator too, and sorry about that dude, but I guess we got footage of what happened…"

Slaught was just staring at him now. "They didn't notice?"

"Well, I had it tucked outta sight, and why would they, there was only the one camera ready to go. It was just a fluke."

"And can you see if it worked?"

"Well, yeah, I could check on their laptop. All of ours are out of batteries right now. I could probably get it, but maybe that isn't such a good idea right now?"

"Get it."

Seeing the look on Johnny's face he just said, "Okay."

"Don't say anything to anyone else. Nobody needs to know right now, got it?"

"Yeah, sure Johnny. Might be a while, okay?"

"I'm not going anywhere."

—

The funeral should be held at dawn, that's what Auntie Verla had said. That squared okay with pretty much everyone because nobody wanted the body sitting in the chapel for another day. Chumboy had woken up his Auntie in the middle of the night, telling her he had an awful job for her, and she said, "Who is it?" just like that.

When Chumboy brought her into the chapel and pulled back the plastic, she just said, "Poor little girl," and told him to get her a bucket of clean water and some washcloths.

Auntie Verla and Susun washed the body. When they were done, Auntie Verla told Susun to go find Johnny, said he was probably making the coffin. Susun said, "Why do you think that? I thought he'd gone somewhere with Jeff?"

"Maybe he did, but he's the kind of man to make a coffin."

Susun asked, "What kind of man is that?"

"The kind that is always busy when he should just stand still."

Susun finally found Slaught at the far end of the work bay, door thrown open, his back to her, staring out into the thick turquoise band pushing up into the grey sky. The room was freezing even though Susun had grabbed her parka before she'd gone outside. She glanced over at the workbench. The drill was gone. A rough coffin made out of plywood sat on the floor. He'd made quick work of it.

She walked over to him saying, "Hey there," to let him know she was there, not wanting to startle him.

"Hey." He didn't look over at her, just kept staring out.

She stood beside him. It was cold, damn cold. She waited awhile in the silence with him, just following his gaze. The dawn was starting to make itself seen, changing fast, the sky now the colour of baby blankets.

"You ready?" she asked him.

"Yeah, I'm ready. Is it time?"

"Pretty much. You should say a few words."

"Yeah, I thought of that. Not sure I'll be able to."

She risked looking up at him, his face under the glare of the overhead lights. She couldn't recognize the expression. Rage maybe?

She said, "Not really much choice."

"Oh?"

"People need you to, it's as simple as that."

He nodded, then said, "Okay, you're right. I'll come over, but then I'm going to go get some moose, maybe some fish. With all the shit going on our food stores are real low, not much left and lots of people to feed. I'll be a couple of days."

"You're leaving?"

"That's what I said. After the funeral, I'm heading out."

"I don't know if that's the best idea, someone else could go."

"I said I'm going."

"Look, I know you're feeling bad, we all are, but what if they come back?"

He didn't say anything for a few seconds, then took a deep breath, "I'm going Susun, okay? I'll come back as soon as I can, but I'm going."

"Why?"

"Because I have to, it's as simple as that."

CHAPTER FOURTEEN

SUSUN HADN'T HAD EVEN TWO HOURS OF SLEEP when Chumboy came and woke her up, saying they needed her in the kitchen. When she got there Jeff was already up, cradling a cup of tea, and Chumboy was explaining about this family stuck down near the border.

"That fella, Laurent Champagne, he was here before, comes in every now and again, remember, the prospector guy? Yeah, well anyway, he got in last night just after all the shit hit the fan, tells me that his sister's brother-in-law disappeared about a month ago, probably with a little help from Talos Security. Said the guy went out to the family hunt camp and never came back. She's on her own with four kids and they've pretty much run out of everything. Laurent thinks we should bring them in, told her to sit tight and wait for us. Thought maybe you and Jeff could go."

Susun could just imagine what a woman with four kids would need. "Bringing them in isn't going to be easy."

Chumboy sighed. "Shit ton of fuel too, but we don't have much choice. Make sure you bring extra along, just in case. And see if she has any stashed at her end."

Jeff asked, "How far?"

"Far enough, right near the border."

Jeff whistled, "Yeah, that's a ways."

"Bit of an operation, yeah, but with Johnny MIA, and a few of us needing to stick around here to hold down the fort, I think it's going to fall to you two to go collect them. Me, I think you're going to need at least two machines plus a sled or two in the back, they'll have stuff to bring out."

"What's her name?"

"They're Skinners, think her name is Lorraine."

"Alright, better than sitting around here waiting for Armeggedon."

Jeff looked up from his mug, said, "No kidding, waiting for Armeggedon to get ready can be a real bitch."

Muspar thought Laskin was looking way too comfortable, leaning back in the swivel chair, legs stretched out. The guy took up half the goddam room. When Muspar had seen Solanski dragging himself into headquarters and had asked how things had gone, Solanski just shook his head, said things kind of got out of control. Muspar was on his way to Talos before Solanski could even finish explaining.

Laskin was saying, "I told you, they're hillbillies, plain and simple. They invited us in, threw us a party, started playing with

Brit Griffin ·

some of our guns and got carried away, we decided to bail and come back here to check in. Figured we should apprise you as to the women and children aspect of the situation. End of story."

Muspar said, "Mr. Laskin, you had a very straightforward task," but already Laskin was sort of waving his hand and shaking his head, causing Muspar to stop and ask, "What?"

"Really, call me Grier, that whole Mister thing just doesn't sit right with me. And as for the job, no one said it was over. If it was up to me, boss, that place would have been razed to the ground. Mitch thought we should check in, that there were possible PR issues, I didn't agree with her assessment, but a team is a team. So here we are."

"There is always a place for sober second thought," Bob Scott said, "so what was on your mind, Mitch? Did you get to see Slaught?"

"Yeah, we saw him. On the up side, they're very accessible, not too deep into the Territories and highly visible. These guys aren't hiding out. Downside? There seems to be a group of maybe a half dozen active members of the cell but also a lot of civilian enablers, and that really complicates things."

"How many?" Scott asked.

She glanced at Laskin, "How many was it, forty-four?"

"Something like that, give or take a few kids."

Mitch continued, "There's too many civilians there, way more than we anticipated. It was unclear also how many of them were there because they were left behind and needed a roof over their heads, or were actually ideologically committed to the community."

"Ideologically committed?" Scott asked.

"Well, we're not in total agreement with this interpretation of the community but there does seem to be some sort of extremist religious element. Their community is called Lazarus..."

Laskin interrupting, saying, "It doesn't matter what they are, they could worship fucking Baal, whatever he is, but they're wasting a lot of our valuable time," and then standing up, grabbing his jacket, he said, "Look, these bozos are playing way above their weight class, they have shit when it comes to manpower, fire power and fucking brainpower. So I'm heading back up, with or without the team. I am finishing this, getting my money and going far away." Turning to Mitch he said, "I'm heading out in forty-eight hours, whether you're there or not."

Once the door slammed, Scott looked at Mitch. "What's with him?"

Mitch sighed. "The situation escalated more than we anticipated, probably because we underestimated the Wintermen. As we were leaving, Grier lost it a bit, ending up taking out a civilian. He seems to be having a hard time getting perspective on things."

Muspar figured this Mitch Black might be having some perspective issues of her own. "I think you are going to have to do better than that. What the hell are you talking about, he lost it? A professional doesn't lose it, we send some half-assed celebrity out there to do our dirty work, I guess that it stands to reason doesn't it..."

Mitch interrupted. "Look Captain, it was a new set of circumstances when we got up there, we are told to expect something akin to a rogue hunt camp and we end up in a full-fledged community— women, children, bible thumpers. It was incredibly hard to get a bead on what was going on, there were lots of different dynamics and it was, quite frankly, difficult to accept that the whole community could be conspiring to create some sort of faux Waco."

Muspar persisted. "Want to explain exactly what happened, from the beginning, right through to how your boyfriend managed to kill someone?"

She sighed as she looked at him, Muspar thinking she was

sizing him up, weighing in her mind how much she had to give a shit about what he had to say. He could see as she turned away from him, giving him her back, that she'd made up her mind. "No, I don't want to fucking explain."

Muspar couldn't believe this bitch. Standing there in her saran wrap dress, thinking she could say anything she wanted. He was walking, taking his boys and walking, that was the last straw, but Scott was saying, "Okay, whoa people, look. Let's all calm down, we need to be cool and think this thing through. People high up the food chain are watching and expect results, from all of us. Now, we clearly have a serious situation, and I think you did the right thing by coming back and checking in, decisions like that can't always be made in the field. These are decisions that Talos," and looking over to Muspar, "and Police Services need to make together in order to secure the situation, and keep our shareholders happy."

"Your shareholders?" Muspar was incredulous. "I think there are more important things at stake here."

"Well Captain, maybe I need to remind you that those share-holders control a large part of your budget too, not just mine. So let's remember that we have shared interests and objectives and that we should be working towards obtaining those objectives, okay?"

Shared interests my ass. Muspar had no doubt that Scott would hang him out to dry if this crapshoot turned sour, and he was getting a strong feeling that was exactly where it was headed.

Scott was saying, "Now, our fatality?"

Mitch shook her head, "Young female, simple case of collateral damage. But regardless, that place is going to be in an uproar over it. My guess, though, is that the death will panic them, probably undermine the leadership core and create some chaos. That works for us but it might take a couple of days to filter through the group.

I think we should proceed carefully, maybe try to ID some of the other players up there. I don't think we need to rush. Let's face it, they can't really reinforce or re-tool their operation. There really isn't anything they can do to get ready for us, so I think we have a couple of days at least on our side."

"So are we going to stick with the original plan then?"

Mitch shrugged. "It's your call but I think taking out a few of the key players on site, rounding up the rest and bringing them out, it could work but we'll have to keep them under lock and key and away from the public. The PR would have been tricky even without the casualty, but now, well, I guess Talos can handle the PR on that."

"We talking actual families?"

"Some, and a lot of old geezers. The optics aren't ideal."

"Well, we've talked before about how grueling the trip can be, maybe some of them won't survive it," Bob Scott said quietly. "It is more than plausible too that in the arrest process there is more collateral damage..."

Muspar wasn't sure what he'd heard. "What the hell are you talking about?"

"I'm not talking about anything Captain, except a situation that is potentially very damaging to both Talos and the Police Services, as I've already explained to you. My thinking right now is to stick to our original operation for appearances sake, take up the trucks are far as the border, and then Ms. Black here can make a judgement call."

"I don't think I am willing to turn the control of this operation over to some Talos operative who can't even keep her boyfriend on his chain. Those trucks don't come back fully loaded with these people, I will turn the matter over to the Justice department."

Scott said, "You know Captain, Talos is the Justice department, but if it makes you feel better, I think I'll refer this up the line for a thorough risk assessment and I'll let you know the parameters of the operation once I hear back, how does that sound?"

"Don't give me your corporate bullshit. I'm sure I'll be right at the top of Talos's need to know list." He gave Mitch a bleak look, said, "Guess it is too much to ask to have these jokers brought in for trial? Seems like you both have already locked in on execution-style diplomacy."

"The last thing you want is this guy in the court of public opinion," Mitch said.

"Oh, and why's that, does he know all of Talos's dirty little secrets?"

"No, because people would love him, that's why. And you and your little army boys, and Talos, would look like Goliaths to his charming David. That what you want out there?"

"I guess we weren't apprised of Mr. Slaught's celebrity potential."

Mitch said, "Grow up Captain, this is a crappy situation but you have a real problem out there. This guy, he's the real deal and you better accept that reality or you'll be caught in a shitstorm of trouble when Grier and I are long down the trail."

Muspar was thinking he should've been taping this, because this little bitch and her sidekick were going to be in for a big surprise, maybe sitting in jail instead of some high-end resort. He was going to be contacting some people too, but he just said, "Just do your job like a professional and I guess we can all live with the results."

"Whatever. I'm out of here, I have work to do."

Scott was already gesturing towards the door, "Sounds good Mitch, where do you want to start?"

"Pulling together our gear. I'll head down to the supply room, but I'm in no mood for that little creeper to be hanging around."

"I'm sure the Captain can keep his people out of your way, this is a fairly sensitive operation."

"For your information Ms. Black, my so called 'creeper' seems to have vanished. And not to worry, Police Services doesn't want to be seen anywhere near this operation."

Mitch frowned, turned to Muspar, "Isn't that a bit of a security breach, to just have someone up and disappear?"

"Ms. Black, why don't you mind your business and I'll mind mine, we'll get along better that way."

"I don't mean to harp on this Captain, but that piece of shit Skinner was around during our logistics sessions. I think you should at least follow up to make sure he's actually where he's supposed to be. He could have walked out with some sensitive material."

"Oh, he did, my secretary's spare pantyhose and a bottle of her nail polish. The kid's a weirdo, and I don't give a shit where he is as long as it's nowhere near me."

Muspar was sure he heard her swear at him as she slammed the door behind her on the way out. He turned to Scott, "Well, those two are a couple of real professionals. I can't believe you are sending them back up there, but just remember, I'm not putting my future prospects at risk when this thing blows up in our faces."

"For chrissakes Muspar, I think at this stage of the game there are bigger things to worry about besides your career."

"*Your* career maybe?"

Scott said that was ridiculous, told Muspar he should keep a lid on his emotions. Muspar stood rooted to the ground. Scott gestured towards the door but Muspar was shaking his head, no, he wasn't going to leave until he had some guarantees.

"Like what?" snapped Scott.

"I want Laskin in jail when this is over."

"Jail? For what?" Scott was surprised.

"I don't care, murder maybe, but it better be for a long time. Along with his bimbo. They're loose ends that we can't afford. This whole thing, I've had a bad feeling about it all along."

Scott shrugged. "I'll look into it, but that creates complications of its own, I'll mull it over…"

"No, not good enough. I want your word now."

"Captain, you aren't really in a position to start giving orders around here."

"Really? Don't think for a minute that I haven't covered my ass."

"What does that mean?"

"It means I'm taking care of myself and if things tank, you and your A-team are going down."

"Okay Captain, calm down. You're probably right about Laskin, he is clearly having authority issues. Mitch Black might be more complicated. I'll move on the Laskin thing for you, but you focus on the job at hand and make sure that your guys get back out there with Laskin and finish this job."

Susun and Jeff were telling Chumboy that he wouldn't believe what had happened. It was just getting dark when they'd gotten back and they found him in the kitchen trying to fix the fan on Tiny's big broiler. Both of them seemed pretty pumped, in a hurry to see him.

Chumboy asked, "Yeah? What happened?"

Susun said, "We brought back a stray."

Chumboy was wary, saying, "This isn't Noah's Ark, animals here either work or get eaten."

"Not that kind of a stray."

"So what kind of a stray then?"

"A guy called Ricky Skinner."

"Related to Lorraine?"

Jeff said, "Think she's his mom. Hard to tell exactly what he was saying, he was babbling a lot, but it was clear he was from the City."

"The City? I thought it was getting impossible to get out of there."

Susun said he was sort of an odd little guy, added, "Apparently, it was his second time trying. He snuck onto one of the trucks running up what used to be the old highway. Now they use it as a security corridor, runs straight from the edge of the City to the border of the territories with not much on either side of it. This time though he bailed early, then up over the snow fence, wanted to make it to his Uncle's hunt camp. Ricky said it was only a couple of kilometers or so from the old highway and figured he could make it. He'd brought snowshoes with him, and off he went, figured going cross country was his best bet after he got hauled off to jail the last time around."

"Used snowshoes, eh? Couldn't have been bringing much else with him."

"According to Ricky, his Uncle had a well-stocked camp, snow-machines, guns, always six months worth of grub," Susan said, "though he said he had been worried that Talos had already been there and wasn't sure what shape things were in. So he headed straight there and low and behold, some of the shit was still there, but Talos had clearly been there first, razed the main cabin, no sign of his Uncle. One of the shacks was still standing so he stayed there over night, got a snowmachine up and running and loaded it up, then made tracks for his mom's first thing in the morning. Think she was about half an hour away, Ricky said he knew the route by heart. He'd only been there a little while when we showed up."

"He must be beat, maybe Tiny can rustle him and his mom up some dinner."

"It might have to wait until the morning, he conked right out when he hit the pillow, but you'll probably want to talk to him sooner than later," Susun said, "he knows about Laskin's team."

"What did he say?"

Jeff explained the kid was a little incoherent about a lot of things, but it was clear that Mitch Black had made quite an impression on him. "He's seems pretty messed up about the whole thing. Said Mitch wouldn't let him help because he was fat."

"Fat?"

Jeff nodded. "Yeah, that's what he said. He's a bit of a tubby one. Sort of sensitive about it too."

—

Ricky said he didn't want to leave his room yet, that he was still tired, rubbing his eyes like he was trying to prove it to her.

Susun said, "Bet you're hungry, though? And there are some folks who'd like to meet you. We wanted everyone to meet you last night but you were sleeping by the time I checked in on you. But you might be able to help us out."

He didn't think he had much choice but he was nervous, and thought maybe he'd just tell her he was sick. But he was hungry too, so he said, okay, and followed her along a little hallway then down some stairs and into a big dining room. A few people were sitting around a table in the middle.

A big guy stood up, said, "I'm Chumboy, good to see you Ricky," and then shouted over to the kitchen, "Hey, Tiny, get Chubbycheckers here some tea for godssakes."

A man came out with a pot of tea, poured some into a mug,

asked, "How d'ya take it?" but before Ricky could answer the guy had dumped in what looked like a pound of sugar and a quart of milk and pushed it over to Ricky saying, "Now don't bug me again, I'm trying to make a goddam great dinner and you're fucking me up. My cousin brought me a few ducks from your mom's place, said their feet were freezing to the barn floor. So they're going to be our dinner."

Ricky stammered out a sorry, was feeling worried, the men sitting around the table watching him, that woman Susun smiling nice but not taking her eyes off him. He'd told her yesterday he wasn't sure now if he had done the right thing in sneaking out of the City, and then ending up here. He was still nervous about it all.

At first he'd just planned on going to the hunt camp, but when he got there he got scared. He tried not to look at the ash and debris that was piled up across the yard where the main cabin used to stand. He dragged the ladder out of the shed and over to the small barn, climbing up, brushing away the snow, reaching into the opening onto the second floor of the barn. At the edge of the opening he felt it, hauled out the heavy canvas bag and tossed it onto the ground, then checking inside to make sure Delbert's .30-06 was in there. Ricky could still remember the night his Uncle had sat by the fire, carefully wrapping his guns in garbage bags and duct tape, then joking about where to hide them. Ricky could remember where each and every one ended up, and there were plenty hid that night.

He put the ladder away. The big drift behind the barn, that's where the snowmachine was, so he dug down in the snow till he found the edge of the tarp and hauled it off, sending snow flying, some it going down into his boots. He checked the fuel and figured there was enough there, grabbed an extra fuel can from the shed, and then put the files on his Uncle Delbert and the Winterman into the gun bag and headed back out, following the trail that he had taken dozens of times from the hunt camp north towards his mom's house.

She was glad to see him, said she'd taken him for dead. He told her what he had found at the hunt camp, asked her where Bo was, his Uncle Delbert's dog, and his mom said, "I guess they burnt them all up together."

When his mom had told him that she hoped that the folks from the Wintermen community were coming to fetch her soon, that she'd sent her brother to ask them to come get her, he'd panicked, but she told him she thought he should come because they were good people and it was the government or that Talos bunch that was lying, they'd been lying all along. Ricky asked her how she could be sure and she said that's what Delbert thought.

Chumboy thought Ricky had a hard time paying attention, his eyes now unfocused, like he was daydreaming or something. He asked, "So Ricky, you gotta tell me, what made you head on up here?"

Ricky sort of re-focused, peering across at Chumboy.

Chumboy said, "Go on Ricky, tell us your story before your pancakes get here."

Ricky took a deep breath and said, "Uh, well, I worked for Captain Muspar and he had all the files, files about the government and the people, and all the stuff that goes on, know what I mean? Captain Muspar is in charge of the police. And I read it, the file, and after I read about my Uncle, my Uncle Delbert, and saw his death certificates, and I thought maybe, well, I should stop at his camp, that maybe there was a mistake, you know, maybe my Uncle wasn't dead, but he is."

The kid talked like he had no brakes. Chumboy later told Susun he thought it was because Ricky had no punctuation in his brain.

"Do you know who did that to your Uncle?" Chumboy asked.

Well, I don't know for sure..." He trailed off.

"I think the people who hurt your Uncle are the same people who hurt a friend of ours," Chumboy said, watching a sweaty kind of panic move across Ricky's face as he pushed his glasses up his nose. Sure was a jittery guy.

"What did they do?" Ricky asked.

It took a few seconds before Susun said, "Killed a girl, a nice young girl. They shot her."

Ricky's eyes looked like they might pop out of his head, bouncing around from one person to another, blinking a lot, tilting his head, Chumboy worried that he was getting too agitated. He said, "Everything is under control now Ricky, and those people are gone, long gone."

"They killed my Uncle Delbert too, burnt him and his dog and his cabin?"

"Well, if not them personally then it was likely Talos. Right now we're trying to come up with a plan that is going to stop them from hurting anyone else. Do you think there is anything else that can help us out?"

"When I heard Captain Muspar and Mr. Scott talking..."

Chumboy interrupted, "Who's Scott?"

"Mr. Scott is from Talos. He has a big office."

Chumboy nodded, "Go on."

"Well, they talked about something called Project Final Sweep and Mr. Scott said 'From now on there's only going to be resource parks up in the Territories, nothing and nobody else,' and Captain Muspar asked, 'This goes all the way to the top?' and Mr. Scott said 'Yes. All the way. The agenda is to cramp industry's ass to get up there and get moving, but every scrap of settlement has got to be gone. Erased.'" Ricky paused after delivering the information in a flat monotone, like he'd been rehearsing it over and over, like his times tables or something. Then he said, "And that's what I heard."

"Okay Ricky, that's great."

"And I know some other stuff too, like the big Safety Parade that's coming up and that the Captain and Mr. Scott fight a lot, and then I also brought some files with me too, stole them from the Captain. There's stuff in them too."

"Files?"

"Yeah, I took Captain Muspar's files about the Winterman and my Uncle. I sure hope it wasn't the wrong thing to do…"

Chumboy slapped him on the back, said, "Rickyman, you're doing one right thing after another. Keep it up you're going to turn into a damn genius."

CHAPTER FIFTEEN

SHE DIDN'T KNOW WHAT TO SAY WHEN SLAUGHT came up to her, said, "I'd like you to go for a ride with me."

She was with Verla in the workbay. It was dark, and the light in the bay was harsh. She hadn't seen Slaught since yesterday morning, right after the funeral. Before the sun was up, they'd wrapped Kirstie in a green sleeping bag and Mrs. Merrill had said a prayer and Slaught mumbled a few words about Kirstie being a great kid. Larose looked rough, said that he and Shaun were Kirstie's only family, and that Shaun and her had been going out for three years. Lived pretty much as man and wife, he said.

When the funeral was just about over, Shaun had shown up. He'd turned away from the coffin, said he was going to go fuck those bastards up bad, but Johnny had said quietly, "Not now. Not yet," in a way that quieted Shaun down. Larose took his son out of the room, Shaun not even noticing he was being led out, and they'd finished the funeral. Then they'd taken Kirstie out so they could bury her, finding a place deep in the cedars with thick layers of needles. They cleared the layers, then poured some old fuel oil over the patch and setting it alight, watching it burn down, thawing the ground enough to get the pick axes going. Took them four hours, taking turns with the pick axes and shovels, to break through the frozen topsoil and dig down far enough to bury her.

And then Slaught just up and disappeared. When he'd said he'd be going after the funeral she had sort of thought he wouldn't, but then he was gone. So when he just came walking up to her in the workbay she felt like saying, "Where the hell have you been?" but instead she said, "A ride? Where?"

"Doesn't really matter." His tone scaring her a bit, making her think that she didn't really know this man very well. Kind of man that that just takes off, what was that? None of the guys had said anything, maybe seemed pissed off but weren't saying if they were. A couple of the women had taken her aside, asked where he was, was everything going to be okay? She'd finally gone to Tiny, asked if this was like Slaught, to run off like that, and Tiny had said, "He's gone all fucking soft on us," but then Chumboy had said later that Slaught was having some serious Kierkegaard time but he'd be back. She had to ask who Kierkegaard was and Chumboy said he was the daddy of angst and maybe they were teaching midwives the wrong things. "Wrong things? Don't be a smartass," she'd said. "Bet your Auntie doesn't know this guy either," and Chumboy said his Auntie didn't need to but the rest of them did.

Seeing Slaught now, standing there, snowmobile helmet in hand, his face impassive, she wasn't sure it was angst that he was feeling. When she'd heard the snowmachine coming and then pull up outside the workbay she knew it was him, and felt a wave of nerves flood over her. But then she thought, what if it'd been Laskin, what would have happened then?

"Well, I promised Verla I'd help with the, you know, the cleaning. Thought for Shaun we should get it scrubbed up."

Verla said, "I don't mind going ahead without you," smiling and giving Susun a push. "Go on. We'll see you two later then."

Feeling stuck, she shrugged, grabbed her snow gear, and followed Slaught, asking him if she should take someone else's machine and he said no, telling her to just hop on, that they weren't going that far.

He said, "Just hold on tight, okay?"

She climbed on and he revved it up, turning and bombing down the main street towards the south end of town, Susun thinking the town must have looked nice back in the day this time of year, people with their Christmas lights on, probably a creche or something in the little park.

Slaught followed the highway out of town a ways, then bolted up and over a big snow bank to go cross-country, the flying snow taking nasty little bites at her neck. She was afraid to let go to pull the throat of her snowsuit tighter so she closed her eyes as he drove and drove, pounding down along the edge of a lake, patches of it still open, gunmetal water slapping onto the ice, and then they were into a line of scraggly jack pine. Slaught slowed and then killed the engine, pushing open his helmet and looking over his shoulder at her, said, "Great view, eh?"

Yeah, it was great, she thought, the sky a deep cobalt, the snow a few shades lighter. And there was a yellow moon, big and round, pasted up on the sky.

He took off his helmet and she did the same, cradling it in her arms, then clumsily pulled herself off the machine, hearing the snow squeak under her feet. Johnny pushed himself back and swung his leg over, sitting to face her and said, "I wanted to tell you something."

He sounded serious. He wasn't looking at her, just staring up at the sky.

She managed, "Okay."

He waited, just sitting in the silence for a while so she just stood, trying not to fidget, him all sombre and still, both of them now just staring out at the sky.

The stars were coming out now, slipping out bright against the dark. Slaught said, "I always look for Orion, makes me feel good, seeing him up there, doing his thing."

Susun nodded but didn't say anything, surprised that he was talking star gazing, then he finally said, "I've been thinking a lot about killing."

She waited a second to see if there was more coming but he fell quiet again so she asked, "Killing? Killing what?" hoping it wasn't a stupid question.

"Other people. I've been thinking about killing other people."

"Oh?"

"Yeah. Seemed like the time to think it over."

"You've already done it, haven't you, killed somebody?"

"Yeah," he said, "but that was a while back. And then I didn't have time to think about it, I just did it. Been thinking about doing it again though."

"Come on," she said, "let's go back."

"What? You didn't think about it?"

"What do you mean?"

"After you saw what they'd done, didn't you think about it?"

"No, I guess I was thinking about other things."

"Yeah? Like what?"

Was he calling her out? She couldn't hear it in his voice, just seemed like a simple question, maybe he really just wanted to know. She said, "If everyone was going to be okay, if Shaun would be able to put himself back together. And Jordan, seeing that happened and not being able to stop it, not being able to protect someone else, that's hard to climb back from."

There was silence for a bit and then Slaught nodded, said, "Well, it made me think about killing."

"And?"

"Well, I came out here," he said. "I mean, look at it."

And she followed his gaze, the moon going to a pale lemon now, not sure what he was going to say. She said, "It's beautiful. But what does it make you think about killing?"

He turned to her, said, "I don't like the idea."

"The idea of killing?"

"That's right."

"Well, that's good."

"Maybe it is, maybe it's not, but there it is anyway. In my head I can do it, I can see it, each one of them, pop, pop," him making the sound of a gun, "but it's so ugly when it isn't in your head, when it's right in front of you." Again looking right at her, "Know what I mean?"

She put her hand on his shoulder, said, "I do. But let's get back, we don't want to worry anyone."

He just looked at her for a bit, said, "Yeah, okay, I just wanted to tell you that."

He drove back slower, like whatever it was that had been chasing him down the trail had let up. Susun was feeling good for some reason, holding onto to more of him than just the edges of his coat, thinking that whatever had just happened meant something, she just wasn't sure what.

When they got back to the work bay she found herself watching him as he pulled closed the big doors, as he glanced over to where the workbench had been, maybe seeing if all the blood had come off the floor. Coming back towards her, she thought maybe he was smiling at her, but he also seemed business as usual.

"So was that your idea of a heart to heart?" she asked, trying to tease him, but really trying to get a bead on the guy too, not trusting her instincts and thinking maybe she read too much into it.

Frowning, sort of surprised, he said, "No. That was my idea of a date."

———

Chumboy was just saying, "Hey Chubbycheckers, slide that folder over here, let's see if there are any beauty shots of me in there," when Slaught came in. He'd been gone too long and lots of people were beginning to notice. He looked like shit. Chumboy just said, "Hey Johnny, pull up a chair. How was the hunting? Tiny told me you brought him in a dozen sparrows and were pretending to have bagged a moose."

Slaught sort of smiled. "That wasn't what he said when he laid his greedy little eyes on that pile of partridge." Then he looked over at Larose. "Hey, sorry man, about everything."

Larose nodded but didn't say anything, Slaught glad about that. He looked over at Chumboy. "So?"

Chumboy had decided they needed a game plan, in case Slaught didn't come back, or came back and was haywire, so he had called a meeting in his room, which was really the library, or at least that's what Chumboy called it. He slept on the floor on a pile of coats in the far corner and everywhere else was books.

They were all just watching Slaught now as he crossed the room, not saying anything, not explaining where he'd been. Chumboy, worried to shit, had gone to his Auntie and asked her what she thought about Slaught leaving, saying, "It isn't like him, just to up and leave like that, think he's going to be okay?" and she didn't look up from her knitting, her hands flying through some scarf that was lime green and navy blue and just said, "You won't know until he makes up his mind."

"Well, how long is that gonna take?"

"Every man is different."

Chumboy said that wasn't exactly illuminating, could she ballpark the time it might be before Johnny came back. She said, "I'm not a psychic down at the mall, Chumboy."

"Yeah, I know Auntie, but things could get pretty bad soon. Just hoping he'll come back."

"Me too."

"That's it then?"

"No, pass me that yellow wool there, I don't think this scarf is happy enough."

She'd once complained that only the women and children would wear her scarves and Chumboy had said, "Well Auntie, the colours, I mean come on," and she had said she thought men were all colour blind anyway, what difference did it make, and Chumboy said men weren't that colour blind.

He sighed, passed her the tight ball of wool. "That is one ugly scarf Auntie, who's it for?"

"Johnny."

Watching now as Slaught pushed a stack of books to the edge of the small table and leaned back, stubble on his chin, eyes bloodshot, Chumboy figured he could use a happy scarf.

Slaught said, "Okay boys, what have you come up with?"

There was a nervous looking guy there, Slaught assumed he was Ricky based on what Susun had told him. Larose and Jeff were there, sitting on milk crates against the wall. Chumboy was leaning against the wall, arms folded across his chest.

197

"So Rick's been telling us some stuff about our Mr. Laskin you might want to know Johnny," Chumboy said.

Slaught said, "Oh?"

Ricky blinked, looked questioningly over at Chumboy.

Chumboy said, "Oh, sorry Rickyman, this is Johnny Slaught. You might know him as the Winterman."

Slaught said, "How'ya doing Ricky, heard all about you, heard you got some great info for us."

Ricky was just sort of staring, so Slaught prompted, "Laskin, tell me about Laskin."

Ricky swallowed hard, said, "I recognize you from your picture."

Slaught said, "Yeah, what picture?"

"The one in the file. Says lots of things about you."

"Any of it true?"

As Ricky just kept staring at Slaught, mouth turned down like he was concentrating on a math problem, Chumboy tried, "Hey Rickyman, tell Johnny here about Laskin."

"Uh, okay. Well, he's a pretty famous guy and all. Mr. Laskin was a regular on I-TIME before things got real bad, now it's only on once and a while, when we get the energy-hours. His show is called *Man Up* or something like that. I've only seen it a couple of times."

"They hired an actor?" Slaught couldn't believe it, thinking of the surveillance footage Jeff had shown him, Laskin saying "This isn't a party, jerkoff, it's a fucking home invasion" like some badass from the movies, playing a part.

"Well, he's an actor I guess, but he does real things, he does extreme things, done all kinds of adventure things."

"Like what?"

Ricky was about to continue but Shaun came in, dragging a crate over beside his Dad and sitting down. Slaught nodded at him. Man, the kid looked bad.

Shaun spoke up right away. "We know they're coming back, right? So what's there to talk about? Let's just finish it, meet 'em at the top of Thibeault Hill and blast the fucking shit outta them."

No one said anything and Shaun said, "Fuck, guys, come on."

Slaught said "Christ, Shaun, we don't have the people or the guns for that, or even a way of knowing when they're coming."

Shaun looked across at his Dad. "Well, what are we going to do, just roll over? After what they did?" almost shouting now. "We gonna go hide? Call the cops? Run away? For fuck's sake, these guys murdered Kirstie."

Larose just shaking his head, and Chumboy said, "Shaun, we got to make sure that nothing like what happened to Kirstie is going to happen to anybody else, we got kids here, and old people, we have to really think this thing through."

"I'm not afraid of those bastards," Shaun red in the face, his Dad's hand on his sleeve and him not noticing, and Slaught seeing the image from the tape, Shaun bent over, blood over his face, moaning, and Kirstie crying. He wished to Christ he hadn't seen it, it was like a stain inside his head. He could only imagine what was inside Shaun's head.

Slaught said, "Yeah, I know Shaun, I know you aren't, but we're fighting a battle we didn't expect, not just with Laskin, but the government too. That's a big fight."

"I don't care if it's a fucking war, Johnny," Shaun answered, saying it like a challenge.

Chumboy interrupted, "If it's a war, we need a strategy."

Slaught looked over at Chumboy. "Yeah, guess so. Like what's his name, sunzoo?"

"Sun Tzu," Chumboy corrected, "and no, all that shit's too vague."

Shaun stood up. "For fuck's sake, we aren't going to fix this with some book."

There was a few seconds of silence, Shaun then exhaling loudly, like he'd been holding his breath for a week and said, "I'm fucking outta here."

Slaught grabbed Shaun as he pushed past.

"Don't do anything crazy man, understand?"

Shaun tried to get past him, but Slaught didn't move. "We're in this together, and we'll figure it out together."

"Yeah, is that what you were doing when you took off, figuring it out together," Shaun now yelling, staring back at Slaught, "'cause that wasn't how it felt. Some people thought you weren't coming back. They were scared."

Slaught had been waiting for that. He could almost feel people holding their breath, saw Ricky's eye's darting around, Jeff looking down at his feet. Slaught said evenly, "I had that coming. I just needed to clear my head, think things over, I can't do much to change everything that's happened, except not fuck it up again."

Shaun didn't look back as he left, saying, "You're well on your way."

Slaught figured the kid had a point. He'd been going over things again and again since Shaun had shown up in the doorway, bloodied, incoherent. He should've known, by their gear, by Laskin's smirk, he should have known they meant business. He was so off the fucking mark he couldn't even put it into words.

Slaught knew Chumboy could see it all over his face when he said, "Hey, you couldn't have known they were out of control."

"I read it wrong Chum, playing at it."

"Wear it if you want bud, but we all read it wrong. We didn't know what we were up against, but now we do. And you're right, we're in it together."

Slaught said, "The hard part now is to get back on track, and I guess we gotta figure that we're taking on the government. So that is a lot of bullshit to battle…"

"No, you're taking on Talos. That's worse."

It was Ricky who spoke up, sitting on his milk crate, squirming every now and then as the plastic dug into his bum.

Slaught said, "Take on Talos? Guess so, but all they'll have to do is get a few special ops guys in some choppers up here and bomb the shit out of us."

"Well, then, I guess the question would be, like, why haven't they?" Jeff asked. "They got all the military-industrial, evil empire shit in their back pockets, so why didn't they just do that in the first place?"

"Yeah, that's a good question." Slaught thinking, "Maybe the expense of sending up choppers, maybe they don't have any, who knows. Maybe they don't want people to really know what's going on…"

"…or that we're even up here anymore," Jeff said.

Slaught was mulling it over, figuring that up here, in the middle of nowhere, they were sitting ducks that nobody knew or cared about. But also thinking of that stain in his brain, if other people saw that they might see Talos in a different light. Might see the monster. Maybe they should get Talos the beast onto this I-TIME crap, see what happens.

"Maybe we need to get our perspective out there, on that I-TIME, let people know," said Slaught.

Larose was shaking his head. "But Ricky said you've been on this I-TIME thing, as a terrorist or something, there's probably a lot of people who think we're criminals. They'd probably just as soon hang us out to dry."

"That was sort of what went down for the Scottish nobles who were riding with Bonnie Prince Charlie way back when,"

Chumboy offered, "went marching through Scotland, sacking and winning, got to England, weren't greeted like the rock stars they thought they were, got a bad case of the jitters, and hightailed it back to the Highlands."

"Then what happened?"

"Wasn't pretty Johnny, the British kicked the crap out of everyone and old Charlie had to sneak out of Scotland in a dress."

"Thanks for that Chum, that was extremely helpful."

"I don't know anything about that Scottish guy," Ricky said, "but Mr. Scott is worried about you guys, and he is sending Talos in to get you."

Slaught asked. "How do you know that Ricky?"

"I heard him, I heard him say that he didn't want anymore warm bodies down in the city because everything was falling apart, and he didn't want anyone down there knowing there were warm bodies up here."

The room fell quiet for a minute, Slaught glad for the time to think, letting his eyes roam over Chumboy's walls, every inch of which was covered by posters, magazine articles, pictures from ads.

Pointing to a poster tacked up between a children's drawing of a big red tow truck and a photo of Madonna in her black corset, Slaught asked, "Who's that?"

Chumboy looked over his shoulder to see the image of a man on a horse, pipe jutting out from the balaclava that hid his face.

"That's Subcommander Marcos, that Zapatista guy," he said, turning around to see the poster better. "Led the uprising in Chiapas, Mexico, late 1990s."

"Did he win?"

"Sort of, I guess. And he wrote some trippy shit on revolution and all. Most the time I can't tell what he's talking about what with the Four Horsemen and quoting Shakespeare and all the deconstruction and chupacabras. Guess I have to start reading more."

"Chupacabras?"

"Goatsuckers. Some sort of werewolf creature that sucks the blood of goats."

Slaught told Chumboy he thought he was reading more than enough, asked him what this Marcos guy actually did.

"Traveled all over Mexico fighting for the poor. Raised himself sort of a guerilla army, most of them using wooden guns. Fought their way through small towns and then straight into Mexico City to confront the government. Think he even had a return stint, you know, came back to keep fighting later on."

"Yeah?" Slaught interested now.

"Ever big cojones, him," Chumboy said, then added, "I prefer Hannibal, tying torches to the cattle so the Romans thought he was leaving, and then sneaking out the other way."

"You like the sneaky guys, eh?"

Chumboy nodded, "Sneaky can be smart."

"I think the time for sneaking is over for us Chum. We need to head for open ground."

"So we're going with the Subcommander then are we?"

Slaught stared at the picture for a second, said, "I like his gear."

"Better than sneaking outta town in a dress?"

"That's for sure. But no pipes. I mean, who the Christ smokes a pipe anymore?"

Chapter Sixteen

Slaught pushed back from the table. "So. Ready to rock 'n 'roll?"

Chumboy answered, "I'm always ready."

"Got the list?"

Chumboy pointed to his head, tapping the side of it, "It's in here, every last item, including the cloth diapers for our new age witches in the infirmary."

"Noticed you've been lurking around the infirmary a fair bit since those witches arrived Chum." Larose was grinning. "Saw you bringing over a stack of books for them."

"I was just exchanging some information on healing plants with Melinda. New mothers need to know that stuff, but I guess you wouldn't know too much about that."

"And you do?"

"Turns out, Harv, I do. Darla is a bit of a traditional healer, learned about the plants from her Uncle Leonard. That man, he knew his shit about the plants. And of course my Auntie Verla taught Darla a fair bit too."

"Darla? That would be the wife you never mentioned?"

"Didn't want to make you boys jealous, can hardly imagine what it's like to not have the love of a good woman waiting for you. Guess that's why you've been hanging around the witches yourself, eh Harv?"

Larose said, "That's bullshit."

Slaught was shaking his head, smiling, thinking it almost felt like it did before all the shit went down, said, "Can we get our asses in gear, and don't forget the toy guns. I want lots of those. They were on the list."

"Getting bored, are we?" asked Chumboy.

"Just get the guns, okay?"

"Come on, you really want me to be dragging wallymart specials across the tundra for you? Me, I got priorities, I gotta get diapers."

"Just get as many as you can, alright?"

"Why?"

Slaught was shaking his head at Chumboy. "You sure know how to piss me off, don't you? Let's just say you aren't the only one who reads, okay?"

Chumboy was heading towards the bay. "Fine, but there's no way I'm riding into the great unknown with a plastic bb gun."

"If it's good enough for your Zapatistas, it might just be good enough for us. We need to get some public support, unleash some propaganda of our own to counteract this Wintermen bullshit Thought about maybe stealing a page from your Marcos fellow there, using those wooden guns as a way to let folks know we aren't some sort of heavily armed threat."

"Hey, you've been reading ahead," Chumboy complained, "but maybe you didn't read far enough, or even look at the pictures. I hope you noticed that it's a real AK-47 Marcos has across his chest. Did you?"

"Yeah, well, Ricky and Jeff are taking care of that."

"Not breaking into a government bunker?"

"Nope, Uncle's hunt camp."

"I don't think you're focused Mitch."

She looked over at her shoulder at Grier. They'd just finished a final equipment check and had headed back to their room. Grier was pacing a bit, like he was winding himself up for something. Christ almighty, he was sure stressed. But he had a lot of nerve slagging her.

"That right?"

"I know maybe your confidence is shaken, babe, but you gotta get back on the horse."

"Bad day at the office, Grier?"

"Sarcasm doesn't really help at this stage of the game Mitch."

"Oh, what would? Pouting? 'Cause you have that totally covered."

"We can talk about me if you want, but I think there are some serious issues we have to address if you are going to be part of this final op."

"If?"

"Well, to be honest, I think this has gotten a little personal for you, and I think that might be clouding your judgment."

"Grier, why don't you worry about your own issues, like having a tantrum and popping little Miss Bible Belt, and let's just get on with it before one of us says something we might regret."

"Mitch, you know we've both had the training, we both knew it could happen eventually."

"What's that, Grier?"

"You're attracted to a target. Now that's okay, but you need to know when to step back."

She took a minute to draw in a deep breath. She really didn't want to get into it now, they didn't have a lot of time to get things together and get back out there, and Talos was cramping her ass for a wrap up. "Grier, not now, okay? We have a job to do."

"That's my point, Mitch."

"Nothing interferes with me doing my job."

"Well, that's what I always thought honeybabes, but you're making me nervous here. I don't think your head's in the game. I don't know if you should be heading back into the field without resolving this."

Patronizing dick. She grabbed her bag and shoved some of her clothes in it, tucking in her Browning as well, hoping Grier didn't see. And she had no intention of heading back to Lazarus, not straightaway anyway. She was getting ready to teach that sonofabitch Slaught a lesson he'd never forget. Not much for details, Grier had probably completely forgotten about the tracking chip she'd slipped on Slaught's snowmachine. But Slaught was on the move, and she was more than willing to meet him halfway.

Grier said, "I think you'd feel better if you just admitted that you were horny for him."

She kept her back to him, waiting a few seconds, then said, "The first time he looked at me, well Grier, horny doesn't come close to describing it."

There was silence. Mitch grabbed her bag, headed for the door.

She glanced over her shoulder at Grier. "You know, you were right, I feel way better. How about you?"

Jeff followed Ricky for what seemed forever before they crested a small ridge and Ricky turned sharply to the left, taking them down a long tree-lined trail that ended with a few small buildings. Jeff killed his engine, pulled off his helmet and took a look around. "What the hell dude, this is messed."

Ricky was already off his machine and heading for the small building that sat beside the pile of ash and snow. Ricky stopped when he got to the door, looking back. He wasn't sure if Jeff was actually asking him something, but he saw him sitting on his snowmachine just looking around the camp, shaking his head. Jeff yelled over to him, "I've seen some haywire places man, but this is seriously whacked."

There was a school bus painted flat black up on blocks across one end of the clearing. About five different car bodies in various stages of decay were scattered around the yard. There were three outhouses, one on either side of the clearing and one set back a ways into the bush. A couple of rusted out barbecues lying in a tangle on the snow just a ways from the heap of charred beams. A smallish cabin and woodshed sat some hundred yards from the main cabin, far enough away to save them from the fire. The woodshed was full of wood scraps, snow drifted up high along its sides and icicles dangling along the edges of the roof. A couple of deer heads were sitting on top of the log piles, glassy eyes staring.

"This was your first stop, eh?"

And Ricky said, yeah, he had needed some of his Uncle's things. He also said he wanted to make sure.

"Make sure?" asked Jeff.

"Yeah, you know, uh, make sure that, uh," Ricky stammered, not sure how to say it, "you know, that it was true, that my Uncle, was..." He trailed off, so Jeff said, "Murdered?"

Ricky said, "Yeah, I guess so, eh?" as he held open the door of the shed for Jeff.

"Should we start a fire and warm up?" Ricky asked.

"No, no time now Ricky, let's find the guns first while we have daylight and then worry about getting comfortable for the night, alright?"

Ricky, standing in the middle of the room, said, "Makes me feel bad being here."

"Yeah, I can see that."

"It's all that's left behind, you know? It used to be such a great place, with my Uncle and stuff. We had fun here, coming up in the fall, moose hunting, I'd get up in the morning, and it'd be cold, and my Uncle Delbert would be up making the coffee. It was the best."

Jeff was nodding, thinking this would be the last place he'd want to be if it was cold. Then he said, "Okay dude, enough memory lane, let's go search for your Uncle's stash, you're making me depressed."

"Won't take much searching," Ricky said, suddenly grinning. "What kinda camp needs three outhouses?"

CHAPTER SEVENTEEN

SHE HAD LEFT EARLY, WANTING TO CHECK IN on the new mom and baby, see if they needed any help getting to the meeting. Johnny said everyone had to be there, no exceptions. It would be her first outing from the infirmary, Susun telling her to stay put for a week, saying "You need to cocoon with that baby of yours, just cuddle up and don't think about anything but each other."

"Hey, Susie." It was Tiny, leaning in the doorway between the kitchen and what was lately called the Meeting Room, Tiny bitching that before it was perfectly fine to call it a dining room.

"I guess this is it, eh?" she said.

Tiny looked grumpy, said, "What? What's this supposed to be?"

"The big plan."

"Big fucking plan, my ass."

"What does that mean?"

"It means we're in deep shit Susie girl."

"I thought that was obvious," answering him, but not really paying attention, seeing Slaught come into the room with Chumboy and Larose, looking all calm, leaning into Shaun as he passed by to say something to him.

"Hey Slaught," Tiny shouted, "if you and your two ladies in waiting are done socializing, can we get this bastard of a meeting on the road?"

Slaught nodded over at Tiny and headed up to the front of the room. Larose stayed with Shaun, and Chumboy drifted over to Susun and Tiny. "Ever cranky you," Chumboy said to Tiny, and then to Susun, "When does Ricky get back?"

"Tomorrow. He sure didn't want to go, though."

"I think he's scared to come out of hiding, thinking that Mitch Black is going to reappear somewhere."

"Yeah, well, she's pretty scary, I know how he feels."

"Bullshit she's scary, that woman can't even peel a goddam onion," Tiny said.

Chumboy told Tiny that women like Mitch don't need to cook because they eat their men alive, but then Tiny told him to shut the hell up because Johnny had cleared his throat and was waiting for people to stop talking. "Gotta hear this," Tiny muttered.

Slaught started off saying "Good day folks," like he was welcoming people to a show or something, "and thanks for coming out. I know we've been through some rough shit this last week and people might have something to say about it. Now some of us, well, we've been talking this thing over and we're going to put a few options on the table here. If anyone thinks it's bullshit and has another way of doing things, speak up. Loud. That clear?"

People were nodding.

"Alright then," Slaught started. "So we got bad trouble. Those folks who were here, Laskin and his crew, were some sort of special Talos outfit, probably sent here to get rid of a few of us. I think we, well, I think I, was a little naive in thinking we could handle them. Should've known better, after seeing the things I have but...well, what has happened is done, I can't fix that." Slaught noticed a few people glance over at Shaun then look away quickly—maybe the young lad shouldn't have come today. A few of the women at the back were sort of huddled together, looking like they'd been crying. There'd been a lot of crying over Kirstie.

Slaught looked down, trying to gather his thoughts. "Can't change what's happened, but we can try to fix what's coming down the pipe, 'cause I don't think it's going to be pretty. Those guys have every intention of coming back."

"When?" someone shouted from the back.

"This is crazy," someone else muttered. Too many people for Johnny to see who it was that was talking.

Johnny shrugged. "My guess would be sooner than later. But we're thinking that they are going to have to bring trucks, so they can move most of us out of here. Ricky Skinner, he came up from the City. He was sure there'd been a truck contingent to the requisition forms that had come through for this operation and I don't see any other choice. There's over fifty people here now, and might be more along the way that they want to clear out, so they can't do that on snowmachines. They need those trucks. From what Ricky tells us, they use the outpost there at the bottom of Thibeault Hill as their staging ground, so the old highway route seems most likely. Does that make sense to everyone?"

No one had much to say, couple of people leaning into their neighbour to whisper something. Then Shaun spoke up. He was standing near the back with a few of the other young guys and his Dad. "I don't think they're gonna need the trucks Johnny."

Slaught could hear the challenge in his voice, asked, "Why's that Shaun?"

"'Cause they're just gonna come in here and kill us all."

That set off the crowd, most people muttering things like "Don't be ridiculous" or "Calm down, you're gonna upset the kids." Slaught stole a glance over at Larose. His face was impassive. Johnny took that as a bad sign, thinking probably Larose agreed with his kid, otherwise he'd be telling him to shut the fuck up and sit down.

"Well, Shaun, I think you might have a point. I guess after the other night we gotta anticipate a worst-case scenario and have a plan for that. But I think for now we need to assume that they aren't going come in here all postal like."

"Why?"

"Because they aren't going to get here, Shaun."

"Yeah, why's that?"

"'Cause we're going to stop them. Right at the bottom of Thibeault Hill."

Shaun said that sounded good to him and maybe they should take a vote. Slaught wasn't too sure what exactly they were all voting on but he figured it might help move the meeting along. "Okay, show of hands?"

Slaught figured everyone must have a pretty good idea of what he meant, even if he didn't, because it looked like his plan had unanimous support. Even Mrs. Merrill raised her hand.

Slaught was thinking this was a fairly crazy situation, figured too that most people were probably relieved that the showdown with Laskin was going to happen elsewhere. "I'm not going to lie to you, we are flying a bit by the seat of our pants, and things could get haywire, but if you're willing to give it a go, then I think we have a chance of beating these bastards back. I think just to be on the safe side, we're going move as many of you as we can out of the hotel, and the rest of us are going to do our best to make sure they never get here in the first place. If any of you want to hightail it on out of here, hide out elsewhere till this thing is done, got for it. Just let us know where you're headed so we aren't worrying about you down the road. How does that sound?"

"Is this going to be it?" old McLaren asked. "We want these sons of bitches to go away and stay away. Leave us alone, once and for all."

A few people said yeah, and others were nodding.

Slaught nodded too. "You're right on the mark with that. We got a few ideas about how to do that."

"Are we going to war with the city?" It was the new mom Melinda asking, holding her baby tight and looking worried, glancing over at Susun. Susun asked, "Do we have a position on violence?"

Shaun stood up and said, "Yeah, we're for it."

"That's the most ridiculous thing I've ever heard anyone say." Mrs. Merrill was fussing in the back. "You should be ashamed of yourself, there's children here."

"Well, they didn't take a drill to your head, did they? Or shoot your girlfriend right in front of you. I don't remember seeing you there so what do you know about it? This is fucked up, seriously fucked up." He was yelling at her by the time he finished and Mrs. Merrill's cheeks were pink and flushed and Slaught was wondering if this meant the vote was off.

"Whoa a minute here," Slaught holding up his hands. "Shaun, you got some strong feelings about this, I understand that. But we can't go off half-cocked on this. And we also gotta let everyone have their say without trying to shut 'em down, alright? Those rules are for all of us. We need to have a plan and stick to it, but I also don't want anybody getting pressured into something. If it takes all day, we'll stay here all day."

Jordan stood up, pushing a chair out of his way. Slaught noticed his hair was a dark blue-black, all spiky now. Must've been Susun's work, he remembered her saying something about hair therapy. Jordan was looking over at Melinda. "It's not really an issue of whether we are for or against violence. Jeff and I've been talking, trying to get our heads around all of this. To be honest, violence, like, it really scares me. Guns scare me. Sometimes you guys scare me. But those guys from Talos are completely mental. So whether we like violence or not, we gotta prepare for the worst, unless we want to pick up right now and go down to the City. And hope we don't get thrown in jail." He shrugged. "Well, that's what I think."

"I'm scared to go to the City." It was Melinda, looking like she was going to start to cry. Her nose was a little red already. "I don't want baby Grace anywhere near that place. When the winter leaves, and I know it will one day, I want Grace's daddy and me to have a garden, and a little house of our own, and I want us to decide how to raise her."

Jordan nodded. "I understand how Melinda feels, and I know for me, my future isn't in the City either. Not by a long shot. I mean, I'm hardly a fighter, but I just can't see any other way. And it would have come to this sooner or later. Talos wants the stuff up here, the mines and the dams. And they don't want us here."

"You're right about that," Shaun said, "and everyone knows where I stand. Me and my Dad are staying."

Susun was shaking her head, saying, "It's too scary, why can't we go hide somewhere, avoid them altogether, we've never even talked about that."

"Can't see how running and hiding would work," Slaught said. "The logistics of it alone—like you said we're almost a town now. We can't just pick up and move. Some of us could maybe sneak off, maybe me, Chum, Larose and his crew, head for the rez—I guess you could argue we're the ones they're really after—but I don't trust them, especially not after what happened to the folks on your bus there Susun, or to Kirstie. That being said, we have to make this decision together."

Susun said, " Most of us ended up here because we didn't want to be stuck in the City, not because we wanted to be freedom fighters."

Chumboy leaned forward so he could see her. "Hey, some of us are here 'cause we wanted to go fishing and be left alone, so what? It doesn't really matter why or how any of us got here, we're here now. Most of us didn't realize we were doing anything wrong by being here, by wanting to stay. But I think that position is off the table now. And that's how these things go—Talos wants everything, even our little bit of everything, and they're going come take it unless we stop them. That is the story. That is always the story."

Slaught felt people's eyes turn from Chumboy to him. "I guess that's true. It's usually about someone trying to take things away from someone else. Now I think we got a pretty good thing going here, it's becoming a town, a place where people like Melinda could raise a family, especially if and when the winter goes. And in the meantime, we are starting to build a place for people that they can have a say in running, and I think this place is worth fighting for. So folks, we got to make some decisions now. We have negotiating, fighting, and some of us high-tailing it out of here hoping to take off the pressure. That's it. A, B, and C."

Old McLaren rose slowly to his feet. "Do we have a chance if we fight?" He sort of surveyed the crowd. "We all agreed to take the action we did with that bastard Laskin and his bunch. I think now we'd be fooling ourselves if we think they are just going to round us up and put us in jail for a few months. Don't think that's going happen. And we all knew Kirstie."

A general murmur went through the crowd that Slaught

figured seemed to indicate people agreed with that position, but it was hard to be sure, still some folks looking out and out terrified. And he could feel Susun's hard blue eyes on him, pinning him, but he was trying to look anywhere but at her. Then she said, "But what if we can't fight?"

"What do you mean, 'can't'?"

"Like they come in and just bomb the hell out of us."

"We gotta do the best we can."

"I'm not into trying. I want this to work."

"I'm staying."

Everyone looked to find the voice. Chumboy's Aunt, sitting in the corner, knitting, didn't even look up as she added, "I think this place belongs to all of us. We give it up, they'll just want more."

Slaught figured that was about as big an endorsement as he was going to get and said, "I think Aunt Verla is right. We've made a home here and I think we have a legitimate claim to this place, unlike Talos. The way I figure it, they just want to come up here and do what they've always done, gouge what profit they can out of the land and then walk away when there's nothing left. I just think now is as good a time as any to make our stand."

Susun still looked uncertain, said, "I just hope we can do this."

Slaught said, "Susun, we'll be having Christmas here, okay?"

"Okay, but they aren't going to be sitting around for weeks waiting for another go at us. We have to get ready, have a plan."

Slaught said, "Well then, why don't we get this place organized so it looks like a command centre and not a tea party in a church basement. Everyone, get your own things sorted out and everyone pack a small emergency bag, just in case. If you need anything, Max can help you out. Max, take two guys down to that storeroom and get it together, we need to know what we have and what we don't. Susun, could you go with Mary and Mrs. Merrill and head down and make sure all our seniors get what they need? Sound like a plan?"

People were already moving, Slaught figuring they were just relieved they had something to keep them busy. He could feel Susun still standing there looking at him as he was walking towards her, not quite sure what kind of look she was throwing his way. When he got up to her she said, "Guess we're going all the way then."

He said he guessed so.

She said, "So it's not the end times?"

He smiled then, remembering what he'd first said to her, her standing there all strung out, telling her they could get to making some babies. He said, "No, not yet, but I'm watching for the signs."

Chumboy asked, "So what are the signs telling you now Johnny?"

"We need a Plan D."

Susun said, "I hadn't realized we actually had plans to go along with A, B, and C."

"We don't really. But I've been working on Plan D in my mind for a while now, think its almost there."

Chumboy said, "That's a good thing Johnny, cause I think soon enough they're going to be here. Auntie says so."

CHAPTER EIGHTEEN

HE'D KNOCKED LOUDLY, SOUNDING IMPATIENT, and Grier had yelled for him to come in. Muspar pushed open the door, saying, "What the fuck are you doing down here, shouldn't you be getting ready?" Laskin explained that he was finishing up, told him to have a seat, he'd be right with him.

Ignoring Muspar, he tried to carry on with his stretches. Muspar was breathing loud though, and it was starting to freak Grier out, distracting him. He'd rather listen to Muspar talk than hear him wheezing, fat old bastard.

He asked, "So any developments in the plan?"

"Everything's set," Muspar said, groaning a bit as he lowered himself into a chair. "The same core team is ready to go, plus a twenty man squad joining you to follow up, waiting at the end of the highway to mop up once we get the word. We'll send in the ploughs a few hours behind you guys, follow up with the trucks.

Should be a cakewalk, if nothing goes wrong or we don't have any rogue actions by Talos. I've talked to Scott about that, think I finally got through to him."

Grier was grinning, wiping a towel through his hair, all spiky and messy, feeling good again. "That's great Capitano. Now more important matters, did you sign out my Glock?"

Muspar nodded, said it wasn't really his job to be requisitioning guns. Also asked what was so important he had to come over in person to see Laskin. "When I got your call, I have to say I was surprised, we haven't exactly seen eye to eye on this mission. I wasn't sure what information you might have on Talos that you would be sharing with me, but I'm ready to listen."

Laskin ignored him, asked, "Did you bring it?"

"What? The gun? Yeah, its here in the bag."

"Plus the Osprey and the ammo?"

"Yeah Laskin, I picked up all your shit for you, though why the hell you need a silencer I have no idea. There isn't anyone left up there to hear you. Now what's on your mind about Talos? You said something about some disturbing news."

"Toss them over, want to see how it feels."

"See how it feels? It's a goddam gun, how do you think it's going to feel?" Muspar complaining, but still taking the gun from his bag and passing it to Laskin, then slapping a box of ammo and the silencer on the table between them. Laskin handled the gun, loading it up, said, "Gotta love the Glock," and then, "Nice one, eh?" and Muspar said that it was an okay gun, but could Laskin just get to the point?

Laskin just smiled, attaching the silencer and raising up his arm, pointing to different corners of the room and pretending to fire, making little plouff, plouff sounds.

Muspar said, "Quit pissing around with that thing."

"Like I said, just getting a feel for it. You have to know your gun to use it properly."

"Then why don't you use it on the right guy this time, instead of on some teenage girl."

"Whatever you say boss," said Laskin, unloading most of the clip into Muspar's chest.

Grier looked down at the body, thinking it was a long time coming. The guy was a liability. He knew Scott thought so too, telling him on the side that Muspar was thinking of pissing up the works, Scott saying if Muspar went up the chain it would be a major clusterfuck for Talos. "Imagine shares hitting the shitter if word got out that Police Services was lowering the boom on what until now had been our show. That sorry excuse for a government wouldn't have to shut us down, our shareholders would do it for us."

Grier had gotten the message. He called Muspar up, knowing there was no way way the Captain would be able to resist the offer of dirt on Talos. Muspar had hauled his lardarse over in record time.

Now blood was pooling out under the lardarse onto the carpet. He'd have to find some other digs for the night, maybe leave a note for Mitch. She'd be pissed about the carpet.

Chumboy was telling Susun about the time he ran into a black bear when he was out blueberry picking with his Auntie. They were in a clearing that was thick with the berries when there was some rustling in the bush, and his Auntie had stood up and said, "Chumboy, there's a bear." And it was a big fella, must have been close to four hundred pounds, only twenty feet away.

"So what happened?"

"Well, first I looked around for a stick or something, but I really didn't want to bend over, at least standing up I looked pretty big. I asked my Auntie to give me her buckets to bang together but she wouldn't."

"She wouldn't? What do you mean she wouldn't?" Susun couldn't believe it.

"She said, 'Chumboy, you run that bear off, these are my blue-berries, I'm not picking them a second time.'"

"So what did you do?"

"I decided that the only advantage I had was to be bigger and meaner, so I threw my arms over my head, starting yelling and took a step towards the bear."

"Was that smart?"

"Apparently not, because basically the bear did the same thing, coming right at me. He was up on his back legs in no time. Well, then it was pretty much eye to eye. And then he starts clacking his teeth at me, and I swear we could almost reach out and touch each other."

"You have got to be kidding. You must have been terrified."

"I was, but I was also stuck, so I start clacking my teeth too, though he was better at it, and Christ he had those beady little eyes just staring at me, and then he blew at me."

"Blew at you?"

"Yeah, and ever stinking breath, that bear. That was almost enough to make me turn tail to run, but I knew Auntie couldn't run that fast so it didn't seem like an option."

"What was your Auntie doing while this was going on."

"Oh, she was still picking her blueberries. Anyways, so me and this bear are pretty much nose to nose, so I lean back, and then just drive him in the nose."

"You punched the bear?"

"Well, what else was I gonna do?"

"Did it work?"

"Yeah, I mean it wasn't a knock-out punch but it threw him off balance and he sort of fell back, shook his head a couple of times and backed off a bit. He was clearly pissed off, started hitting the ground, but I just stood there, yelling at him until he got bored and went back into the bush. The next night my Auntie served me the first piece of pie."

Susun was laughing, mostly because of Chumboy's big, shit-eating grin as he finished the story. He asked her how things were coming along and if his Auntie was giving her any trouble. "No, she just sits in the corner, knitting, I sort of wonder if she's thinking I sound crazy with all my preparations."

"Why wouldn't she? We're all crazy."

"I hope this works Chumboy."

"Oh, it'll work. It has to, we're the good guys."

"You think we can win?"

"I don't think it's going to be *Hang 'em High* material. Me, I'm thinking that fighting Talos is going to be like fighting that bear."

"How's that?"

"Gotta watch for the chance for that sucker punch. It's the nature of any Plan D."

Ricky thought he was having a nightmare.

He was lying in his sleeping bag on the cot in the corner of the shed. He and Jeff had found the guns and piled them onto the

sled attached to Jeff's machine, and then Jeff had made them some supper. When they'd cleaned up, Ricky realized he didn't really want to go to bed. He was spooked, being so close to the burnt out remains of the main cabin, thinking that his Uncle, and even the dog, were just piles of ashes buried in there. And the cabin was so dark he hadn't been able to see where Jeff was lying not four feet away. Made him think of the last time he'd gone out with hunting his Uncle Delbert. Delbert had said they had to get to their spot early, get hunkered down before the deer came out, said before the dawn the deer just looked like ghosts, that you needed time for your eyes to adjust to be able to see them. So he followed Delbert into the thick black of the morning, stumbling across the field, not seeing anything, the sky and the ground and his Uncle, and even himself, just blackness.

Thinking about his Uncle made him feel worse, and he tossed and turned on his narrow cot until Jeff had finally gotten up, Ricky feeling bad that maybe he'd woken him up, but Jeff said he'd keep an eye on the place, was going to got outside for a bit and take a looksee, and that Ricky should try to get some sleep. But he still had butterflies in his stomach.

He had started to think about that, picturing butterflies inside the pink lining of his stomach and they kept turning into dark, hairy moths as he drifted off to sleep, and so he'd already resigned himself to bad dreams when he heard a slight creak across the room, sounding like the door, then a shuffling sound, and he was thinking maybe an animal had got in. Maybe Jeff hadn't shut the door tight enough. He was trying to think of what kind of a animal it could be when he heard a voice say in a slow whisper, "Well, hello there, thought we'd take a minute to reconnect before the fireworks begin, maybe have some of our own. How about it?"

Ricky froze. It was her. He was sure of it. He tried to stifle his breathing. It was too dark to see anything, the blackness thick inside the cabin, so he knew she couldn't see him. She must've listened to the sound of his breathing to find him. Or maybe he'd been snoring. Except he didn't think he'd been asleep, but maybe he wasn't really awake right now, and that was what was messing him up.

"Hey, don't worry, I'm not here to trick you, or capture you and haul you back, though I guess I could right now if I felt like it, but that's not what I feel like at all," and Ricky heard the sound of a zipper. He tried to think of which side of his pillow he'd tucked his flashlight under, but he couldn't think straight. He was wondering if she had a gun and she said, "You awake? Oh, don't worry about your little friend outside hearing us, he's way down the trail. I'll be finished with you by the time he heads back."

He heard some more rustling, staring up at the sounds, trying to discern exactly where she was. She sounded close. He could hear her touching the edge of the table beside him, could almost see her sliding her hand along, feeling for the top, then the sound of something hard being set down. A gun?

" Johnny, don't be shy, talk to me, I'm getting cold standing here like this."

Ricky had a lot of thoughts all at once when she said that, but he didn't have time to really sort them out before the door blew wide open and Jeff's big Coleman flashlight illuminated her and he said, "Duh, no wonder you're cold. You're not dressed for the weather."

And there she was in the harsh white beam, her down-filled overalls unzipped and hanging around her waist, wearing a white wife-beater, big boots still on her feet, coat lying on the ground.

Ricky still wasn't sure if he was stuck in a nightmare, because from where he was lying she looked massively tall, and the flashlight cast dark shadows across her face, making the rage absolutely terrifying when she looked down at him and hissed incredulously, "It's you? You fucking little dirtbag."

Ricky scrambled up, bumping into her and stretching around her to grab the gun off the table. She leaned to grab at him, but he was off balance, and already tumbling away. She tried to land a kick, but he had fallen out of reach. For a second she looked panicked, looking to see where her gun had gone, then seeing Ricky holding on tight to it, not pointing it anywhere in particular but not letting go of it either.

Jeff, shotgun in one hand, flashlight in the other, said, "Whoa, dude, nice move, wait till the boys down at the shop hear about this," and Ricky wanted to tell him it was an accident, that he he'd just grabbed the gun without thinking, but then he said, "Be careful, she's very dangerous."

Jeff said, "Don't worry, I know," and then he said to Mitch, "Uh, and Ms. Black, time to get back into your onesie, okay?"

She was still pretty white with rage, but Ricky saw her face change and she said, "What's your name, again?" as she reached down for her fleece jacket and set it on the cot, hiking the overalls back up onto her shoulders.

Jeff said, "Keep your pole dancing moves slow, okay?" and Mitch sort of smirked and asked, "Is that how you like it, nice and slow?"

"So, like, you know this routine of yours? Not getting any traction here, I play for the other team, and Ricky here, well, he is just plain terrified, so could you just zip up and step outside please?" And then he looked over to Ricky, telling him to get his stuff together asap, and then he adding, "Like that means real quick, okay?"

Jeff gestured with the gun for Mitch to move away from the bed and over towards the door. Ricky grabbed his stuff and followed Jeff outside. There was no light out there, the blackness almost a physical presence, no stars in the sky tonight either, Ricky following the light of Jeff's lantern as they hiked the short distance to where Mitch had stashed her machine near theirs. Standing there in the bush was scary so Ricky snapped on his flashlight. It shone straight into Mitch's eyes and she told him to fuck off, but he left it there, staring at her for a minute, and she told him to fuck off again, only louder. Ricky dragged his flashlight off her face when Jeff said, "On her sled, shine the flashlight there. See her parka? Pass it over to her, just throw it if you want."

Ricky threw it at her and she caught the parka, shook the snow off and pulled it on, her hand headed straight into the pocket.

Jeff held up a set of keys. "These what you are looking for?"

She didn't say anything. Ricky found that even more worrisome.

Jeff asked, "So how far away are your buddies right now?"

"I don't know. May I please have my keys?"

"Don't worry. When we run into your friends, we'll be sure to let them know you're waiting here at your little love nest."

"You're just going to leave her here?" Ricky asked.

"Got any better ideas?"

"Ricky isn't the kind of person to leave someone here to die," Mitch said softly, looking over at Ricky, "are you Ricky?"

Ricky didn't like her saying his name, it made him nervous, but he thought it might be wrong to leave her behind, it was real cold, so he looked to Jeff who said, "Okay, I'll take Johnny's sled, leave my piece of shit here for Ms. Black." He tossed his set of keys into the snow by the dogwood scrub. "That'll give you something to do to kill the boredom, eh?" and then to Ricky, "You get to ride her sled, dude."

He tossed the keys over and Ricky caught them in his left hand. That, Ricky figured, was a sign. He had never, ever, been able to catch keys like they did in the movies, even when he was practicing tossing them to himself.

Jeff said, "Back up Ms. Black, give Ricky some room there," then to Ricky, "Don't worry about her, she can sit here in the cold and think about what she did to Kirstie. That should keep a bitch like her warm enough."

CHAPTER NINETEEN

CHUMBOY HAD PULLED HIMSELF OUT from underneath the machine and was wiping his hands on a towel. The towel was so greasy that Larose said, "Maybe you should try washing up with something that is actually clean."

Chumboy held out his hands, turning them over admiringly, then said, "No, I don't think so. Women love the smell of gasoline on a man."

"Sure they do."

"No, it's true, women love it, drives them crazy. Reminds them that you're a man who can get things done."

"Then how come all that male cologne stuff smells like flowers and shit?"

"Well, technically, it's not flowers. Male cologne tends to offer scents reminiscent of bergamot or musk, things that make the modern male feel closer to nature."

"You're full of shit."

"You see, Larose," Chumboy continued, ignoring him, "the new breed of urban male that emerged at the beginning of this century had no choice but to resort to faux natural scents. He was attempting to reclaim his lost manhood by covering himself with scents that he believed would convince females he was still virile."

"Where does he get this shit?" Larose asked Slaught.

Slaught shook his head. "We going to stand around talking horseshit all day or get ourselves ready? It's D-day tomorrow gentlemen."

Chumboy said, "Oh, my Auntie told me to tell you that Mother Nature is smiling on you."

"That so?"

"She says it's real warm out there today, but D-Day is going to be a cold bastard."

"Your Auntie said that?" Larose asked.

"Not in so many words Harv, but what she did say is that the hill is going to be a mess, getting all sloppy today and then seizing up. Think if our luck holds, getting those trucks up that hill is going to be harder than getting to Mitch Black's heart. So let's finish up these sleds boys and send some prayers to the weather gods."

The three of them had spent the day checking the snowmachines, making sure everything was good to go. Jordan had come in part way through, asking if he could help, said sitting around waiting for the end times was making him crazy. Slaught put him to work moving in more wood for the woodpile at the back end of the shed, saying he found it hard to believe it was going to warm up at all, they'd been feeding the firebox steady and could still see their breath in the workbay.

He was just about to start helping Jordan when he heard machines coming up the road. He swung open the big doors and

Jeff and Ricky pulled in, parking and cutting their engines. Slaught frowned, seeing Ricky riding one of the creepy black sleds with the demented looking happy face.

"Where'd you get that puppy?" Slaught asked.

Jeff told them about their run in with Mitch. He had them all laughing by the end of the story, but pointed out that Mitch Black's attempt to makeover Delbert's shithole into a lovenest was terrifying at the time, not just for Ricky, but for him too. Jeff nodded at Ricky, "We played it cool though, didn't we bro?" and Ricky nodded, and then told them that he'd caught the keys in one hand, and that's why he was riding her machine.

Jeff said he had something to show Slaught, reaching into his pocket and bringing out the rice-sized transmitter that Mitch had attached to Johnny's sled. Jeff said when he'd seen her show up he figured she must have been tracking the sleds.

Johnny said, "Check 'em all."

They didn't find any others, Chumboy saying Johnny must feel pretty special. Slaught asked Jeff what they should do with it. "Definitely keep the little sucker for now. Got nothing to hide about being here right now and it worked once sending her on a wild goose chase."

Then Jeff asked where to put the stash from Delbert's hunt camp, pointing to the filthy canvas bag that looked like some old army rucksack.

"That your haul?" Johnny asked.

"The motherlode, direct to you from hillbilly heaven," Jeff said, opening the bag then nodding over at Ricky. "His Uncle had acquired some seriously demented firepower."

Chumboy whistled. " Whoa, what was Delbert thinking?"

"Whatever it was, he didn't get a chance to put it into practice—the place was torched. Those Talos boys did a number on it."

Chumboy rummaged through the bag. "We could start a war."

"I think we already have, Chum," Slaught said, then added, ""Nice work on the guns. Why don't you two wash up and get some food. Jordan can haul these out of here."

Jordan was complaining about how much the bags weighed as Jeff and Ricky headed off. Jeff shouted back that he'd send Max over to help. Slaught tossed Jordan the gym bags crammed with the plastic guns. "Sort these out too, bin the real ones and stash them all some place outta sight. Don't want some of those little ones going all Montana militia with these."

Max and Jordan repacked the bags and then hauled the four out across the snow, Jordan pretty much dragging his, leaving a thick band of track behind him. He had to stop and brush the snow off in the doorway, then caught up with Max. "Hey, slow down man, these are heavy!" but Max said there was lots to do and they should get a move on. Jordan followed him down the short hallway to one of the storage closets and started emptying the bags onto the floor outside while Max unlocked the door and tried to make room on the big metal shelves. He kicked some empty bins over towards Jordan, saw him tossing the guns into piles so told him to watch it, they weren't toys, and Jordan frowned, "Some of them are, right?" and Max said, "You can tell by the weight Jordan. Just be careful, okay? You have to be careful around guns."

Jordan said Max sounded like somebody's mother and that he was more than welcome to do it himself since the guns were giving him the heebs anyway.

Max ignored him, surveying the rows of shelves, said, "There's too much shit in here, honestly, with all these friggin' diapers and crap, there's no room for anything."

"We can't leave them out here."

Max sighed. "Well, let's try and shove a least the real ones in here. I'll haul out some stuff and then we'll take the ones we can't make room for to the maintenance room. There's some shelf room there. At least it has a lock." He tossed a black marker over to Jordan, said, "They like things labeled."

In big black letters Jordan scrawled REAL and FAKE on the lids of the bins. Max pointed to the latter and said, "Put the Slaught specials in here, okay?" Jordan shrugged, began loading up the bins as Max hauled some gasoline cans around the corner to make more room. Then they grabbed two of the bins and headed for the maintenance room.

As they'd stashed them beside the toilet paper, Jordan was still complaining that they were too heavy and why did he always get the shit jobs. Max told him to quit whining and then felt bad after what Jordan had been through so he asked him if he was getting nervous.

"Nervous? No bro, I'm not nervous, I'm fucking terrified."

—

Slaught said, "We got a slight hitch."

They'd just finished filling up the machines, Larose cursing, saying they were getting low on fuel, and then adding, "A hitch? Yeah? Is this a new hitch or just one of the fucking hundred facing us right now?"

Chumboy laughed. "Ever testy bastard, you."

Larose didn't answer, just said again, "What's the hitch?"

"Tiny says we are seriously running out of grub. Big time. Said we were into, and I quote, emergency rationing. There's no time for a proper scavenge trip. I got that moose waiting about two miles north of here but one of us is going to have to bring it in soon. It's a helluva job."

"There's got to be someone besides us to go?" Larose worried about going to Thibeault Hill a man short. They were pushing their luck already.

"Got no other experienced guys. Couple of the older guys got the know-how for the moose but not the gumption, not for hauling out that sucker. Can't ask Shaun, think we need to keep that young lad focused and not leave him on his own. God knows what he'd end up doing. Max and Susun are going to be holding down the fort. Then someone's going have to stay back with Tiny to butcher the thing once we get it back. Maybe Jordan? Just too big a job."

Chumboy raised his eyebrows. "Big job indeed. We gonna volunteer or get drafted?"

"We gotta decide together."

"How?"

"Not sure," Slaught said.

Chumboy said, "Draw straws."

Slaught looked at Chum. "You think that's the best way?"

"It's the only way."

Slaught didn't look convinced so Chumboy added, "It's fair and it's blind. Otherwise one of us is going to feel like shit for backing out of the job, right? This way, its completely random and none of us has to make the decision."

"Alright. Fine with you Larose?"

Larose nodded, "Sure, why not. Everything else around here is pretty fucked up and random, why not this too?"

Chum handed Larose three toothpicks from his pocket and Larose broke two off to different lengths. He buried them in his fist and tucked them all down so they were even. "Short straw stays. Ready gentlemen?"

Chum took one, then Slaught.

"Showtime," Chumboy said.

Slaught opened his fist, then Chumboy. Chum's was longer. Larose showed his. His wasn't broken. Chumboy whistled. "Not an outcome I would have anticipated. Guess you hold down the fort Kemosabe."

"Maybe just as well," Larose said, "case something we didn't count on happens."

Slaught shrugged, looking maybe surprised himself that he wasn't going to the hill. "Now that'd be a shock wouldn't it?"

—

"Action!"

When Jeff yelled for them to start, the dozen or so folks lined up in the workbay squared their shoulders and stared forward into the camera. Jeff had said they had to be unflinching, that was the word he had used, and so even though the balaclavas were itchy and hot, nobody flinched. They stood behind Johnny, watching the back of his head as he delivered his lines. Afterwards, Mrs. Merrill had said to Mr. McLaren that she thought Johnny had done a pretty good job.

"It was the way he ended his speech, after we'd all taken off our balaclavas and dropped those silly guns to the floor and said our names, when he said, 'So, this is who we are and where we live. We're not hiding anything. Now that we've shown you what we're like, that these guns Talos says we have aren't even real, now we're going to show you the real face of Talos, and what real guns can do,' I liked that."

They had tried the shot first with the kids up front but the three boys, maybe around seven or eight, couldn't stand still, and Jeff said the fidgeting was distracting. Susun suggested getting the kids to stand in the background against the wall, but the kids begged to be in the shot, saying they wouldn't move a muscle but Jeff said they weren't in a position to promise the impossible and stuck them against the back wall, then looking through his camera said, "Hey, they look good back there, love that Bob Marley t-shirt Sheldon."

It took about two hours to get everything right, then Jeff and Jordan went off to put the thing together. Slaught asked them if they were sure it was going to work.

Jeff said, "Well, if we don't run out of batteries for the camera, maybe," and Jordan added," Just don't expect Fellini."

"I was hoping more for James Cameron," Chumboy said, but Jordan just snorted and said, "Please."

After they left, Slaught asked Chum what "Fellini" was?

"Some famous Italian director. I think Jordan was trying to impress us."

"Doesn't work if you don't know what the fuck someone's talking about."

"I rarely know what he's talking about. How'd he take the news about staying behind?"

Slaught said, "Fucking jubilant until he found out he had to help butcher a moose."

"What's the plan then?"

"I'll go out get the moose. We can butcher it down in the bay. I got the boys setting up Harv's tripod. You guys should head out in time to be at the hill before dawn. Block the road then get the hell over to the outpost and do the Fellini."

As Slaught was saying it he thought it didn't sound so bad. He'd woken up in the middle of the night, lying in his cot, listening to his own breathing, thinking how fucked up everything was. He'd thought about that day on the loading dock, looking around at the supplies and guns and deciding he didn't want to be part of the bullshit anymore. He decided he wanted a place of his own, with rows of firewood in the yard, fixing up his cabin so it would be a good place to live. And now this, going to fucking war over a run down hotel with a mittful of guys and some very scared people that were just strangers a year or so ago.

Chumboy asked, "So if it gets too dangerous, folks that want can just sit tight and turn themselves in when the cavalry arrives, hope for the best?"

"Cavalry? Thought that was a good thing when the cavalry got there."

"Not so good for us Indians."

"Right," said Slaught, "guess not. And what about the rest of us renegades?"

"Head north."

"The rez? Yeah, maybe."

Chumboy frowned. "You don't sound too sure about that. Not planning on going down in flames are you?"

"No Chum, but it isn't going to come to that. We'll be having Christmas here."

"You sure about that?"

"I promised."

"That's right, you did."

CHAPTER TWENTY

LASKIN KILLED HIS ENGINE AND TOOK A QUICK LOOK over his shoulder, wondering where the fucking trucks were then realizing he didn't really give a shit. From the top of the hill he looked back down what at used to be the main, cross-country highway, a deep four-laned chute that had been blasted out of the rockface lining either side. Laskin figured it had probably been a couple of years since any machine beside a snowmobile had tried to get up what the locals had called Thibeault Hill back in the day.

He'd told Talos that bringing along the trucks was a bad move, that nothing was left of the highway to even plough. But Police Services demanded the 'safe removal of non-criminal civilians' so Talos had agreed on paper to having the trucks written into the action plan. But Scott had been pretty clear that this wasn't a rescue mission and to not worry too much about what Police Services wanted anyway. Now staring up at the sheen on the hill, he guessed it didn't matter, those trucks weren't going anywhere, not with that ice.

Below he could hear the revving of the trucks as they tried to find some traction. One of the snowploughs had already slid sideways down the hill and was face first in a high snow bank.

Christ Almighty.

He headed back down the hill.

A truck was sending the snow spitting outwards under its big tires, digging in deep before the back tires even reached the icy surface. Laskin barked at the driver to shut the fucking truck off.

Laskin grabbed his flashlight and shot the beam up the hill. The thing glistened like a goddam skating rink.

"Wow," Miller said, "I didn't know it had gotten that warm. Look at it. It'll be near impossible to get those big ploughs up there."

Laskin turned to him in irritation. He saw Turner and Miller watching him.

"I don't need a fucking weather report."

Miller asked, "Any other way of getting those ploughs up there?"

"No, there's no other way up the hill or you wouldn't be standing here with your thumb up your ass would you?"

One of the drivers approached them, shouted over the din, "Want me to contact Muspar? I could head over to the outpost."

"I don't think that would be too fucking helpful right now," Laskin snapped, thinking of Muspar lying there in his own cooled blood, his body probably now thick and waxy, then saying, "You guys take one of the trucks that can still move over to the sand silos there," pointing. "See 'em, down the highway there on the right? Start working on the hill and see if you can get anywhere."

Then the drivers were complaining, one of them saying, "Well, how long do we have to sit out here? We aren't exactly able to check into a motel or anything you know. It's damn cold."

Laskin told them to shut the fuck up while he figured it out. He wasn't a goddam babysitter, and now with Mitch fucking off on him, he wasn't in the mood for anything but getting Slaught into a body bag. Just as well the trucks were stuck; he hadn't really planned on bringing them along anyway. Best to keep them busy down here, giving him a chance to get up to that shithole and take care of unfinished business. Now with Muspar out of the way, Laskin wasn't feeling too committed to honouring the terms of that agreement. He figured Talos wasn't either.

"You sit here until we get back. How hard is that to understand?"

"You mean we're going on?" asked Miller.

"That's right, Miller. Now let's move out. I want this done. These bozos can catch up once they get moving."

"But what if they don't get moving. How are we going to get everyone out of there?" Miller asked. "We can't bring them out on our snowmachines, and there weren't that many sleds up there by my count, only a dozen or so. And there's kids too, Mr. Laskin. I don't see how it's feasible."

"Think Talos ever thought it was feasible? They know there's no road up here. So open your fucking eyes, okay?"

Laskin just walked off, barking at them to get a move on, they were heading out. Miller caught up to him. "So, sir, really, what is the plan?"

"Are you completely fucked up, Miller?"

"No sir, I don't believe so."

Laskin was shaking his head. "We don't bring them out. Problem solved."

Miller was just staring at him now so Laskin said, "They want to stay so fucking bad, fine, there's enough assholes in the City already."

"There're probably enough machines to get some of the women and children out sir."

"Don't give me that women and children shit, Miller. There aren't enough sleds, end of story. You don't have the stomach for it? Go help those sorry bastards back there sand the highway. Maybe one day you'll get your trucks up there for your big rescue."

"Have you briefed the team on this?"

Laskin looked at Miller's face. These cops were something else. All yes sir, no sir, except when it counted. He'd be so fucking glad to be done with these jerkoffs and back on his own. From now on man, that was the way it would be, go it alone or don't bother. "Yes, I briefed Talos. That good enough for you and your mother?"

Miller hesitated, then asked, "Do we have clearance for changing the operation from Police Services, sir?"

Laskin had already been walking away but he came back fast at Miller, grabbing him by his parka. "You question my command again and I'll leave you behind too, understand? Now do your job before I write you up, you fucking wuss."

"Well, can you see anything?"

Chumboy and Larose were hunkered down in a rock cut half way down Thibeault Hill. From where they crouched off to the side, they had a view of the lower part of the hill as well as the scatterings of buildings along the other side of what used to be the main highway.

"Looking at them right now," Chumboy said. He had the night vision goggles they'd taken from Laskin's team.

"No way."

"Yes sir, just the way Ricky said. You just don't want to believe it."

"How many?"

"Again, the Rickyman was right on the money, seven sleds, four trucks."

Larose took the night-vision goggles from Chumboy and asked, "This going to work?" and then said, "Hey, these are cool."

"Nice toy, eh?"

Larose said that Chumboy sure liked that gadget shit.

"What if I do? Anishinaabe brothers are allowed a little high tech you know."

"Yeah, well, what does your low tech knowledge tell you about that red streak spreading across the sky there?" Larose asked.

Chumboy figuring he was talking mostly for the sake of talking. Larose pointed to the horizon, "See, look at that, it's going to be a red sky in the morning, man. That's not good, right?"

Across the sky, thick charcoal clouds were emerging from the night, sliced by a single thin streak of dark red. Chumboy told Larose it looked liked the scar that ran across his mother's belly. She'd given birth to him by c-section, had said otherwise it would have been like trying to drive a Ford pick-up through a doghouse.

"That doesn't tell me much about the red sky, Chum."

"You a sailor?"

"What?"

"It goes, red sky in morning, sailors take warning. Are you a sailor?"

"No Chumboy, I'm not a sailor," Larose sounding testy, sitting back on his haunches.

"Then you got nothing to worry about, okay?"

They fell into silence, listening to the creaking of the trees, the birches slapping their tips together, cackling up high. Chumboy heard the engines revving up again and took a deep breath before he turned around to look down the hill, said, "Lock and load buddy," as if they were in some sort of movie.

Larose said, "Ever think about that day at the warehouse, that guy shooting that kid in the back and how we all just stood there, almost knowing it was coming, or that something bad was coming, and saying things like, oh come on, give the kid the gloves. I can still see the kid turning, smiling, as if he was thinking that things like that didn't happen in real life."

"Well buddy, we aren't standing around tonight now are we?"

"We could die here Chum, I mean it. I was just a parts guy. What the fuck do I know about any of this guerilla shit?"

"Look Larose, that day at the warehouse, we all made a choice. If we'd made another choice, some of us might already be dead, some of us might be in jail, and the rest of us would be trawling dumpsters for wasted Taco Bell shit and thinking Lysol was a fine merlot. We'd just be shit on the streets of the City."

Larose thought about it for a few seconds, said, "Yeah, fuck, I don't know."

"Look, its like that Dillon dude said in *Alien 3*, when it was coming down to the wire, and they were deciding if they should go after the alien beast, and he says, 'You're all going to die. The only question is how you check out. Do you want it on your feet or on your fucking knees, begging?' Essentially, Larose, that is the choice facing us."

"Wasn't it Ripley who said that?"

"No, it was Dillon."

"Sure?"

"Yeah, I'm sure, but you're missing the point here."

"No, I got the point, I'm not a fucking moron, I just think you're wrong about who said it."

"Larose, that is ridiculous, I've seen that movie at least twenty times."

"You kidding me?"

"No, I'm not kidding."

"Oh, shit, where are the sleds? I can't see them anymore. I can't see Laskin anywhere. Shit, shit, shit!" Larose was scrambling now, getting into position.

"Them trucks have been raising a ruckus, can't hear shit over them. There's a chance they could have slipped by us. Or they could be down behind the trucks, hard to say."

"Fuck. What now?"

"Well Harv, not much we can do about it."

"But Johnny is counting on it taking at least a day for them to get up, between the ploughing and the speed of the trucks. But with the sleds? Shit, they could get there in a couple of hours."

"Well then, we better get our job done and get back up there fast as we can, eh?"

"Maybe we should just go back. What about Jordan? He can't handle any of that shit on his own—Christ almighty, we should have left Shaun back there too. I think we should head back."

"No, we've come this far, I say we finish it right. Jordan can get a hold of Johnny if he needs to. And this might be our only chance. Anyway, I think things are gonna be okay."

"What the fuck could lead you to that conclusion, Chum?"

"My Auntie said we needed a miracle."

"No kidding, that's exactly what's fucked up about all of this, Chum."

"You know, that's your problem Larose. You only have one way of thinking about things."

"That so?"

"Yeah, see if the answer lies in a miracle, well, you don't get a miracle when things are going okay. You get a miracle when you're desperate. So now we qualify."

"That's some messed up thinking, Chum."

"Well me, I figure we kick start this chain of events and see what happens. We can sort out our theological differences later."

Chumboy swung back around and up, peering over the bank with the binoculars. "This makes me think of another line from the movie."

"What's that?"

"I say we grease this rat-fuck son of a bitch right now."

Larose took a deep breath. "Let's go then."

He grabbed the beacon and flashed it twice, and from down below, over by the wreck of the strip mall, two lights flicked back at them.

They watched as Jeff hauled the string of crap out across the road with his snowmachine. They'd counted on Laskin's guys still running their trucks and not being able to hear much of anything over the big engines, and it was likely they couldn't see past the glare of the floodlights. Still, there was a lot of gambling going on with this one, especially now since they weren't sure exactly where Laskin and his crew were.

Jeff, Shaun and Ricky had spent the last couple of hours pulling together a shitload of old butane and propane tanks and empty gas cans, tying them into a thick length of rope and jimmy-rigging in a bunch of sticks of crap dynamite and flares. After securing the rope to the back of the snowmachine, Jeff hauled it across the bottom of the road in the dark. He then left the snowmachine and ran back all hunched over, just like he was in the movies. Larose waited, counting softly in the dark, imagining the three of them scrambling up through the snow trail along the edge of the cliffs until they were far enough away. Then two flashes of the light. Good to go.

"You're up," said Larose. Chumboy swung his rifle across his back and said "Keep an eye on me. If you don't, my Auntie will kill you."

"Yeah," said Larose, "she mentioned that."

—

Ricky crouched down beside Jeff and Shaun, breathing hard after scrambling up the embankment deep with snow. After listening to the guys arguing about what would work and what wouldn't, and soaking the rope with everything from kerosene to Tiny's homemade hooch, Shaun said he was sure it would burn like a bastard. Jeff has also set a couple of plastic jugs full of fuel on the snowmachine for good measure. Ricky wasn't sure what to expect. Would it start slow or blow up? They were catching their breath, Ricky listening in the dark, wondering if he'd be able to hear the shot from Chumboy over the roar of the trucks and clanging of metal below.

Shaun said he thought he'd heard it, and they waited as a few seconds dragged by. Then things sort of happened fast after that.

The idea had been to drag the junk across the road, hitching enough potential explosive trash to it that it would blast a deep gouge into the snow to stop the trucks getting up the hill. Then all they needed was the magic of Chumboy's remote flare gun. Chumboy told them he used them back in the day when working summers fighting forest fires, using them to start control fires to slow things down. Said if he could get within a couple hundred feet he could hit the plastic milk jugs, figured it might just do the trick, starting some flames going that could then spread along the rope. With the rope burning down through the snow, all the debris and crap along it would sink down too, creating a big fucking melted mess that would stop anyone going up that road for a least another twenty-four hours or so. They'd also thought it might pack quite the psychological punch, making Laskin's team re-group, thinking that there might be some more guerilla action along the trail. Johnny said if they could just create enough of a delay to allow for the public airing of their propaganda masterpiece, it might just to the trick.

Watching from his position up the hill, Ricky saw the fire eating its way along the rope and then following it back towards the abandoned convenience store that sat at the end of the strip mall. The fire was grabbing everything in its path as it tore along towards where the rope ran out just past the stack of empty propane tanks sitting in front of the store. He'd glanced over his shoulder and could see the fire licking up around the racks of old propane tanks.

He was still thinking it was a bit of a letdown when the rack blew, a hard, violent cracking sound sending the tanks skidding up and outwards over the snow, causing Ricky to slip, turning too fast, leaving him sitting on his ass watching the red and orange dancing around the blue flames. Scrambling up in the dark, he was glad Jeff has insisted they get up the hill right away, Ricky thinking at the time he'd like to stay down and watch it go up.

Jeff said, "Holy shit, did you see that?"

Shaun whistled, said, "Went up like a fuck-ing a-tomic bomb."

Ricky scrambled up and just kept moving.

Chapter Twenty One

Laskin stared down the street. No signs of life. He barked at everyone to proceed slowly towards the hotel, to keep their eyes open. "Let's give these shitforbrains the benefit of the doubt and assume they might have posted sentries to protect their precious fucking Lazarus."

They'd made good time, Laskin saying that they could rest all they wanted once Slaught was dead. Until then, the clock was ticking down and they'd keep moving. Soon after they'd crested the hill after starting out, Miller had bombed up beside him, pointing back down the hill, Laskin turning and seeing the sky lit up. Miller stopped, killing his machine. The others did the same, half turning to look back. Laskin bellowed at them to get the fuck moving, saying they still had a good hour and a half of riding to go, it was no time to be pissing and moaning about some dumbfuck who'd probably blown himself up smoking while gassing up his truck.

So they'd followed Laskin through the dark and the cold, arriving in the town just as the thin red sliver running across the sky started to bleed into the grey clouds. They'd left their machines around the corner at the top of the street, moving down slowly along either side, building to building. Behind Laskin was Turner, wheezing a bit as they pushed their way through the snow ridge that had been pushed back along the edges of the street. Turner pointed down the street, past the bulk of the hotel on the corner to the crooked shadow of an old, wooden building.

Turner asked, "What's that thing anyway?"

Laskin looked at him over his shoulder. "Don't you fucking pay attention to anything? This was a mining town. That's a head-frame." Then he added, "Imagine what a shithole this must have been, a fucking mine in the middle of town."

Across from the headframe, the big floodlights over the workbay were out. That was good. Laskin could see only a few dull lights burning inside the hotel. Everyone still tucked in their little beds, just the way Laskin wanted them. He was pumped to go in, catch them by surprise, and leave them wondering what the hell hit them. Miller had said he wasn't sure that was exactly a plan but Laskin told him to shut the fuck up.

"Okay, Turner, you're up, so quit sitting there with your head up your ass, get your fucking sensor out and get up there and tell us what we got."

Turner set off awkwardly in the snow, sending Laskin back a sour look as he went. He didn't get too far before he slipped off the hard-packed trail and plunged down to his knee in the snow, cursing and hauling his foot back up onto the trail, muttering loudly that this was fucked up big time.

Laskin shook his head, thinking that Turner was a big lardarse. If he'd had a proper team he wouldn't be stuck out here for a second time around. He'd worked with a couple of A list teams in the past, especially back in the day before Talos had taken over, when free-lancers had more of a role, but Talos called the shots now. Fucked everything up. Man, he was ready for some serious R&R.

Turner came back huffing and puffing. "Crazy thing, sir, can't get a reading. Maybe it's too cold?"

"Too cold?"

Miller said he'd give it a try, hadn't had trouble because of the cold before. Turner just shrugged. Laskin stared at the building, the impulse to just hammer Turner hard to control.

"Fuck it. We're going in. Burke and Leclerc, you two go and check out the workbay down there. The rest of you assholes come with me and be on your guard. No more fucking sucker punches."

Laskin slipped around the side of the hotel and pushed open the door quietly, the team slipping in behind him. The hotel felt empty. He told them to stay a few yards apart, then sweep through the dining room. After that it'd be room by room.

They were part way down the first hallway when Miller whispered, "I got a live one right up ahead, sir."

Laskin saw the darkness of the dining area and tried to remember where the lights were. He hissed, "There, on your right. Turner, hit the lights."

"Shit" was the only thing Turner could come up with when he heard the gun cocking at his head.

"Getting sloppy?" Mitch said, flipping on the light switch.

Laskin could feel the guys watching him, decided to play it cool, only said, "Where the fuck did you come from?" and then turning to the guys, the bunch of them just standing there gawking, said, "Why don't you guys do your fucking job for a change and keep searching?"

"Don't think you're going to find much," Mitch said, pointing over her shoulder to a big hand painted sign tacked up on the wall. 'Shop Closed. Gone Fishing.'

Laskin said, "Look anyway, turn this fucking dump inside out. I want to know where those bastards are, unless of course you have the inside line on them."

She shrugged. "Just got in here a while before you, had been waiting for a bit of light. Saw lots of tracks around the perimeter but that's about it. Maybe it's worth a look."

"Okay guys, beat it, and come back with something I can use," Laskin said, dismissing them with a jerk of his head and then turning to Mitch. "So, did you get yourself into a situation darling, or just off sight seeing?"

"Miss me?"

"Oh yeah, missed you on the long ride up here, thinking it was a fucking amateurish thing to do to run after the schoolyard crush."

He saw her face tighten.

She said, "There you are, all dressed up for your ambush and all you get is me."

"Some consolation prize you are. You here on your own?"

"Looks like."

"Yeah, well, your Talos toadies are here with me. Turns out they're a bit more professional than their boss."

"You know Grier, if you were any good at your job, maybe you would have gotten your big fish already. So unless you've given up, maybe we should start tracking these people down."

"How long have you been here?"

"I told you, just a few minutes."

"So that's leaves a good day and a half unaccounted for."

"Okay, whatever, I can see this is going nowhere. I need to check in with my boys. Maybe when I get back we can skip our little spat and then get back to work. So where are they?"

"You aren't going to bolt after your boyfriend again are you?"

"Oh Grier, if I didn't know you better, I'd swear you were jealous."

Laskin said they were at the workbay out back, watched her leave, then noticed Solanski and Turner had come back and were standing staring at him. "Start looking the fuck around you two assholes and find me something."

They walked the length of the dining room, checking the chairs, shelving unit and even the dishes still left in the sink, but all of them knew there was nothing that was going to tell them anything except following those sled tracks, which no one really wanted to do. Turner muttered to Solanski that he'd rather be any-where but in this shithole and that the place stunk of sardines.

Laskin shouted over at them, "Hey, more action and a little less fucking gossip."

Solanski said, "Well, there just isn't anything here besides cookie crumbs and empty chairs. Not really sure what you expected to find here. They're gone, probably for a while, and who knows where Slaught is. Did Mitch say if she saw him?"

"Solanski, you mind you own fucking business and let me handle the big boy stuff, okay?"

Miller returned form the other rooms saying, "Not much to go on sir. Looks like maybe only some of them left and they didn't leave in a hurry, things seem pretty tidy, looks like people had time to pack some stuff up, some personal items seem to be missing from the rooms, but, ask me, I think they plan on coming back. Lots of stuff left behind that people would normally take, family photos and stuff."

Laskin turned on the other two. "That, you morons, is what I was talking about, some useful information."

Mitch came back and said she'd checked out the first floor plus the chapel, that Leclerc and Burke were up on the top floor.

"Nada," she said, but Grier didn't bother looking over at her, so she said, "Okay, you want to know where Slaught is? I don't have clue. I never saw him, just one of the guys from here and that little piece of shit from training, Ricky."

Turner said, "Ricky? You saw Ricky the Retard with them?"

Mitch shrugged. "I don't really know what the deal was but he was with that Jeff guy. Just around the border area in some burnt out hunt camp."

Laskin ran his hand through his hair, looking exasperated, but she was thinking it was more of a performance for his crew, that right now he was raging inside but was putting on a show, then he said, "Seriously, Mitch, please explain exactly how you managed to bump into those fellas?"

"There's no need to be so testy Grier. It's a bit of a story though and I think it might just be a bit more pressing to finish searching the building."

"I disagree."

Mitch couldn't believe it. She'd seen the petulant side of him before but this was whacked. She was wondering if he was even fit to finish up the mission, talk about compromised emotionally. "Fine, I'll explain the whole story to you, okay?"

"Can't wait."

Taking a deep breath, she said, "When we were down at Police Services Muspar mentioned in passing that Skinner wasn't around, thought maybe he'd bailed. So low and behold, I check his locker and all his winter gear and his security passes were gone. But he's not too clever because he left a couple of his little scribbles on some papers, including info about his Uncle's hunt camp right near the border, just inside the Territories. Plus he had some stuff about Slaught. Then I checked the tracker I'd put on Slaught's sled and, lo and behold, the coordinates lined up. Thought it was worth checking out."

"Why are you telling me this? This is just bullshit. You telling me you took off after that little shit? That rummaging through that kid's locker was a priority? You have got to be kidding."

"I figured he was either pulling a Lone Ranger and was heading off to nab the guy himself, or else he was going to trade info, probably with Slaught. Either way, I figured I should grab him and haul his ass back before he mucked up the works."

"Didn't occur to you to get another opinion?"

She shrugged. "I didn't think I'd be gone that long."

"I see, and that's how we make judgement calls when we're part of a team?"

"Spare me the lecture Grier. Scott approved the change in plan. I work for Talos, not you. Can we just move on, okay?" Lying now, but knowing Scott would back her up regardless.

"So why did it take you so long to get up here? You easily could have met up with us at the border?"

Mitch didn't say anything.

"Oh, don't tell me, the dweeb janitor got the jump on you?" Laskin was almost laughing now, smirking at her, added, "You must really be slipping, Mitch."

"Grier, we are going to drop this and finish the mission, okay? That's the priority. Every minute we waste here they could be further away. Time to move on."

"No Mitch, we can't move on. I think you were out of line."

"Grier…"

"No, it's no different than if any of these assholes had pulled a stunt like that." Laskin waved his hand towards the guys who had stopped and were now just watching, Mitch knowing they were loving the fireworks, him going after her like that. "You'd have had their asses for that."

Mitch felt the knot in her stomach tighten, decided enough

was enough, moving towards Laskin, seeing Miller involuntarily taking a step backwards, but she could tell Laskin couldn't help himself so he said, "I think you wanted to get to Slaught, thought Ricky might be onto something, and chased him up the fucking tundra like a groupie."

"Fuck you, Grier," Mitch said, slamming her gun hard across his temple, watching him spin sideways and then crumple up. She'd been waiting way too long for that one. Felt good. She turned to the guys. "You can stand around babysitting this waste of skin or you can help me to find that son of a bitch. Coming?"

Jordan pushed the cord back into his laptop. This, he told himself, would be his last try to get the damn thing working. He was crammed into the small maintenance cupboard off the main hallway, trying to jimmy-rig the surveillance system. Everyone else had gathered all their supplies and moved into the old Coniagas headframe across from the hotel. They'd made the decision to move everyone across the road and then down into the old shaft below the building. It wasn't too deep and had stayed pretty dry, and down around the fifty foot level were tunnels running under the road and across to the hotel. The guys had found the tunnels when they'd gone down scouting around for silver to trade. Slaught had said the timbers were still solid and holding, but the silver was long gone.

Once safe down the shaft and into the tunnels, folks were supposed to wait there until they heard from Chumboy. There hadn't been any word yet and people were getting anxious. Jordan couldn't handle the stress so he decided to catch up on installing their spycam, Slaught having told him that it wouldn't hurt to have a few more of the things around just in case. He had mostly given up hope on getting it to work, so when the picture sprang onto the screen as he popped the cord in again, and he saw Mitch and two other guys walking past him down the hallway, he at first thought it was a mistake.

Shit. No mistake. There she was.

He stared at the screen, considered pulling the plug so he didn't have to watch. Shit shit, damnit. He pushed himself back a bit into the small space and felt his breathing start to speed up, feeling like he was hyperventilating.

Calm down dude, calm down. Breathe.

He closed his eyes, trying to think, and when he opened them again he realized she was no further than fifteen feet from where he was crammed into the cupboard. The group was dressed in their outside gear, Mitch popping up her hood as she went by. They'd be outside in no time, then only yards from the headframe. It had seemed like a perfect hiding spot just in case. Well, 'just in case' was in the building.

He snapped the laptop shut and held his breathe, picturing them passing by the door. He waited until they were out of sight then plunged his hand into his backpack, feeling around in the dark. A few screwdrivers, his Swiss army knife, good god, why him, of all of them? He was clearly the least equipped to deal with her. He kept rummaging though, a few extra USB jacks and, at the bottom of the bag, dusted in crumbs, the walkie-talkie. Thank god.

He listened carefully and then switched it on. It crackled loudly. Jordan hit the off button. Crap, that sounded loud. They'd be dragging him out by his feet any minute.

He tried to think. Okay, so he was hiding in a closet and his friends were about to get executed. All right, he had a small knife, a few screwdrivers and a lame-ass walkie-talkie. He stared at the walkie-talkie, remembering Johnny saying to him, "If it makes you feel better staying here, take this—worst case scenario, call me in." Jordan figured this was definitely a worst-case scenario. If he was lucky, Johnny actually had the other walkie-talkie on him and was actually within range. He held his breath and turned it back on, praying for a miracle.

Chumboy had gone through the doors first, they'd agreed to that, the rest waiting outside till he gave them the sign. They had met up with Shaun and the boys at the junction of the main highway and the old airport road. The airport had been converted into the region's last outpost when the government had finally established the border, making the road the last maintained official transportation route, everything north of it was left to ruin and ratshit. They hadn't said much when they'd met up, except Shaun had said that that was one fucking-A sniper shot Chumboy had and did they see it go fucking nuclear out there.

Larose said it was kinda hard to miss and they better hope for their sakes that it didn't bring Laskin running back to see what happened. He was wondering about that now, standing outside the sliding doors, his feet starting to seize up from the cold, heart pounding so loud he thought he was going to puke, right there in the snow. What a fucking disaster he was turning out to be. Even Ricky was doing better, punching in the security code for the gates like an old hand, Chumboy saying, "You got the magic memory Rickyman."

Then Jeff had stepped inside the unmanned security hut and shut down the security cameras without much fuss and the rest, Chumboy had said, was going to be a cakewalk. Larose said, "Yeah, let's hope they have toy guns too." Then Shaun lifted up his pump action saying, "I'm not packing a toy."

"For shit's sake Shaun, you know the drill, we're supposed to be unarmed."

"Fuck that."

Jeff intervened. "Dudes, let's just get this over with and try not to completely mess this thing up, okay? Shaun? Just stay on the chain."

Shaun just nodded but Chumboy, shaking his head slowly, stared at him for a few seconds before turning towards the doors. "If I don't come out after five minutes, Shaun gets shit in my will."

Shaun muttered, "You got shit to give anyway," as the door closed behind him.

And now they were waiting, Larose wondering if he really meant five minutes, or if they should wait that long, a lot could happen in five minutes, it was up to three minutes now and everyone was looking grim. Maybe since this was the last outpost before the territories, it'd be crawling with security. Maybe they'd shot Chumboy with a silencer or something.

Four minutes. What the fuck was going on in there, Larose whispering maybe someone should go in after him, but Jeff said no, they were supposed to wait, they'd wait and then the doors slid open and Chumboy came out with a can of coke in his hand.

"You know, you don't have this shit in ages, and you think, man, is it ever going to taste great when I finally have a nice, cold can of the stuff, and then it's the same old crap. What a fucking let down."

"So?" Larose feeling like he was going to explode.

"So, obviously the vending machines are not guarded, so the immediate coast is clear. I figure they must be in the office, which means there aren't too many soldier boys in there. Maybe just a pencil pusher snoozing in there, otherwise he'd have noticed that his surveillance screens are down."

Chumboy turned to head back inside but nobody was moving. "Uh, guys, show time, ready or not. Shaun and Harv, take the far set of doors, Ricky and Jeff, come in behind me. All set?"

And then they were in, the main area of the small airport empty and hollow sounding, their boots smacking on the ceramic floor. Chumboy headed towards the closed doors past the baggage carousel. He held his finger to his lips and slowly turned the handle of the door, saying as he went in, "Hey buddy, rise and shine, I stopped by Timmie's and picked you up a double double."

Sure enough, a guy was stretched out on the beige vinyl couch along the far wall, a picture of a small bush plane and a smiling crew hanging over it, his surveillance monitors scratchy and grey. The guy turned, rubbing his eyes, and Chumboy said, "Sorry about the whole Timmie's thing, that was a lie, but I knew it would get your attention. Now could you please fire up your system here, we have a public service announcement we need to make."

Slaught was glad to be done. It was a worry being away so long. He'd spent the day quartering the moose cow and dragging it out of the thick bush to load onto his sled. He was tired now, resting on his snowmachine. The wind was up, bleak streaks of ashen cloud against the pale mauve sky. Slaught was thinking that it was good to be out in the bush, in the silence, just taking some time to clear his mind. Then a loud crackling sound erupted behind him.

His hand went flying to the rifle lying on the seat of his sled. He stared towards the source of the sound, then scanned the area around him. Slowly, he turned, looking behind him, following the curve of the snow in behind the now blackening spruce, past the red sticks of dogwood poking up along the edge of the trees. Nothing. And then that fucking noise again, and again he jumped. Christ! It was coming from his backpack.

He recognized the crackle and hiss of a walkie-talkie, grabbed the pack, pulling it open, hearing the cackle again, distorted, pulling out his extra mitts, his matches, axe, flashlight, then finding it in the front pocket of the pack. It crackled again.

Sounded like "help."

Slaught switched on, said "What?"

Then there was silence. Slaught tried again. "Who is this?"

Silence. Then crackling, and what Slaught took as, "Who's this?"

Slaught peering at the walkie-talkie, thinking what the fuck is going on, "Jordan?"

"Yes," he said, then the whispering, making it hard for Johnny to make out exactly what he was saying but he caught, "Help... they're back... Hurry."

"Who's there?"

"Them."

Shit. Them. That was fucking quick.

Slaught grabbed the axe and matches and threw them in the pack, jammed his rifle into its holder and said, "On my way. Sit tight."

Jordan, glad to hear it, didn't have much choice.

CHAPTER TWENTY TWO

"I CAN'T FUCKING BELIEVE IT." Laskin rolled over, nursing the welt along his temple.

He took a deep breath, pulled himself into a sitting position, back to the wall, trying to fight off the growing sensation of pain behind his eyes. He wasn't quite sure how long he had been on the floor. Five minutes? At the most it might've been ten. He wondered where that bitch had gotten too.

He was on his feet but not feeling too steady. He could hear boots coming back towards the kitchen.

It was fucking Miller and Turner.

"Uh, sir, just checking back with you. Ms. Black has Solanski and the Talos guys outside taking a broader sweep. Going up the street, checking other buildings."

"How long have I been out?"

"Half hour maybe, sir."

Laskin didn't say anything, still paying attention to the throbbing in his head, trying to focus on his watch. The two men stood looking down at the floor, Turner shuffling from foot to foot.

Laskin hissed, "Stop with the fucking noise."

Turner froze, watched as Laskin raised his head, the purple scar on the side of his head livid. Turner said, "Sorry sir, would you like me to get you something for that?"

"No you fucktard," Laskin spat. "I wanted you to get me Slaught. Now get back out there and find him and bring him to me. Alive."

Miller said, "I don't think Slaught is here sir, not sure any of them are. I mean, we're talking about around forty people and so far, we've been top to bottom and haven't found anyone. I think maybe we're too late."

Laskin "I don't give a flying fuck what you think Miller. Find him. Or find me some of those breeders and brats so we can start hauling one out every five minutes to shoot until one of them tells us where Slaught is, got it? Forty people just don't vanish. Now get out of my face and get going. I'll be there in five."

———

Miller found Mitch out front of the hotel, reporting back that Laskin seemed more aggressive than usual, and was wondering if his head injury could be further impairing his judgment, and Turner said, you mean making him more of a miserable bastard than usual, and Mitch told Turner to shut the fuck up and let her think.

"Okay, Solanski, Burke, take the perimeter and keep checking for any indication of a mass evacuation. Watch for any tracks out of here, maybe even up on the street, there could be people in any of those houses. You three, get back inside and locate Laskin. That is a priority. We don't want this situation escalating, so be careful. Under the circumstances, I think it's best if we take Mr. Laskin out of the picture until we can assess his condition. Got your stun guns? Use them."

Miller asked, "So, technically, are you second in command?"

"No shitbird, technically I'm first in command. I am Talos as far as you're concerned, and Talos is in charge, got it?"

Miller nodded, headed back towards the side door of the hotel. That woman was such a ball-breaker. He wasn't sure who he loathed more, her or her raging partner. This was the most useless, fucking assignment ever. Once inside, he paused to catch his breath, sending Turner back into the dining room, telling Leclerc to take the second floor. He headed up to the third floor, hitting the top of the stairs and moving down the skinny hallway, kids' pictures along the wall, coloured bright reds and blues. He was getting a real bad feeling abut the whole thing. The Captain had been right, it had disaster written all over it from the get go. He'd felt good when Muspar had taken him aside, told him to stay on his toes and report in if things started going off the rails, but now he just felt burdened by it—what the hell should he do? Take on that bitch? Not for the world.

He heard something further down the hall and pulled out his stun gun, keeping it down at his side.

"Mr. Laskin?"

"In here."

He followed the voice, found Laskin leaning against a desk, a big picture of Madonna behind him on the wall. The walls of the small room were covered with pictures cut out from magazines and newspapers.

Laskin turned a sour look on Miller, "What do you see?"

Miller shrugged, feeling unsure as to whether to go straight at him and take him out, or talk him down and take him back to Black. Laskin tossed a book on the desk, then grabbed another, and another, throwing them just past his head. "Military history, all of them, every single book. Look," he pitched another one across the room, hard, "The Art of War."

"Have you read it?"

"No, I haven't fucking read it Miller. I don't read fucking books, but I have heard of it."

Miller said cautiously, "There's probably a history buff in the bunch, some stodgy professor or something."

"I don't fucking think so Sherlock, I think we've been had."

Miller decided he'd try to reason with the guy, see if he could get him to leave the room, then maybe get him from behind. "Look, it might make us feel better to think that these guys were serious contenders, but the reality is Slaught was a snowmobile dealer, and Commando a bush thinner. End of story."

"I'm telling you, these guys are the real thing."

"Come on, look, there's lots of different books here, some on cooking."

"What if it's a set up?"

"A set up?"

"Scott, or Muspar, remember that little shit Ricky, infiltrating us maybe, playing both sides, maybe there's something there..."

"Sir, why don't we go find the others, and lay out our plan for rounding these guys up, whatever they are."

"No, you and me are going to go find those nice people, drag a few out onto the main street and start shooting. That should wrap things up pretty quick, get this thing over with. I'm tired of this fucking around. How the Christ do you hide forty people?"

Miller looked at the welt running along Laskin's face, the guy's colour high, his face all blotchy. He looked like a fucking maniac. "Our orders were for arrest and containment, maybe relocation, of our non-combatants, sir."

"What the fuck do you know about our orders? You know shit. That's what you know about anything, absolute shit. Your orders come from me, period."

"All due respect sir, there are families here."

Laskin glared for a second, then smiled. "I don't care. Someone is going to break. Your choice if it's a kid or Grampa Bob. Now let's go."

"Is that what Captain Muspar requested?" Miller asked, watching carefully as Laskin's eyes narrowed.

"You have one more strike Miller, that's it."

Miller stood his ground, but he was feeling uncomfortable, just wanting to get the hell away from Laskin, said, "Sir, Captain Muspar is the ultimate authority for our end of the operation. Maybe we can check back and confirm my orders?"

"You sound like a goddam school prefect. I don't know who you're trying to kid, but this wouldn't be the first time the Service has had to take out civilians, it's been going on under the radar for the past couple of years. And right now, Muspar's out of the picture and Scott's just worried about covering his ass."

Miller said, "What? Not sure I understand you, sir? How is the Captain out of the picture?"

"Grow up Miller, okay? You wanted to volunteer with the big boys, so start acting like one and fucking obey direct orders, alright?"

"I'm afraid I can't, sir. I can't kill civilians."

Laskin pushed into Miller's shoulder as he moved past him, said, "But I can."

Miller took a deep breath and said, "Under Section 6.3 of the Civilian Security Code you are a rogue officer, and I am relieving you of your command, sir. I'm afraid I will have to take your weapon, I'm calling this in to Captain Muspar."

Laskin stopped, stepped back a few paces and looked at Miller who was standing almost at attention, shoulders back, a serious but expectant look on his face. He was saying, "Your weapon please..." when Laskin said, "Yeah, here it is," and pushed his gun into Miller's forehead and fired two rounds.

There was a few seconds of silence as the echo of the rounds died out and then Miller fell back, knocking over a chair stacked with books, his face a slurpy mess.

Shaun and Chumboy were sitting out on the baggage carousel. It was kind of crowded in the office, so Chum had said to Ricky and Jeff, "Get to it boys, and Harv, keep an eye on buddy there."

Chumboy was still complaining about the pop and Shaun said, "Well, what did you expect?" and Chum said, "More, I always expect more," and then the bathroom door opened and a security guard walked out tucking his shirt into his belt, and Chumboy said, "Shit, I didn't expect that."

The security guard came up short when he saw them, confusion, maybe a bit of fear, flickering across his face as his eyes shot over to the open door of the office. Chumboy saw the guard's hand move towards the gun on his hip and also felt Shaun's gun move but Chumboy reached over and he placed his hand on it saying, "Now, now Shaun, no need for that," smiling at the security guard, saying, "Your friend is just helping us out a bit in there, probably best if you go join him," and he slid his gun up, pointing it at the guard, and gestured towards the door calling, "Room for one more at the party gentlemen?"

They took the guy's gun and walked him into the office, Chumboy saying, "Have a seat with your buddy. We shouldn't be taking up too much of your time," and then to Jeff, "So how much longer will it be, it's getting claustrophobic in here."

Jeff, nodding, said, "Patience."

Ricky said, "I'll be glad to get back."

"No kidding, have ourselves a big moose burger. Man, doesn't get much better than that."

The guard snorted. "Don't know where you've been buddy, but this is a game preserve, there's no hunting here."

"Well, we've been living free as birds up here in your game preserve for some time now."

"There isn't anyone up in the Territories."

Chumboy was about to answer when Shaun said from the doorway, "Just try it asshole," leveling his gun at the second guard. Ricky straightened himself out and Chumboy looked at Shaun, "Steady there."

Shaun said, "He was reaching for his gun on the desk there. Guess next time it'd be best not to leave it within reach like that."

Chumboy shook his head and looked reproachfully at the guard, "Billy, don't be a hero." And Jeff laughed, said, "Yeah, don't be a fool with your life," and both Chumboy and Jeff laughed and the guard said, "This isn't a joke you guys, this is a federal installation. You're in big shit and it's just going to get worse. Whatever it is you are up to, I'd stop now and just leave, we'll give you a head start before we call it in, but this isn't going to turn out good for you guys."

"Like I said, its just a simple public service announcement."

Jeff said, "And as they said in olden times, it's a wrap. I-TIME, here we come."

"Okay, time's up, mind hitting the john for a few minutes while we finish up fellas? Right this way." He gestured with his gun and they stood, going through the door, Chumboy saying to the guards, "Go shut yourselves in your stalls and count to fifty. Then you can get back to counting sheep and it'll be like we were never here."

He pulled the washroom door shut. "Everyone but Shaun leave your guns on the baggage thing and let's hit the road."

There was a knocking from inside the door.

"Hey, you guys?" It was the first guard.

"Yeah, what's up buddy?"

"You serious about living in the park?"

"You bet," Chumboy answered.

"Maybe the wife and I will come up once this all blows over, got room for a family of four?"

Chumboy looked at Larose and smiled. "Our first recruitment drive."

"Hey, and one more thing?"

"What's that?"

"How come you're carrying fake guns?"

"For shit's sake," Larose muttered. "He made us from the get go."

Chumboy said through the door," We're postmodern, that's why."

"What does that mean?"

"Look it up in the dictionary."

"Don't have one."

Chumboy shook his head. "Well, then definitely drop in to Cobalt and see us. We got it all, moose burgers and dictionaries."

CHAPTER TWENTY THREE

MITCH WISHED SHE SMOKED. Standing in the center of what was once the main street, sharp wind dragging snow across the hard-pack like it was tumbleweed, she was thinking it might be good for her nerves if she could just pull one out, suck on its heat. She scanned the far horizon, eyes moving down from the tree line to the buildings along the street, seeing the snow banked up against the doors, windows frosted over—there was nothing to indicate any of the other buildings were being used. They just looked cold and abandoned and mute. What a fucking shithole.

She retraced her steps back around to the side of the hotel, looking over towards the workbay. From what the worn out, faded sign said it used to be the fire hall. Good Christ, where the fuck was everybody? She walked back up towards the side door of the hotel, her eyes following the tracks that lead down towards the workbay, the trail worn and wide from the constant traffic. Snow on either side unbroken. She took the path, looking at the tiny houses tucked up behind, the ramshackled auto garage, the old headframe on the corner directly across from the hotel.

The headframe. That's right, this had been a mining town at one time, and now her snow pirates were illicitly trading their high-grade silver down along the border for gasoline. She stopped and turned towards it, a small angular building, blinds down over the big windows that ran the length of its front. She moved closer, ploughing through the hard crust of snow that went up over her boots, stopped a few yards from the rear end of the building, then smiled. There it was, exactly what she'd been looking for, a barrage of tracks trailing down along the backside of the building to a small backdoor.

Fucking busted.

She plunged on, made it to the narrow passageway between a huge pile of firewood and the building, tried the knob. Locked.

She made her way backs towards the workbay, breathing hard but feeling better than she had in a while, thinking about the look on Slaught's face as she stepped into the room, saying something like 'come out, come out wherever you are,' or maybe not be that playful at all, just say 'finders, keepers Slaught.' Or maybe just shoot whoever's next to him, ask 'miss me much Johnny?'

It took her a minute or so to find what she was looking for, headed back over to the door of the headframe, the weight of the crowbar feeling good in her hand. She thought for a minute of going in through one of the big windows, sending the glass flying, but decided against it. Too messy. So she slammed the bar down onto the doorknob, snapping it off, slammed the head into the door jam and popped it open.

The room was empty, the cement floor icy in the cold. She stepped in carefully. Snow. Snow tracked in across the floor and around the corner. She moved to look behind the big counter that ran along in front of a large, timbered doorway leading into the back of the building. Tracks all the way.

But no bodies to go with them.

She stood, staring into the empty space where the tracks led. Either up or down, no other way. She moved around the counter and through the doorway.

"Fucking morons," she said, pulling open the wooden barrier that enclosed the top of a shaft. She looked down, yelled, "If every last one of you isn't up here within five minutes I'm going to blast the fucking shit out of you."

Silence.

"One grenade ladies and gentlemen, that'll be all it takes."

She heard some murmuring, shuffling of bodies. She went back outside and fired a shot into the air to get some of her team over to the headframe, then went back in, standing back, arms folded, smirking as the first head appeared.

—

Slaught stopped in the small ridge of spruce. He'd heard a single shot about fifteen minutes ago, had waited a bit then made his way carefully down the slope in behind the old MacMillan garage across from the workbay. He was hunkered down, could see over to the workbay but not much else. The big doors were flung open, so they must have already searched in there. He wondered how far they'd gotten.

He slid down the small hill, peering out around the building until he could see the hotel. It looked quiet, only a few rooms up on the second floor had lights on, casting a dun-coloured glow against the curtains. The lights in the dining room were now on. He moved back away from the building, tucking in behind the wreck of a truck sitting across from the workbay. He pulled out the walkie-talkie.

"Jordan?" whispering.

Nothing.

Trying again, "Hey, Jordan, you there?"

"Johnny? Yeah."

"What's going on?"

Some spitting and hissing came back at him that he couldn't make out.

"What?"

"I think they've found them. I think they brought everyone into the maintenance room."

Shit.

Slaught asked, "Where are you?"

"Me?"

"Yeah."

"The repair panel in the hall, under the stairs."

Johnny thinking for a minute, trying to figure out what he meant, then remembering the small door along the hall, picturing Jordan crammed in there.

"Stay put. Don't move."

"Okay Johnny, but make it quick, I can't feel my feet."

Slaught shut off the walkie-talkie. Crouching in the silence, Johnny couldn't remember a day so cold in a long time. His legs were feeling cramped, the cold starting to work its way through his parka. It was time to end this, he just wasn't sure how to do that yet. If Jordan was right, there were forty some people crammed into that maintenance room. Tight fit. Jordan was out, so were the guys down in North Bay, so that left folks pretty much on their own. He was glad at least Susun was with them. Susun. Slaught remembering her asking if it wasn't dangerous, taking everyone down into the old Coniagas shaft and him saying, no, used to be a grocery store back in the day, the grocer storing his meat down the shaft to keep it cold. Then he was thinking about what a couple of guys had told him about the Coniagas, that there were drifts running off that shaft and under the Fraser hotel, that you could get underground from the headframe into the back end of the hotel.

The maintenance room was in the back end of the hotel.

Slaught stood up, took a deep breath, shoved the walkie-talkie in his pocket and headed for the headframe, thinking it was high time for a miracle.

—

When Slaught pounded on the thick wooden hatch he was pretty sure no one would hear him. He'd found a length of old timber lying nearby and had taken it, grabbing it by the end and shoving it up at the hatch. He was hoping to hell it was the maintenance room he was trying to break into, and hoping too that the hatch wasn't covered by six layers of linoleum. He pounded a few more times, listened, wasn't hearing much then heard some scrapping overhead, now feeling his heart racing, and then the sound of shifting dirt around the hatch, then a slice of light.

The hatch flew open, Mr. McLaren and Susun peeking their heads over the edge.

Slaught looked up, said, "Hey."

Susun smiled and McLaren said, "Now how the hell are we going to get you up here?"

"I was thinking about getting everyone down."

McLaren persisted, "Gotta be be a ladder around somewhere Johnny, take a look."

"Yep, you're right," Slaught was saying, hauling the ladder over to the opening, throwing off his parka to be able to maneuver better, McLaren grabbing the top of the ladder to steady it. Slaught said, "Hope it holds."

McLaren and Susun watched as Slaught hauled himself up

cautiously, McLaren grabbing Slaught by his sweater to help pull him up over the edge.

"You okay?" Susun asked.

"Never been better, how's everyone here and what's the plan?"

There was a barrage of whispering from the crowd of folks, jammed into every corner of the room. Johnny held up his hand. "Whoa, one at a time."

Max was beside Susun now. He looked miserable. "We don't have a plan yet. We've come up with a few scenarios but nothing that makes any sense. It's the same bunch here and they're in a nasty mood, especially since you and the guys weren't here. And they were pissed on not finding Ricky. And Jordan's missing."

"No, Jordan's okay, holed up in the repair closet up the hall there. He's the one that let me know what was going on here. Okay, so we're in a bit of a jackpot, but that doesn't mean we're not coming out of it. Let's just take this one step at a time. First up, any ammo here?"

Max, even more miserable, pointed to the bin marked "Fake" in purple marker. "Just your postmodernist bullshit hardware, Johnny. Everything else is safely stored in lock up."

Slaught frowned.

"Chumboy?"

"No word yet."

"Okay, well, let's make this room as safe as we can. Let's break down the shelving and make some more room in here. Stack everything you can find in the front part here, might give us some shelter or buy some time anyway. Then everyone back down below. Nothing else, it will slow them down. Let's do this quick too, who knows when they might be back."

Johnny surveyed the mess of blankets and bins, taking stock, then asked, "Hey, where's Tiny?"

Susun shrugged. "He was outside when we headed across to the headframe, said he needed more time. Haven't seen him since."

"Hmm, maybe he's holed up somewhere like Jordan, eh? Once I get out there I might turn up a few folks. Anyone else missing?"

"Chumboy's Auntie."

Johnny was surprised. "Wasn't she with you guys in the head-frame?"

"No, I think she went to help Tiny," Susun said, then added, "This isn't looking so great, is it?"

"Well, I think if we play this right we have a slight chance of getting out of here in one piece."

Susun shook her head, lowered her voice. "Johnny, I'm not sure everyone can get down there."

"Well, we need to try. I'm thinking that anyone who can manage it should get the hell down that ladder and across to the headframe. I'm heading out into the hotel now."

"How are you getting out? They're not stupid, the door is locked."

"Well, I'm going right out that locked door thanks to you. After you pulled that stunt in here, I had Harv put it back on with the smallest screws we could find. If we push hard enough on that door, chances are it'll just pop off. The issue is, then what?"

Susun said that they could hardly fight their way out of there with his toy guns and Johnny said they were pretty fine looking toy guns, and maybe they could bluff their way out, at least till they could reach some snowmachines.

"Chumboy and the guys have most of the good sleds. There are some here but not enough. Not for everyone."

Johnny nodded, thinking, and then said, "Okay, well let's get folks moving and take some water along too. I'm getting a move on before they come back."

Susun said, "I'm going with you."

"Me too," said Max.

Johnny said, "I appreciate that, but we gotta have some defense in here too."

"If it comes to that, Mr. McLaren and I can handle things," said Mrs. Merrill.

McLaren added, "You'll have a fight on your hands here if you try and say no. We'll be fine. We'll get people going across the drift."

Slaught said, "Okay, Susun and Max, grab a gun. They may not be the real deal but they're all we've got and you'll feel better holding onto to 'em. Max, you try to make it to the storage lock-up, grab whatever you can find and get it back up here to these folks. Susun and I are going to get Jordan and then try to stall them."

Susun stared down woefully at her gun. "When I was little, toy guns were obviously toys. I think my brother's was bright green and cheap plastic. This thing is offensive."

Slaught said he found the fact that they didn't fire real bullets to be offensive at the moment, and then to Max added, "Max, you get a move on and get some firepower back here. McLaren, have someone waiting at the bottom of the hatch, Max can toss a few down to you. If there is anyone who can't get down that ladder then you're going to have to stay with them Max, understand? As soon as you are back here with the hardware and ammo, fire a couple of shots, okay?"

He nodded. Slaught moved towards the door and looked over at Susun. "Ready?"

She nodded, said, "Listen. No heroics. You be careful, eh?"

He stopped and looked at her, taking the edge of her shirt collar. "Why are you always wearing my clothes?"

She felt his hand brush against her throat, said, "I like the way they smell."

He stared at her for a bit too long, and then turned and asked Max to come help him with the door, saying, "Praying now would be a good idea Mrs. Merrill," and with that the two pushed and, after a few heaves against the metal, sure enough the door popped open, Max slamming into Slaught who stumbled but steadied himself, saying, "No turning back now, sure that got their attention. Let's pop that door back up and go stir the pot."

After replacing the door, Slaught and Susun disappeared around the corner with Max heading off down the hall.

Slaught hugged the wall, inching down the hallway, stopping to listen every few yards. Susun was close behind.

Slaught leaned his head around the next corner. The hallway was empty. About half way down was the repair closet. It seemed like a long fucking way.

"Okay Susun, I'm going, cover me."

"You're joking, right?"

Slaught hefted the AK-47 in his hands. Probably weighed about a quarter of what a real one would. A good 2-by-4 would probably have been more useful.

"It's a question of mind over matter," he answered. "Humour me alright?" Then he started down the hall.

Susun peeked around the corner as he reached the closet, heard him whisper, "Jordan, it's me, let's go," and pulled on the doorknob. Jordan slumped out, Susun covering her eyes, thinking he was dead, but when she opened them, Johnny was hauling Jordan up, his legs numb from being cramped up so long, and then the two Talos guys came around the corner at the far end of the hallway.

Susun yelled, "Johnny," and Jordan made for the closet as Johnny straightened slowly to face them. They were the same two as before. The first, Burke, said, "Dump your weapon! And you," gesturing to Jordan, "back the fuck away from the door."

"I can't stand up, my legs are shot," Jordan said.

"Then crawl," Burke answered. "I don't really give a shit, just back up."

Slaught thought maybe they were pushing them back towards the maintenance room, but then he thought maybe they were just getting some distance so they could shoot them without getting splattered with blood. "Listen guys," he started, but the second one, Leclerc, said, "Shut the fuck up and drop your weapon. And get that bitch to step out into the hall and get over here, now."

Slaught didn't say anything, feeling Jordan sort of scurrying back behind him. Leclerc shouted, "Enough bullshit! Drop the fucking weapon or we shoot your miserable little sissy."

He leveled his gun at Jordan and Slaught said "Alright, alright," and tossed the gun down, the sound of plastic hitting the floor making the two guys frown, and then Burke brought his gun up and aimed at Slaught, saying "You fucking morons," and Susun pulled the trigger on her gun, thinking it was just like when you were in the passenger seat of a car and you slammed on the brakes, knowing it wouldn't make a difference but not being able to help yourself, it being instinct, and the guy down the hall let out a scream and crumpled up and Slaught yelled, "Again Susie, again!" and so she fired again and Johnny dove forward, slamming into the Leclerc's legs, knocking him flat and sliding into the wall.

Jordan scrambled on the floor, reaching for Burke's gun. He noticed the guy's eyes were blue, noticed too that the guy was dead. He pushed the gun over at Slaught who stretched out his arm to take it and slammed it into the side of Leclerc's head a couple of times.

Susun came down the hall, looking a little ashen, and Slaught said, "That's a pretty impressive case of mind over matter," and then, "You okay?"

She nodded, "I'm okay, I just hit the brakes, know what I mean, I wasn't thinking." She stepped gingerly over the guy now bleeding from his knee onto the shiny hall floor, saying, "Guess we should find the others."

Johnny nodded, smiled at her. "Thank God that the guy who sorted the guns was an idiot."

"That idiot was me," Jordan said.

"Well then, thank God for you Jordan."

CHAPTER TWENTY FOUR

LASKIN SHOUTED, "WHAT THE FUCK NOW?" as two shots went off deeper in the building.

Solanski heard the shots too, then followed the sound of Laskin's voice.

Laskin was yelling some more. "That's four shots, what the hell are those fucking Talos people doing, skeet fucking shooting? Get them back here pronto. I'm so goddam sick and tired..."

Solanski entered behind Laskin, said, "Been looking for you. Have you seen Miller at all, sir? Is that who you were talking to?"

"No, I wasn't talking to Miller, I wasn't fucking talking to anyone, do you see anyone in here. And as for Miller, he had an accident. I hope those shots are the Talos boys getting some results out of the hostages."

"I haven't seen the Talos guys sir. I was going to ask you where they were. I'm not hearing back from them at all."

"Well, if you're looking to hold their hands, they aren't here. Now why don't you make yourself useful and follow me to wherever our hostages are so I don't waste any more fucking time."

Solanski had his hand resting on his stun gun, wishing he'd pulled it before he came into the room. Laskin wasn't looking too good, his face was shiny with sweat. "Just where I was headed sir. Ms. Black asked that we locate you so we can have a brief update."

"Solanski, no more bullshit from anyone, especially Black. What I want is Slaught. And those religious freaks are going to give him to me. So let's go start the party."

"But Miller, sir, where is he?"

Laskin said, "What is with you fucking wusses anyway? Fucking one-track minds. I told you, Miller is indisposed, okay, so unless you want to be similarly indisposed, I suggest we head down to meet and greet the hostages."

The satellite phone on Solanski's belt started blinking. He adjusted his headset, said his name but then shook his head, "Sorry sir, I have to step outside for a second, no reception." He crossed over to the front doors and pushed them open, snow banking up and tumbling in along the edge of the doors as they dragged outwards.

Laskin waited a few seconds. "Screw this, I don't have time to listen to you talk to your mommy. I'm out of here."

Solanski stuck his head back inside. "Hold up, sir. It's Mr. Scott from Talos, sir."

"Tell him I'm sort of fucking tied up now."

"Mr. Scott says he wants to talk Ms. Black."

Laskin said, "Well, she's not fucking here is she?"

Solanski moved away from the door, half shouting into the phone, "The reception isn't great here sir, but Mr. Laskin says he's busy looking for Slaught right now and will check in later, sir."

Solanski listened, then said, "Repeat that, sir?" Solanski listened, slowly shaking his head, said, "Okay sir, yes sir, got it, yes."

Solanski took a deep breath, stomped the snow off his boots and came back inside, pulling the door closed behind him. He looked over at Laskin who was popping a new clip into his gun. "He says Slaught has been on I-TIME for the past 15 minutes. And so have you—blowing away that girl down in the workbay."

Laskin said, "What the fuck are you talking about?" his face turning a hard white, Solanski sort of backing away, asking, "So what now, sir?"

Laskin said he'd already fucking told him, they were going to start dragging out the hostages and shooting them until someone coughed up Slaught.

Solanski said that maybe in light of this recent development it might be a good idea to revise that plan, said that Scott ordered that the mission be aborted and they were to get back to the City. Laskin told him to shut the fuck up or he'd shoot him too, then he walked out of the room.

Solanski figured there was no point looking for Miller anymore. He pulled out his walkie-talkie. "Turner, you there? Turner?"

Turner grunted, "What?"

"We're fucked."

"What?"

"Shit's hitting the fan, Turner. A tape of Laskin killing that girl just aired on I-TIME. Part of some sort of Wintermen propaganda bullshit, aired right in the middle of the Safety Parade. We're probably in it. Scott's pissed beyond reckoning. We're done, done like fucking dinner."

"Scott? Jesus. How the Christ did that happen?"

"The hillbillies must've had cameras in the workbay."

"Guess they weren't such hillbillies."

"And that's not all."

"For chrissakes Solanski, you're killing me."

"The Captain's dead—they found Muspar in Laskin's room, took one shot straight in the chest."

"Fuck me," Turner said.

"It's already done, Turner. Scott says abort and head back. There are arrest warrants out for all of us."

"Should we tell Black?"

"Christ, I don't know. Think we can trust her?"

Then he heard Laskin say from the other side of the room, "Trust her? You have to be kidding. I wouldn't trust her anymore that I trust you two bitches."

Solanski heard Turner say something through the static but he ignored it, saying to Laskin, "Listen sir, we have to sort this situation out here..."

"Is that what we have here, a situation?"

"Yes sir, I think we do. Mr. Scott definitely thinks we do."

Laskin spit. "I don't have the time to flay you alive as much as I'd like, so I'm just going to shoot you—after all, time is money."

Laskin left Solanski slumped over a table, Turner calling his name over the walkie-talkie as Laskin left the room.

—

Mitch had grabbed Max by his hair, shouting at him that he better tell her what the fuck was going on or she was going to smash in his ugly face so bad he wouldn't be able to tell he had acne. She'd found him down the hallway from the big storage closet, and it took her about four seconds to get the gun off him, another two until he told her about the two shot signal he was supposed to fire when he got there, told her Slaught was waiting for the all clear from the weapons lock up, not sure what else to do since he had a gun jammed into the side of his neck.

She wanted to know where Slaught had come from, and Max had said he'd been hiding out in one of the houses up on the hill behind the hotel, not wanting to mention the headframe or Thibeault Hill.

She'd blasted off the two shots and then hauled him down the stairs and along the short hallway, her fingers twisted deep into his hair, him scrambling, half crab walking, half being dragged. When they got to the lock up, she pushed him against the chain mesh door and wiped her hand on her black snowpants, said, "You're a greasy little prick."

He just watched her, trying not to cry. Then she said, "Open this fucking door."

Max pulled himself up and dug in his pocket for the keys. He could barely hold his hands still to unlock the padlock. She shoved him inside and said, "I want something small and light, none of that bush shit, okay?"

"Like you mean a gun?" he asked, but that just seemed to piss her off, and she grabbed the edges of the doorway with either hand and swung her leg up, shoving her boot into his back, shouting, "Hurry the fuck up."

Max started to haul bins down off the shelves, tossing the lids aside but mostly he was finding first aid stuff and toys. Mitch came at him again, catching him in the ribs as he rummaged through a purple bin loaded with shells, sending him flying against the shelving. "Stop this bullshit. I want some firepower Junior and if it isn't here you better find it fucking quick."

"This is the only place we keep guns."

"Fuck you, this place is full of goddam toys! You telling me you keep your Barbies under lock and key?"

Max hesitated, but then said, "Chumboy said the kids are the worst."

She looked at him for a minute and Max shrank back. Christ, she looked like a mean animal, and he watched her as she moved to the far end of the row, reached out and grabbed a metal pipe off the rack. "I'll tell you right now you piece of crud, kids aren't the worst."

—

They heard Max, not sure if it was a yell or a scream, and Susun plunged forward towards the sound but Slaught caught her by the arm and said, "Hang on."

"Did you hear that?"

"Yeah, hard not to, but us charging in without thinking might mean all of us will be hollering for mercy together, and that isn't going to help Max is it?"

Jordan and Susun were both staring at him now, frozen, listening hard and then there was Max again. It was definitely a scream.

"Alright, then, slow though, no charging in, it's probably a trap. Right?"

They both nodded. They inched their way down the corridor, waited a few more minutes making sure all was quiet, and Slaught leaned his head around the corner to see down the hall that led to the security lock up.

When he didn't say anything, Susun put her hand lightly on his back and whispered, "Johnny, all clear?"

But he didn't answer, found it hard to speak, just staring at the body. Susun leaned around him and looked, saw Max crumpled up on the floor, said quietly, "Johnny, I think he's breathing. We best get him somewhere safe," and gave him a soft shove. She heard him finally breathe and then he was down the hallway, checking Max's pulse. Susun knelt, gently feeling around his limp head.

"He got a serious clobbering."

"Think we can move him?" Jordan asked.

Slaught could hear the fear in Jordan's voice. Slaught looked up at him, said, "We're going to be okay. Max is going to be okay. But we can't leave him out here. Think you two can get him back to the maintenance room?"

"But you … ?"

"I'll gotta to settle this once and for all. It was going to come down to this anyway and there's no point any more folks getting hurt. Chum and the boys should be getting back sometime soon— I'm figuring within the hour. If we can hold things together till then, I think we might just make it."

"Watch yourself," Susun whispered, and then held her gun out to him.

He shook his head and pushed it back towards her.

"Keep it," he said. "You might need it. Jordan, you carry Max. Susun, you hang on to that and stay right beside him. Keep your eyes open. It could've been Laskin or Black in the storage room. My money's on Black."

"What do I do if we run into either of them?"

"You do what you did before Susun. Don't talk, don't think, don't second guess, just hit those brakes so hard you're going backwards."

—

"You think it's a good idea to wait here?" Tiny asked.

They were sitting in the dining room now, the body of Solanski lying across a nearby table, the soft patter of blood that had stained the floor below him now dried up. Chumboy's Auntie had said they should find a safe place where no one was likely to be looking. When she saw the body she said, "Guess they've checked in here already," and stepped past the body, said maybe they could play cards while they waited it out, but Tiny said he wasn't really in the mood and she said, "You're a grumpy man. It will help with your nerves."

They'd been out back when Laskin had arrived, Auntie Verla having offered to show Tiny how to make real bannock, saying bannock would be good because it was nutritious and you could sprinkle sugar on it and the kids liked it. A few big batches of bannock and they would have been all set for a day or so if they were cooped up. She said you really had to make it over an open fire so Tiny had started up the fire pit and they sat in the snow turning the bannock and Tiny had asked her if she knew bannock was really a Scottish food and she said, "So what?"

The sound of gunshots made them decide to move inside, figuring eventually they'd be noticed even though they were tucked in pretty good at the back of the hotel, Tiny wanting to hurry but Auntie Verla insisting they bring in the bannock that was finished, Tiny kicking snow onto the fire to put it out. Now they were sitting in the half-lit room, Auntie Verla playing solitaire, the sound of the cards snapping down sounding like explosions to Tiny.

"What's the matter with you? Aren't you scared?" he asked her.

"Yes, there is a dead man lying on the table over there."

"Well, maybe we should hide, get outta here. We're like sitting ducks."

She snapped down a three of hearts. "It's worse to be chased."

"But we aren't being chased, not yet anyway. If we got going we might avoid that."

"As soon as you run, you are being chased. You go if you want to."

"Well, I can't leave you here alone."

Her small hand slid a two of hearts on the row of cards and she looked up at him. "I take back what I said about you being grumpy."

Tiny sighed, "I can play Go Fish, but it's the only card game I know. I hate cards."

"I play Go Fish." She gathered up the deck and began to shuffle the cards. Then she dealt two hands.

Tiny picked his up, looking his hand over, trying to remember exactly how to play, thinking it was an goddam abnormal thing to do, to die playing Go Fucking Fish.

"Any Queens?" she asked.

"Go Fish."

Auntie Verla was reaching for the stack of cards when Laskin, back flat along the edge of the door, inched into the room, then stopped when he saw them, said, "I don't fucking believe this. You're playing cards?"

Over Auntie Verla's shoulder, Tiny could see him. He looked hot, cheeks an ugly flushed tone.

"Stand up and get away from the table," Laskin barked, bringing up his gun, "hands where I can see them."

Tiny did as he was told, Auntie Verla pausing to gather up the cards, and Laskin said, "I don't have a policy against killing old bitches. Hurry the fuck up."

Tiny scowled, "Hey, don't talk to her like that."

Laskin's gun came up, level with Tiny's face. "Small man syndrome making you a nasty little bastard, eh? Shut the fuck up or she goes first." Then he gestured with his gun, "Move around beside him on the other side of the table, and keep your hands out."

Auntie Verla got up, resting her hands on the table for a minute then shuffled around to where Tiny stood. They stood facing him now and he asked, "So where are they?"

"Who?" Tiny frowning, wondering himself where Slaught was, thinking too that Chumboy and the guys should be getting back anytime now if things had gone okay.

"Don't screw with me, understand? You have nothing now, nothing. I have the gun, see," he said, holding it up, his voice mocking, "and I'll use it. If I were you, I would come clean if you don't want to join Solanski over there. I don't have all fucking day either."

Auntie Verla looked at Laskin reproachfully and shrugged. "Johnny went moose hunting."

"You get one more answer old lady and then I'm going to start breaking your scrawny little fingers."

"Hey, that's enough," Tiny protested.

"Gonna stop me? I don't think so."

Auntie Verla said, "He won't have to."

Laskin looked at Auntie Verla. Tiny could see the guy was ready to snap, barely able to control himself. "Why's that granny?"

Auntie Verla shrugged, said, "You just can't help yourself."

"What the fuck does that mean?"

"It means you're your own worst enemy."

Tiny saw Laskin's hand tighten on the gun but also a flicker of uncertainty in the guy's eyes. Laskin said, "I think you've got that wrong."

Tiny thought his insides were going to burst and his mouth was so dry he couldn't swallow, but Auntie Verla just looked back at Laskin and said, "No, I don't think so."

Laskin bellowed and slammed his gun down. He leaned forward to grab her from across the table but slipped. He tried to regain his balance by pushing the gun against the table to stop his fall but he already had too much momentum and the gun popped out from underneath his body and discharged on the way down, sending a bullet straight into his foot.

Laskin howled, his eyes darting over to the impassive face of Auntie Verla as he spun down. Tiny scrambled around the table and dove for the gun. Laskin tried to swipe at him but his foot felt like it was burning and he couldn't focus, but he could see Tiny with the gun and heard the old woman say, "Shoot him in the other foot too," and Tiny backed up a bit and fired, and watched the colour drain from Laskin's face as he slumped onto the floor.

Tiny grabbed her hand and said, "Maybe we should go?"

"Okay," she said, and she picked up her deck of cards from the table and Tiny said as they were leaving the dining room, "So what was going on there, how'd you do that?"

"Do what?"

"Come on, you had him totally spooked."

"Oh, it's all in his head. He thinks us Indians have powerful juju."

"I think maybe he's right."

"That's just crazy talk."

—

Slaught had found it hard to breathe as he approached the storage lock-up. The sound of a gunshot brought him up short. He thought of Susun and Jordan hauling Max back, figured from the sound of it the shot had come from behind him, the dining room maybe, or somewhere near the maintenance room. He turned and headed that way, coming into the hallway. It was empty and quiet.

Slaught tapped lightly on the maintenance room door, said, "It's me."

At first there was no answer, Slaught frowning, but then he heard Jordan call out, "Come on in."

Slaught, still frowning, pulled on the door, it falling back on him clumsily, him dragging it aside and looking in and of course there she was, sitting up on a small table, swinging her legs. "Hey, glad you came, I was just thanking Max for helping me find everything I needed for some close range target shooting."

Slaught scanned the room, saw Max lying against the wall, a coat under his head, Susun beside him. And there was Jordan with three of the older folks. The rest of them must be underground. Well, at least there wasn't wholesale carnage yet, meaning Black probably really only wanted him. Maybe she'd leave the other folks alone. But he figured Laskin was still out there somewhere.

"So what's the plan?" he asked Mitch.

"You tell me?"

"Don't have one."

"Well, you did kill one my boys, and the other one is next to useless right now. That isn't going to look very good on me back at headquarters. I will have to do something about that, won't I?"

"Where's your boyfriend?"

"I'm considering myself single for the moment."

Slaught could feel everyone watching him. He asked, "Everyone okay?"

Jordan just nodded but Max's eyes were glazed.

"You're just taking right over, aren't you Johnny?" Mitch said. "Always such a leader."

He looked at her, her long legs swinging like she was waiting for a date on her granny's porch, leaning back on her arms. She was smiling at him, noticing him looking her over, but Slaught said, "Let's go Mitch." He knew he was taking a chance, but right now he just wanted to get her out of the room before someone or something pissed her off and she started shooting.

"What about little Miss Muffet?" she asked, jerking her head towards Susun.

Johnny said, "Let's go," and he nodded towards the door.

She raised her eyebrows and said, "Just like that?"

He looked right back at her and said, "Yeah, just like that."

She slid off the table. "Alright then, after you."

Johnny gave Susun a reassuring look and headed out the door. He kept walking away from the room, hearing Mitch say, "Where is it we're going?" sounding curious, thinking they were playing at some sort of cat and mouse thing.

He turned to face her, his mind drawing blank, he had no idea what to do, her walking towards him, her hips moving slow, like she was in no hurry at all, totally in control of the situation, and she was close enough for him to smell that musky scent she had, and to see her dark, almond eyes sort of smiling at him, her head cocked to the side, about to ask him something, when his fist shot out and caught her, full bore, on the side of her face.

She sailed back hard against the wall and hollered, "You dirty fuck!" her gun flying from her hand as she grabbed at the side of her jaw, her lip cracked open and bleeding, Johnny not really believing he'd punched her, his hand stinging like shit. He grabbed at her arm and spun her forward but her hand came up under his chin, slamming him, and it surprised him, taking the wind from him, him sort of tipping backward and she swore and slammed him again in the throat then wrenched her arm out of his grip. She staggered free of him and he thought she was going to run but she turned to face him, wiping the corner of her mouth with the back of her hand.

"You pathetic shit. So that was your plan, hitting a woman?"

Chumboy's voice from down the far end of the hallway said, "That might be a bit of a stretch, I mean the 'woman' part."

She jerked her head around, seeing Chumboy standing, still in his snowmobile suit, gun leveled at her. She said, "I think your friend can handle this by himself."

Chumboy said, "Uh, I don't think so."

Larose, Shaun, Jeff and Ricky were crowded in behind Chumboy, Jeff saying, "Holy shit dude, she's right there," as if maybe they hadn't noticed.

"I think we got this," Chumboy said.

"You don't have shit," Mitch said, then seeing Ricky peering out from behind Larose, said, "I don't fucking believe it. What is that piece of shit doing here? He your town mascot?"

Chumboy said, "Don't mind her Ricky. Why don't you and Jeff

go check on the others?" and then to Johnny said, "Good to see you Slaught."

Mitch said, "He's right Johnny, it is good to see you, but sadly, I have to leave now."

Maybe because there were so many people crowded in around Chumboy it took her a minute to see Turner directly behind Ricky. Slaught saw her smirk, followed her gaze to spot Turner, said, "Hey Chum, behind you."

Chumboy said, "Thought I smelt him," then looked over his shoulder. "Hey, Turner, there's a few of your machines gassed up and ready to go. Interested?"

"Fuck that," snapped Mitch. "Turner, why don't you try using that gun instead of keeping it stuck up your ass?"

Slaught could see Turner looking at her, thinking, his eyes red and tired.

Chumboy said, "Mine's the best offer you're going to get today, that's for sure. I'd take it if I were you."

Turner zipped up his jacket. "I'm outta here."

Mitch barked, "Turner! Don't even think about it."

"Too late," he said, and he was out the door.

Slaught said, "Guess you're on your own."

Mitch moved towards Slaught, an awful look on her face, both fury and smugness fixed in her eyes. Slaught looked down the hall at Chumboy and Larose. "Suggestions?" he asked, but she just kept walking, passing by him and staring at him as she went, drawing her hand across his chest, then heading down the long hallway.

Chumboy said, "I just saw my Auntie in the dining room. She said to let her go for now."

"Yeah? You sure about that?" Slaught asked, his eyes on Mitch's back.

"She's been batting a thousand so far," Larose said.

Slaught shrugged, saying, "Okay then," and started to walk slowly backwards towards Chumboy and Larose, not wanting to turn his back on her, watching her disappear around the corner, not even looking back, probably heading outside.

"Is it over?" he asked Chumboy.

"No, sorry. My Auntie says it ends in the snow."

"Shit man," Slaught answered, shaking his head, "it always ends in the snow."

"She also said to tell you it also begins in the snow. Said you'd understand."

"I'm not even close to understanding, Chum."

CHAPTER TWENTY FIVE

BY THE TIME THEY PULLED UP, LASKIN WAS TRYING to dig his
snowmachine out of a big drift, working on his back, clawing at the
snow, his feet looking like they were wrapped in towels or something, seeped full of red. Mitch was up and using some sort of small
shovel to dig away the snow. The machine was on its side, ploughed
into the backside of a drift.

Earlier, Tiny had filled Slaught in on how Laskin had managed
to shoot himself in the foot and how Chumboy's Auntie had said
to do the other one too. Chumboy said his Auntie knew what it
took to get a job done right. From what they could tell by the blood
tracked out and across the road, Laskin had then dragged himself
out the front doors of the hotel. Looked like Mitch had picked him
up on her way out.

Eventually, they'd accounted for the three bodies that were
lying around the building and Slaught asked where the other Talos

guy was and Shaun said, "Loaded up and ready to go. Jeff said the best bet is to haul him back down towards Thibeault Hill. Said from the sound of what he's picking up on Solanski's sat phone, the Territories are going to be crawling with Police Services in no time, said the government is sending in the army and Talos's security operations have been temporarily suspended. Think our little video did the trick."

Slaught and Chumboy had waited while Tiny made them a pot of coffee and gave them some of the bannock, saying, "You better fucking appreciate this, I almost died making it." Then Jeff and Shaun did a final sweep of the building and a complete head count and everyone was okay.

"Time to go, before the snow starts," Chumboy had said. Slaught was glad Susun wasn't there because she'd worry about him going out after Laskin. She'd gone to check on Max and said that she might lie down for a few minutes afterwards, said her head was buzzing. But she also said she thought Johnny was looking great, that she was glad he was okay. He said he felt a hundred years old and thought his hair had turned grey, said he'd come find her after she'd rested and she'd said, "Don't worry, I won't be wearing any of your clothes," and he raised his eyebrows and she just smiled.

Out on the trail, it was Turner they found first, one shot through the back, slumped over his machine about ten minutes out of town. Within another ten minutes Laskin and Black came into view, just past a clump of bare birch mixed in with some cedars that had turned a faded rust colour. She had her back to them, digging in the snow. Slaught had hoped they'd be long gone, but here they were in the snow, overhead the clouds like soot, dark and turbulent, a big one bunched up like a fist. Large, white flakes had started to fall, Slaught thinking in a few days it would be Christmas.

Following Chumboy, he pulled his machine around to the

side, giving themselves a decent view of both exits from the clearing. Chumboy pointed down at Leclerc, yelled over at Mitch, "Got a universal soldier over here. Think he belongs to you."

Mitch didn't stop her shoveling, acting as if they weren't there. Laskin fell back into the snow, cursing.

Slaught pulled his pump action up just so they could see he wasn't ready to take a bullet from her at this stage of the game, but Mitch just turned and made a face, sort of pouting, and said, "A little help here, please?"

Chumboy looked at Slaught and crossed his arms.

"Think you're on your own. Hands on the hood while we chat though."

"Look, Grier's hurt, okay. He can't walk."

Chumboy asked, "Now whose fault would that be?

"Well, what are we supposed to do?"

"You could carry him," suggested Slaught.

"Give me a hand. We tipped over because he's fucking dead weight. We're hardly a threat to anyone."

Chumboy laughed and said, "Not sure Turner would agree."

Mitch rolled her eyes and said they were being jerks.

"You got fuel?" Slaught was asking, already moving back towards his own machine.

"Yes."

"Enough?"

"Enough for what?"

"To get to the border."

Nodding over at Laskin she said, "I'm not sure he'll make it all that way. I'll be carrying a lot of extra weight with Leclerc too."

"Not to worry, soon enough there'll be lots of Police Service fellas out scouring the Territories for you, you won't have to wait too long."

Mitch looked over her shoulder at Laskin, but he didn't say anything. She asked Slaught if he meant a search party was out and he said, "You could call it that. Guess your boytoy there caused quite a shitstorm by plugging some Captain in your loveshack. I think you'll have company soon enough. Oh, and then there is the small matter of our home video going viral on his beloved—what's it called?—I-TIME? Guess your buddy didn't get a chance to really fill you in."

Mitch turned and asked Laskin how he felt about being such a fucking asshole but he didn't answer, just lay there in the snow. Mitch sighed, "Look, he's in bad shape."

Chumboy said, "My Uncle Hank once broke his leg when he hit a rock outcrop. The machine came down, smack, right on his tibia. He made himself a crutch from a nearby tree, then hiked over 50 kilometres back to his camp. And it was cold that day. Plus he was 68. So buck up."

"Spare me the lecture," Mitch was saying, turning her back and moving closer to Laskin and starting to dig again. Slaught figured she was banking on them coming round and helping, but he just said, "Yeah, well, sorry to interrupt. Guess you won't mind us leaving your Talos minion with you. Saves us the trouble of hauling him down to Thibeault Hill."

She nodded to her sled, said, "Well, at least pull him over here."

Chumboy shrugged, climbed off his machine and unhitched the sled, pulling it around to Laskin's machine. As he bent over to hitch it to the back of the machine he felt the cold metal on his temple and he said, "Damnit, that is the second time some girl got the drop on me. "

She said, "Straighten up big boy. Slowly."

Chumboy slowly stood up, the gun following him like it was glued to his temple. She had one hand on the collar of his coat, pulling him towards the gun, making it dig into his skin. Slaught was off his machine but hanging back, gun leveled, trying to figure out what she was going to do, guessing he should've figured she'd have firepower. He must've gotten distracted when Chumboy was at the sled. Fuck, couldn't miss a beat with these two.

He said, "Listen, we were walking away from this, maybe you should too."

"You know I won't hesitate to make a mess of your friend's head, right?"

Slaught said, "I could mess you up pretty bad too."

She was still holding tight to Chumboy, said, "I don't think you're the kind Slaught," but then Chumboy went limp, yelling "Johnny, now," but Mitch was pulled downwards and off balance as Chumboy fell. Slaught fired high over the tangle of Mitch and Chumboy, not being able to tell one dark snowmobile suit from the other.

Slaught was moving towards them, watching Chumboy trying to push her off. The snow was deep, clumped up around Chum's shoulders, stopping him from getting traction. Slaught was focusing on trying to keep his gun steady when he saw something shiny, and then there was Laskin plunging a knife into Chumboy's leg, Chumboy bellowing something fierce. Slaught was pushing through the snow, trying to keep his balance and move fast, the crust of the snow giving way as he pounded towards Chumboy, trying to spot Mitch's gun in the scrabble of bodies and shouting and blood.

He saw her hand, red from the cold and snow, still holding onto the gun that seemed to be flailing back and forth with a power of its own as she tried to find a way to make it count. He watched as the gun came up, her now leaning across Chumboy, steadying her gun hand on his shoulder and fixing the gun on Slaught. He came up short, staring, thinking 'it ends in the snow.' He hadn't thought it had meant this, this chaos of blood and yelling and that bitch winning and dragging herself back down to the city to start over. No, that wasn't what he'd seen. He'd seen something else.

And he'd seen it so clearly in his mind that he wasn't sure if he was dreaming or hallucinating or something else altogether, but it was like someone had turned a movie on in his head right then, because he was seeing it now, right in front of him in the clearing, watching Susun swing the thick trunk of cedar across the back of Mitch's head, sending her pitching forward, then smashing it down on Laskin, hitting him time after time till Chumboy finally shouted, "You got him, really. He isn't going anywhere now." And then she was just standing there, the branch hanging loose in her hand, dressed in jeans and a big sweater, her saying, "I didn't think it was going to end this way."

Slaught said slowly, "That is exactly how I thought it would end. I just can't believe it happened."

And she told him after she'd gotten Max settled in the infirmary she had felt bad and restless, had a crawling awful feeling all over her, and had gone to see Auntie Verla. Verla had told her to go right away to a place where she could find some peace. So Susun had headed back to the cedar tree where she'd first seen Chumboy's Auntie, because she thought that it was a place of power. She had stopped her machine, was taking off her helmet when she heard the snowmachines and Chumboy yell, and there was the thick severed branch lying right there in front of her. So she climbed over the snow ridge to where she'd heard Chumboy and saw it there, the blood and the snow and there was the branch in her hands. And it was like she was invisible because no one seemed to see her so she just walked over and whaled Mitch over the back of the head.

Mitch was on her knees, hands cradling her neck, moaning.

Laskin wasn't moving, his eyes were closed, his face pasty. Chumboy pulled himself up, grabbed Mitch's gun and glanced over at Laskin, said, "Ever sick looking, him," and then feeling the sting in his leg added, "the bastard."

Slaught tossed a few flares towards Mitch, said, "Here, try these, it might make the cops' job a bit easier. After all, snow's coming. Sure they want to get this over with as fast as they can."

Mitch tried to look over at him but winced, said, "You can't leave. I can hardly move."

"Leaving is exactly what we're doing lady," Slaught said. "We're outta here."

Laskin groaned, maybe tried to say her name, but Mitch snapped, "Would you at least shut the fuck up if you aren't going to help?" She rubbed the back of her head, turned to Susun and said, "You're quite the little bitch aren't you," then said to Chumboy, "Would you shoot him, please?"

Chumboy looked down at the gun in his hand and then at Laskin. "What? Shoot him? No, I'm not going to shoot him."

Mitch cursed, moving so fast she had the gun out of Chumboy's hand and into the side of Laskin's head before any of them knew what was happening. Laskin opened his eyes, said, "No fucking way," and she leaned back a bit, said "Bye bye baby," and shot him. Then she shot Leclerc. She looked up, saw the three of them staring at her, said "What? Don't tell me you're going to miss them? I sure won't, don't need to be hauling any deadweight around the countryside, especially not if I'm billing myself as the lone survivor of a fatal exchange of fire."

Chumboy was shaking his head, said, "Talos might think you don't know how to play nice."

"These are rogue operatives that I just took care of, Talos will be thanking me for containing the situation,"

Slaught asked, "So you done with your little killing fields routine?"

"That's it gentlemen, this has been a total fucking shitshow and I'm out of here. I'm taking Turner's sled and heading out, hope you have no objections."

"As long as you don't come back."

Mitch said, "This would be my last fucking destination of choice, don't worry."

Slaught shrugged, then noticed Susun, still standing there with the thick branch in her hand.

"You want to give me that? Don't think we'll be needing it now. You could just drop it there."

It was like she was coming out of a trance when she focused on him. She looked absolutely beautiful, eyes vivid, her colour high with the cold, looking like she might cry too, but she didn't, said instead, "I think I'd like to keep it, at least to show Auntie Verla."

He said, "It's a cool trophy for sure. Maybe we could mount it over the dining table or something."

He saw a faint smile cross her face and she said, "I'm pretty sure I'm in love with you."

"Fucking right you are. I say we head for home."

Mitch turned, said over her shoulder, "Oh for chrissake, don't make me puke."

Slaught ignored her, holding his hand out to Susun, asked, "Is that my sweater?"

She took his hand and trudged back through the snow with him to his machine.

Mitch said, "Aren't you at least going to give me a ride?"

Chumboy just laughed at her, told it was a good day for a walk. She said to cut the bullshit, but they both got on their machines, Susun sliding on behind Johnny.

Mitch yelled, "Where the hell do you think you're going?"

Slaught turned, thinking it does begin and end in the snow, pointed over at Chumboy and said, "I don't know where he's headed, but me and Susun, we're going home to start making some postmodern babies."

About the author

Brit Griffin co-authored a non-fiction history (*We Lived a Life and Then Some: the life, death and life of a mining town,* Between the Lines, 1996) that was listed as a must-read on the 2011 CBC Cross-Country Check-up Summer Reading list. For ten years she ran an independent magazine (*Highgrader Magazine*) on rural and resource-based communities. She is the recipient of two American Catholic Press awards for her writing on family life, and has worked as a free-lancer in print, video and radio. Griffin currently works for Timiskaming First Nation, an Algonquin community in northern Quebec. She lives in the town of Cobalt with her husband, and is the mother of three daughters.